TRUE DOLL STORIES

We Remember

As told to
Helene Simkin Jara

Acknowledgements

This book would not have been possible without the more than 90 people willing to freely tell me their childhood stories about dolls. Many of the said not only was it the first time they ever openly talked about it, but that it was therapeutic for them.
I am deeply grateful to them.

Also, my wonderful editors, Joan Levine, Carol Skolnick, Sharon Simkin Meinhoff and Karen Bell. Lastly, I am indebted to Earl T. Risks for his technical support in publishing this. I couldn't have done it without him.

Note from the Author

I never had dolls as a child. I don't remember being interested in them except when I was around 12 years old and my uncle Sammy brought me one from the carnival where he worked. My mother refused to let me keep it, saying it was probably stolen.

This anthology is a collection of stories people told me about their experiences with dolls. The original idea came to me when I interviewed my Mexican mother-in-law, who used to make clothes for naked Barbies and sell them for five pesos at the flea market in Guadalajara. Hearing her story was very poignant for me. When I would tell people about it, oftentimes their eyes would go off to one side and they would either look off into the distance or down to the floor, recollecting their own childhood and the dolls they had.

Each and every story was fascinating to me. I found myself asking just anyone I ran into, whether at work or the dog park or standing in line at the movies, anywhere really. After hearing about a hundred stories, I decided to put together this book. Some people asked me to change their names and even locations. When you read these stories, you will understand why.

Thanks for reading,

Helene

The Psychological Function of Dolls in Our Lives

"Be patient toward all that is unsolved in your heart
and try to love the questions themselves."
--Rainer Maria Rilke (1875–1926)

Winnicot (1953) introduced the term *transitional object*, to describe the process whereby a child imbues an object with the properties of the caregiver. Often the transitional object provides soothing in the absence of that person. In childhood and into adulthood, we can give inanimate objects human aspects.

Helene's storytellers reveal to us the many ways we use our dolls to symbolize aspects of various personas. They are playful, aggressive, and function as messengers calling us to action. This delightful book invites the reader to begin to think about the way dolls have functioned in our lives and the meaning they have for us.

Helen Resneck-Sannes, PhD,
Licensed Psychologist
Helenresneck.com

Excerpt from "Counting The Children" by Dana Gioia, Poet
Laureate of California 2015–2017:

> "Come in," she said. "I want to show you hell."
> I walked into a room of wooden shelves
> Stretching from floor to ceiling, wall to wall,
> With smaller shelves arranged along the center.
>
> A crowd of faces locked up silently.
> Shoulder to shoulder, standing in rows,
> Hundreds of dolls were lining every wall.
>
> Not a collection anyone would want -
> Just ordinary dolls salvaged from the trash
> With dozens of each kind all set together.
>
> They looked like sisters huddling in the dark,
> Forgotten brides abandoned at the altar,
> Their veils turned yellow, dresses stiff and soiled.
>
> Rows of discarded little girls and babies -
> Some naked, others dressed for play – they wore
> Whatever lives their owners left them in.
>
> Where were the children who promised them love?
> The small, caressing hands, the lips which whispered
> Secrets in the dark?

Table of Contents

ABANDONMENT ....
Constance...15
Geraldine's 1st Story...21
Ja-win...22
Lupe...23
Lynn...24

AROUND THE WORLD.. ....
Annapurna..27
Belinda...29
Marika..30
Pat's 1st Story..32
Veronica..34
Yoshi...35

ARRESTED DEVELOPMENT...
Angela..41
Suzanne...42

ASSIMILATION.. ....
Emilia..45
Isabel..47

BAD GIRLS...
Charlotte...51
Diana...52
Joanne..53
Roxie...54

BARBIES...
Jane..57
Jessica...59
Joanna..61
Josefina..62
Kim...69
Nancy...70

BLACK AND WHITE...
Cheryl's 1st Story... 75
Gina..76
Jasmine...77
Lara..78
Laverne...79

BOYS WITH DOLLS...
Al..85
Brian and the Fatties..84
Diego...85
Lucien..86
Steve's 1st Story...89
Therral...90

COLLECTORS' ITEMS...
Dana...93
Dar...97
Diane M's 1st Story..99
Steve's 2nd Story..101
Wilma's 1st Story..102

COMPANIONS...
Beatrice..107
Dana Talking About Tina....................................109
Francine..110
Melissa..112

DEAD AND GONE...
Daraj...117
Kenzie...118

DOLLS AND THE STAGE..................................
Brian's 2nd Story...121
Wilma's 2nd Story...124

DOLLS' DEMISE...
Carmela..127
Diane G's 1st Story...128
Kari...129
Katie...130
Pat's 2nd Story..131

DON'T BE CRUEL...
Larise..135

DON'T TOUCH..
Geraldine's 2nd Story...145
Johnny..146
Laura Laura..147
Robin's Sister Nina...153

FAKE DOLLS...
Brazilian TV..157
Guys and Doll..158

FIX WHAT'S BROKEN......................................
Diane M's 2nd Story...165

GET ME OUTTA HERE.....................................
Ashley...169
Magdalena..170
Marylou's 1st Story...171

HAVES AND HAVE NOTS................................
Annemarie..175
Cheryl's 2nd Story..177
Chris...178
Elsa (Emilia's Mom)...181
Joan..182

Robin...183
Sy...184
I DON'T LIKE DOLLS..
Bonnie...187
Heidi..189
Marcy..190
IN SICKNESS...
Aaron...193
Jill..194
IT DOESN'T LOOK LIKE ME...
Elena..199
Jacqueline...201
Kelly..202
LOVE ME, LOVE MY DOLL..
Helene...205
NOT A DOLL..
Bill...209
Janine..210
Ron..211
RAGGEDY ANN...
Marthann..215
Rebecca...218
Wilma's 3rd Story...221
THAT WAS THEN...
Mae..225
Muriel..226
UNFATHOMABLE—GRAPHIC CONTENT: *BE WARNED*.........
Marylou's 2nd Story...229
YOU REMIND ME..
Diane G's 2nd Story...245
Erica..247
Maria...255

ABANDONMENT

The stories in this chapter left me with both sorrow and admiration. When my father died, I went into a deep depression. Although he didn't abandon me, I felt abandoned. I couldn't believe the sun still shone, people still looked happy, the buses still ran, life went on. Listening to the stories of these children and how they dealt with that feeling helped me understand the strength of the human spirit. We go on. We find a way. It may take some time, especially as an adult, but as a child we seem to find a way out of desperation more quickly. We invent. We hide. We pretend.

I was at my desk at work one late afternoon when a Swiss woman I knew as a re-entry student came by. She asked what I was doing in my life, and I replied that I was writing a book about people's experiences with dolls in their childhood. I asked if she had a story she could tell me. She proceeded to recount her terrifying childhood for the next 2 hours as I typed on my computer. Her story poured out of her.

Constance

Teaching the Alphabet Wrong

We were children in an orphanage in Switzerland, the German part. It was in a small village. I did have a mother somewhere. She would come and get me once in a while. I was forced to be with her. She didn't like me. It was always a nightmare to go with her. Whenever it was time for presents, like my birthday or the middle of summer, there was a chance I would have to be with my mother.

She once gave me a present for my birthday. It was in a big box full of little plastic cheap dolls, the kind that would cost 2 cents: the ugliest, cheapest, naked dolls. I was shocked. Why did she give me a whole box? One doll would have been bad enough, but a box of them? I couldn't even scream, she hurt me so much. I don't remember what I did with the box. I've blocked that out.

Soon it was my mother's birthday—and I got my revenge. I was alone most of the time. I didn't always come home and I wasn't even noticed. So, I found a beaten-up dead mouse. Probably a cat had chewed on it. I wrapped it up beautifully with colorful wrapping paper and ribbons, way more than necessary, and gave it to her. I watched her unwrap it. She looked at me and said nothing. And nothing happened. Sometimes I wonder how I had the guts to do that. It was never spoken about.

In the orphanage, there was an old woman who lived there who made handmade dolls. She made all the clothes herself. They were gorgeous. She even made her own strollers. The dolls' faces were knitted with thick cotton fabric. She made different sweaters and different shoes with real leather parts. They had hair made of wool—curly, blonde, or different colors...dark and white skin. She made black babies. Once in a while, on a birthday of one of the girls, she would get a doll. One day I did. I feel like crying just thinking about it. It didn't last long. She took it away about a month later. It was devastating. I never found out why it was taken away. I think she regretted giving it to me or maybe she wanted it back.

When I was 6, the orphanage was closed down because the owner was violent towards the kids. I had to live with my mother then, which was far worse. She came and got us with a car. When I say us, I mean my younger brother and me. She had put us in the orphanage. She entertained everyone there. She had a big mouth. I didn't want to get in the car, so she pushed me. Pretty soon, my mother arranged for my brother and I to stay in a house called House at the Sea. It was protected from the government. It was right by a lake. It was almost in the lake. The train went right by the other side of the house. The house was light blue and big with lots of windows and balconies, kind of like a castle with turrets. I lived there alone with my brother who was almost 2½ years younger than me. I was only 6.

At the end of the week, my mother would come and bring food and then we were sort of a family. She cooked and left again. She left me a franc—one for each day of the week—to go to the village and buy food for me and my brother. She lined up the francs in a row on the table. I can still see them.

I didn't buy sausage. I never liked meat. I bought candy. When I was in the mood for real food (I took the responsibility of my brother very seriously), we would go to a restaurant in the village. We would ride down the hill on our tricycles into the village. My tricycle was an old one I found. My brother was given a new one for one of his birthdays. So, we would just sit in a restaurant until the owners would give us food. Sometimes on the way there, people would take us back to our house or sometimes, further away, we would find a house in a neighborhood and we would knock on the door. Then we would invite ourselves in for a meal. It was always an adventure riding into the village.

Living alone in that house was scary. There were mice and cats and no heat. It always seemed like one of the grownups might come back, so it was expected that I clean up the house. My mother expected me to. I would pray to God that God would clean up the house instead of me. I mean, there is a God, right? And everyone says He's helpful. I prayed with my brother for

God to clean up the house. God was disappointing. I didn't clean up. God didn't clean up. There was a little anxiety about that. But, other than that, I began to wonder what my purpose in life was. To clean?

Sometimes, for fun, I would break the big vinyl records I found in the house into little pieces. I liked the sound of breaking. I would make a little mountain of them and put them under the carpet.

In the winter, the snow was so high I was afraid that we might not be able to get back home or that we would freeze before we got there. We didn't have winter clothes. I still sometimes look at my fingers and toes and marvel that I never lost any of them.

When we lived in the house, we would play "orphanage." I would teach my brother what the nuns taught me. One day there was a phone call. It was the public school. Someone said that I had to go to school because I was already 7 or 7½ years old. They said I should have been there already. I was very excited, thrilled to go to school. It was far away from the house. It was an hour's walk. The way to the school was between the lake and the railroad tracks. It was not safe. Not like in this country. In this country, none of this would ever happen.

On the way there, there were lots of things to do. We didn't know what time it was. We would eat something for breakfast and then go to school. The school we went to was very small. There were two or three first graders and one second grader.

Sometimes we were an hour early or an hour late. The teacher told me I had to leave my brother at home. I just nodded and brought him anyway. My mother made it very clear I was not to tell anyone about our home life. The teacher finally accepted it and made a little place for him right next to me. He could do whatever he wanted.

In the evening, when we were home again, life was serious. We would go home and do more than the homework, whatever I thought was important. We would play "school" and I was the teacher. I decided we both had to do homework: the alphabet and math. He claims to this day that I taught him the alphabet wrong. I taught my brother how to tie his shoelaces. At least I did that right.

One day my father came home. There was an old laundry basket in the house and he told me to put all the things I wanted the most in the basket. Then he drove me to a new orphanage. My brother was in the car, but he didn't go to the orphanage. I didn't know what happened to him. I found out later that he lived with neighbors somewhere. He was devastated. Two years later he had to go to school because he was the right age and the police brought him to the orphanage.

As I said, I always preferred the orphanage to my mother's house. They made me go home on weekends. By this time, my mother was married to a new person and living somewhere else. His name was Herr Haeberli. He was an alcoholic. He hated me. Why was he so mean? When my brother and I would arrive on the dreaded weekends, I had to check which room we would get and hope that I could lock the door. There was always tension, always fear.

One time the nuns told my mother that she had to get me some shoes or boots. I had broken sandals, even in the winter. When I got back home, even my mother thought I should have something for my feet. She got me cheap plastic boots. The kind you can buy for 5 francs. They were yellow. When my stepfather came home and saw them on the floor, he screamed, "Who bought those?" Nobody said anything. Then he sent me away. He screamed, "Get out of the house! If you come back, I'll kill you!" I looked at my mother for support and looked at him and looked at her again. I knew what he was capable of doing. I remember when furniture went flying. Once he threw a big TV out of the fourth floor onto the street. I remember when pans flew and hit me when he tried to catch me. I knew he wasn't kidding because I had seen him beat my mother. When I looked at my mother's face, I knew I had to go. She said, "Just go. He said you should go." I was 10 years old. I wandered around in the village at night in the street. I tried to go back to the orphanage, but the train wasn't running that late. I just walked and walked. I finally got to the orphanage the next day.

When he was dying, many years later, I brought him flowers. I wanted to give him something, be there for him. He threw the flowers on the floor and said, "Get out of here!"

Because I hated going home to my mother, I was always selfishly thinking of ways not to have to go. When I was in school, there was a class for cooking. I learned to bake cakes. I baked cakes for the orphanage and tried to convince the teacher to let me bake a cake for a little girl in the orphanage who had asthma. If I baked her a cake and brought it to her, it would delay my going home for a long time. I would go back to my room and pack my bags to take the train, but first I would have to bake the cake. That would save me about 2 or 3 hours. I went on the wrong train on purpose. I told lies so often about taking the wrong train that even I believed them. Whenever vacation time would come closer, I would have nightmares at night. I would be screaming and a nun would come out and sit on my bed. But I never would tell her why I was screaming. I didn't explain. I told you, my mother had always threatened us about ever saying a word.

And so, this last part is for you, Wolfie, dear sweet brother. I'm sorry I used to chase you onto so many roofs. I loved to climb roofs and you didn't, but I didn't realize that you were so scared. I didn't realize it until that day with the kitty. I feel bad about that day even now. When it jumped into the lake, I had to try and save it even though I didn't know how to swim. I had to. I saw you on the ground yelling to me, "Stanzie, come back, come back!" I was drowning. I was going under the water. But when I saw your face and you looked so scared and I heard your voice, I knew I had to get back to you even if I couldn't swim. But Wolfie, that kitty died. It died. Can you ever forgive me?

Wolfie, we've been through so much together as children. Do you remember when Mother's third—or was it her fourth?— husband held that knife to my throat and made me eat meat? He knew I hated it. He held that knife to my neck and I chewed and chewed, but I never did swallow it. I still can't eat meat. I'm so sorry, Wolfie, for what I did to you. I made you play house with me and I held the knife to your neck. I made you be me and I was him and you had to pretend you didn't like meat.

I made you do so many things. Do you realize you were everything to me? Because I had to protect you, I couldn't allow myself to go crazy, at least not until later.

I'm sorry I tried to kill myself. I know Father wouldn't visit me in the hospital because suicide is deeply inappropriate for a Catholic. I was afraid, Wolfie. The fear was like a cancer growing in me. I was afraid they'd find out I had mental problems like the nuns said I did. All I wanted to do was become a nurse so I could help people, people like me. I told myself that if I lived, my punishment would be to have to live in the present. I'm doing that now by begging you, Wolfie, to forgive me. I know you will because you are a priest now. And I hope you know I never meant to teach you the alphabet wrong.

I know Geraldine from being in plays with her. We are both actors. We are both mothers. We both have a tendency to giggle at random. We both have stories to tell. In this book, there are two stories from Geraldine, who was born in Ireland and ran away as a young girl to England, worked there as a nanny and then as a nurse, and eventually came to the United States.

Geraldine's 1st Story

I was born in Dublin. My mother left me for America when I was 8 months old. I was brought up by my grandparents, and when I was old enough I attended school in a convent. My mother would send me packages from America, and the nuns would have me go from classroom to classroom, showing the other students what I got. I was the only one in the school whose mother was in America. Once she sent me an American Indian doll. I was around 7 or 8 years old then. I loved it, but I wasn't allowed to play with it. It had beautiful white and yellow beads and leather moccasins. It was put in a glass cabinet by my grandmother. She would allow me to take it out occasionally, but I understood it wasn't a doll I could play with. It was a real Indian with a beautiful face and light beige leather clothes with fringe around the skirt. Another time my mother sent me a pink and blue satin dress with netting that my grandmother made me wear to school. I was paraded throughout the classrooms in my outfit from America.

My mother would like to have me in her life now that she's alone and she's in her seventies, but I can't do anything about that. I don't need her anymore. I felt that I needed her until I was well into my thirties. My mother wasn't there for my marriage or the birth of my children. I can't bring myself to go and visit her. I don't want to. It's too late now. All the damage is done.

I don't judge her for what she did. My mother had her own problems. I never thought about it much until I was holding my own 8-month-old baby. I looked at my little girl and thought, "How could she have left me?" There is never a reason good enough to walk away from a child. I couldn't find an answer, except complete selfishness, totally driven by one's own needs.

Alexis (Ja-win) worked for me as a math and computer tutor (I coordinated the tutorial program in the community college). He is legally blind, very independent and comfortable with his physical disability. His ethnicity is Chinese–American. He has a deep and booming singing voice, which I had the pleasure of hearing when I came to listen to the final performances in his voice class.

Ja-win

My cousin had a thing about changing her name. When she was little, I knew her as Lucy. And then we didn't keep in touch for various reasons. I heard she was at Berkeley when I was, although I never ran into her there. They told me then that she had changed her name to Sarah. It might have been a biblical thing. And then eventually, after college, she changed her name to Heather. Her birth name was Ja-win. She had a brother whose name was Ja-li. His given English name was Stanley, and now it's Steven. Part of the name change thing involved their mother taking them underground after running away from their abusive father.

Lucy (Sarah, Heather) still has a lot of stuffed animals. Easily 40 of them. She has a lot of junk ... She once told me, *Yeah, it's nice being able to accumulate all these things so Steven and I feel like we've made it.*

Their mother died tragically from a pretty advanced stage of colon cancer. She hadn't gone to the doctor for a while. There were various rumors about the reason why the mother had left the father and taken the children into hiding. One rumor was that he had been a sexual abuser. When questioned further, the mother said, *Does dressing your young daughter up and taking her out to dinner in sexy clothes count?*

When I helped my cousin move recently, she told me she still had her favorite stuffed animal. She said something like, *This one's my mother*. She told me she talked to it every day. It was blue and purple, fairly large ... a bear, or a dog or a mouse. She said she bought it at Macy's. When they rang it up and they were about to put it in the bag, she asked them not to because she said it couldn't breathe in there. They looked at her kind of weird. I suppose that's because she was in her twenties.

Lupe is a student I've known for several years. Her life has never been easy. When I knew her she was a single, struggling mom hoping to further her education so she could get a better paying job and make ends meet. She gladly unburdened herself of her sad story.

Lupe

I had a baby doll when I was 6 years old. It was for my birthday. It came with a high chair and had light brown hair and blue eyes. My very first doll that I didn't have to share with anyone or fight for or give to anyone. I got to buy or make its dresses, to take care of it and feed it. It was fun, but I wasn't able to keep it long. I got moved to another foster home and it got lost. I named her Christine. I had her for a school year, from September to June. The other dolls I'd had before, I had to share with other kids.

Before I was with the last family, I was in other foster homes and I always had to share whatever toys I had. We got to make a rag doll one year from burlap and yarn. It was like a homemade doll. The other girls made their own dolls. I got interested in sewing after that. I kept her longer, up until I went back home with my mom. I got to make her colored eyes. I embroidered them and named her Maria. Her hair was out of yarn, black hair and brown eyes, red lips. She was about 10 inches long. I stuffed her with cotton. I had to change her hair because the yarn would get bad. Since my foster mom had yarn, she let me fix her hair. It was red, purple, green, and back to black.

My real mom threw her away after I returned home. One day I came home and she was gone. My mom said she threw her away because it wasn't safe for my baby sister.

My mom wasn't financially stable, which is why I ended up in foster homes. I was 4 years and 11 months old when I went into a foster home. My mom was arrested (she beat up two cops that night) and did some time. I don't know how long. I was in foster care until I was 12.

Lynn was a friend of one of my best friends. We were at a July 4th barbeque and got into a discussion about my book. She told me this sweet, sad story about her stuffed animal elephant.

Lynn

I never had dolls as a child. I only wanted to play with my three older brothers, much to their dismay. My mother tried to entice me to be more "girly" to no avail. She went so far as to take me over to another little girl's house so I could play like "girls do." That didn't work.

Then she bought me a small stuffed elephant. It was red and white. I didn't want to play with it at first, but since there were problems in the house, I would take it in my room and talk to it, sometimes crying, and holding it to my little beating heart.

They sent me away to boarding school soon afterwards. I took the elephant with me. I felt abandoned and lonely at the school without my brothers and would clasp my elephant to my barely budding bosom and cry for hours. No longer red and white, the elephant turned a yellow color. I believe my tears were so profuse they made the elephant turn from white and red to yellow.

AROUND THE WORLD

It is interesting to me how cultures from other countries compare to the one with which I am most familiar. I took a class at UCLA that compared folklore from around the world. Beliefs about what the sun and moon meant, how humans came to be, who was watching over us and why. It was a relief to read how alike we humans are and also how we differ. I felt lucky to hear stories unique to the countries they represent. The stories demonstrate that we all have the same basic needs, no matter what country we are from. They are a peek into their worlds.

I met Annapurna in a Zumba class. She taught at the university. We exchanged personal stories, as women do, and then she gave me this lovely doll story about her village in India.

Annapurna

I remember the dolls, especially the first one I got when I was a little kid living in India. It was a beautiful rubber doll wearing a lovely outfit, maybe a skirt and a top, beautifully decorated with silky hair. I remember she came from one of my uncles who lived in the now multi-national city Rourkela. I cherished that doll, for sure. But I remember that when I played with it with my friends, pretty soon it was just torn apart; the legs and hands were all gone. And then I realized how ugly that doll was once the parts were ripped off and the clothes were gone.

I never had the inclination to get dolls from the store. I thought ... hmm, this is just kind of artificial, temporary, and there is nothing natural about it. So, what did I play with? We would do these weddings among friends. For example, I remember playing with my friend, her brother and her family, her cousins. She would be the bride's side and I would be the groom's side.

I remember a doll made of mud. We would make it very much like a real wedding. That's 7 days. I remember spending maybe three days. We would do the rituals, and then the bride would come to the groom's house and would stay. The bride's house would be providing food, a feast, and then the groom's side would also provide a feast. My mother would be cooking for all of us. So we'd have real food. Family would be involved. Sometimes we would be cooking with sand. I remember that for the wedding it would be real food. So I always associate dolls with food and a wonderful setting.

Besides that, when I went to my mother's village in the summer, I had a wonderful grandmother, my mother's aunt, who would collect a kind of clay from the riverbanks because our village was just on the side of the river. We would go to the river for a bath. My grandmother would collect the sand and, deep in the riverbank, she would get the clay. I would help her carry it, and she would make me clay utensils to use for the wedding and for playing, like pots and pans. They were beautiful. They looked absolutely like original ones. She was so creative, when I think back. She would dry them for me. That was something I always looked forward to. I would play with them for the rest of the year. They were always my pride and joy when I played with my friends. I would say, "See what I got!" My friends would have those aluminum utensils for playing, but I would have these mud utensils. She would also make me mud dolls, a boy and a girl, and a bride and a bridegroom, all these different figures. That's vivid in my mind. Throughout my elementary school I played with mud dolls and mud utensils.

With the dolls, we did weddings, feasts, people coming from the village visiting their families. We would imitate the rituals we saw our parents doing. It established a wonderful connection, besides friendship. We would call each other uncles and aunts and cousins.

I grew up in a family with my brothers and my mother and father, but we were always surrounded by people coming from the village for different things. So in our household, even though it was a nuclear family, it felt like a joined family because we had company all the time. My grandparents were always visiting as were my uncles, aunts, cousins, and people from the village, so I never realized that some were my own and some were not my own. It was a very intimate setup in that sense. Whoever came was welcome, so I grew up with a lot of people. Always being surrounded by people, I never felt a lack of human contact. I still remember my uncle and grandfather making us sit around and listen to them tell stories from the village. Some stories are very vivid in my mind, like about ghosts and spirits, talking about witches in the village, and about different harvests and seasons.

I met Belinda in a Tai Chi class. I was quite taken with the story of her family's travels in the Middle East and the reaction of the children there to the troll dolls Belinda and her sister collected and cherished.

Belinda

My sister and I collected troll dolls. She was still in grade school, so I may have been a freshman in high school. She was probably in the 5th grade. We took a driving trip through the Middle East. She had a big giant troll and also some little ones with her, not many. We drove through the Holy Land. We drove through Israel and Jordan and Syria and all those countries. My sister would always be hugging or holding one of those trolls. The people over there just could not understand why a child would love something so ugly that might even be the devil. It created a stir everywhere we went. Sometimes they would try to give me and my sister a pretty doll instead. It was a whole different culture. We Americans do crazy things.

I was asked to mentor writing students at the university. To my great delight I was paired with Marika, who is part Japanese American. She shared her doll story with me.

Marika

When we go to Japan with my mom and my brother for the summer, we live at my grandma's house. It's kind of like a suburban area on the border of Kyoto and Osaka. I went out with my aunt to the park, one day, that was right in front of my house. I was about 6 or 7. The park is tiny—two swings and a slide. My aunt's not a very strong-willed person. She suffered from a lot of depression and had been in and out of hospitals. She's not one to fight or get in your face. I was on the swing and a man came by carrying a white plastic bag with naked Barbies with their heads all mutilated. He slowly walked up, stopped in front of me and started waving the Barbies in my face. He never came onto the play structure. He just stayed behind the fence. My aunt was standing with me and he was talking, but I couldn't understand what he was saying because his teeth were so screwed up he sounded like he was mumbling. I guess she understood what he was saying because she kept saying, "No, you can't take her. You can't take her." He kept pushing himself forward with his arm around the Barbie. I was just sitting there scared. He kept trying for a good 2 or 3 minutes and arguing with her. But he never laid a hand on me. And eventually she started raising her voice louder and louder and finally he gave up and left.

There were two dolls my mother tried to give me a few years later. But they didn't have clothes on so immediately I was like, "No!" The main one is called the *Rika-chan* doll and it's like a Japanese Barbie. It's the same body structure but it's not impossibly skinny. The Japanese one's head is bigger and she's shorter and the face is completely different. But I would say it still looks kind of Americanized like a lot of *anime* with the big doughy brown eyes. The hair was brown and kind of wavy and fluffy, not blonde and completely straight like Barbie hair. The structure of the arm movements was the same. It didn't have the Barbie imprint underwear, but I think the fabric was the same.

My mom moved from my grandma's when I was 2, so she had a bunch of stuff there. So she said, "Here! These were my dolls when I was a kid." And I said, "Get them away from me." When it happened with the man, I don't think she realized just how much of an effect it had on me.

I played with Barbies all my life, but when they don't have clothes they kind of scare me. She gave them to me. She had one or two dresses. But the clothes for the Japanese one compared to the American one are completely different. The American ones are flashy and skimpy. And the Japanese one is more like a normal traditional type dress. I didn't have any kimono ones. It was just kind of like a normal over-sized dress. I know the American ones I have are like tiny cocktail dresses with tiny pink ribbons, skimpy straps and bikinis. They were also old, so on the arms it was blue from age. I'm not really sure where that came from. And they smelled "Asian," kind of like mildew. I guess that's because they were just locked away for so long. There's a specific smell of Asian blankets. If you leave them in a closet, they get this moldy, gross smell. That's what the dolls smelled like, so there was no appeal.

I might have taken them when she gave them to me, but I didn't bring them home to America. I didn't want them. I know I didn't play with them. I didn't want anything to do with them. I was like, "Gross, get them away." They came with these Japanese blankets, too. I took the blankets.

Do you know what Groovy dolls are? They're plushy dolls and you can swap their clothes. I used the Japanese Barbie blankets for my Groovy dolls. I made little beds for them. But I didn't take home the actual Barbies.

I make it sound like it's a bigger deal than it was and I guess that's why my mom never cared, you know what I mean? If I brought it up now she'd say, "What are you talking about?"

I'm afraid of hobos, too. I mean, naturally I'm afraid of hobos, but I'm *irrationally* afraid of hobos because of what happened. I feel like I was so little that I built it up so much in my head, but he didn't do anything to me, really.

Pat was a student of mine who told me her story when I mentioned the book I was writing. It was a difficult memory for her.

Pat's 1ˢᵗ Story

My grandfather on my mom's side was from the era before the '50s, which was really authoritarian and stern and, even though he loved us, he was not necessarily the real lovey type of father. He was a patriarch kind of guy, strong featured. I heard all the stories about him when I was younger. He was really old, as I remember him. I was in my early teens, or preteens, like 8 or 10.

Whenever I would go to my grandfather's house, he would say, "Come give Grandpa a kiss." He would demand that I give him a kiss on the cheek. He was really old and I didn't grow up with him. We lived in Northern California and he lived in Southern California, so he was kind of new to me and he would speak in this really stern, strong voice: "Come give your grandfather a kiss." I was a little thrown off by that. So I already had this kind of uncomfortableness going to his house.

One of the first times that I remember was when we were going to spend the night. He had his own room. He lived by himself at this point, so he had his room in the back, and my mom and I slept somewhere else. Anyway, my little sister and I slept in the living room on the couch.

My grandfather collected clowns. He probably had about 80 different types of clowns. He had a couple of old porcelain clowns that would hang from the ceiling. He also had some big sad-faced clowns, and a wall of clown dolls. Some of them were brightly colored. A lot of them had a sad face or this really terrifyingly creepy, creepy made-up face. Some of them had the bodies of real men, like clown-suited men, and they had their legs crossed and looked sad.

I remember during the day when I would go visit, he would be fine. It wasn't like he was ever mean. He was just an old man who I didn't really know. I would just sit there on the couch because he told us we were not to be loud, not to be talking too much. So I would sit there on the couch, basically terrified, staring at this wall of clowns. I was afraid of the whole living room, in fact. And he was old, so he had old clowns.

He had one row of little clown dolls that were like stuffed dolls. They kind of looked happy and they kind of looked like they moved.

So, this one time, my cousin came over, my older cousin, and it was nighttime. He was going to stay over with us. He was always messing with me and just generally terrorizing me in a cousinly way. I told him that I hated the clowns. "Oh, you hate them? Oh, you should see what they do." And I said, "Ha ha, I'm not that afraid of them. I just don't like them." He turned off all the lights and went over to the clowns that were scruffy, fluffy little dolls. He wound them up in the back. There were about 15 clowns in this row, all different colors, but all the same brand or style. He wound them up in the back and they would say, "Ha ha ha ha ha ha," and their heads would roll up and down in a circle. I was completely terrified.

To this day I cannot bear the sight of a clown.

I knew Veronica as a student at the community college. She shared her heartbreaking story about living with her single mom in Mexico.

Veronica

I came from a poor Mexican family. I had one doll. It was beautiful—but only to look at. My mother told me that when I was old enough to take care of my dolls, I could play with it. I remember when my mother decided to leave my father, an abusive, womanizing husband, and had to sell anything of value to afford the trip over the border to the United States. I watched as people I didn't know went into our house, buying all our worldly possessions... including my doll.

I met Yoshi through her son, Fred, who was a re-entry student in his 50s. His mother, Yoshi, was probably in her late 70s. She told me that people were always asking her to write her memoirs. When I asked her if any part of it had to do with dolls, she told me this story, which took place both in Japan and here in the United States.

Yoshi

One year my mother told me we had to go to Japan right away because my grandfather was ill. I didn't want to go. I didn't want to leave my friends. I didn't know Japanese. My brother didn't want to go either, but we had to obey my mother. She also told me that same day that they had arranged a marriage for me for when we came back to the United States to someone I didn't even know. And then, as if to convince me, she took out a Shirley Temple doll in a box saying that this young man, whom she called "respectable," had sent it to me to remember him by. Remember him? I didn't even know him! She told me that the Shirley Temple doll was very expensive and popular and that even in the Depression it was a best seller and would be worth a lot of money someday. What did I care about that? I didn't want to marry someone I didn't know, even if he did send me an expensive doll.

Then she goes on about my Chinese astrological sign, even though we're Japanese, saying that I'm a bull and stubborn like her, that I should be grateful, that not every young man would spend so much money. What could I do? In my culture, you don't talk back to your parents. You do as they say.

When I told her I was afraid to go to Japan because I didn't speak the language, she told me I would learn it fast because I'm so smart. She said they were going to give me one year to advance to the 6th grade. She said I could do it because I was as smart as she was. Oh, I felt so much pressure.

Then my mother told us that when we got to Japan, we'd have to give up our passports and our citizenship! They weren't supposed to know that we were intending to return. And to top it off, we had to keep all this a secret! She said we might never see our friends again if we didn't keep this secret. Everything was a big secret. She wouldn't even tell us when we were coming back.

In the suitcases, she hid the Shirley Temple doll at the very bottom under some cotton sheets and towels, some men's undershirts, three real Panama hats, and two alligator handbags. When I asked her why we needed all that stuff, she said it was for something called the black market and that we could trade these things for food. She looked very serious when I asked her if we really wouldn't have any food, and then she told me to keep my doll hidden at all times. She turned to me and said we would never starve in Japan because we would always have rice and fish.

We were still in Japan 2 years later. I was living in a dormitory and had a secret boyfriend. My mother came to my room one day and told me that she had been to a palm reader. She said he told her that in order for my brother to be successful, he would need to be on land that was very big and surrounded by water. My mother said she knew then that we had to go back to the United States. At this point, I didn't want to go. I was afraid I wouldn't remember English. Mother reassured us that we would be rich in America. She missed her garden and American food. She said that maybe she could even go to school. I was desperately trying to think of ways to stay in Japan because of my secret boyfriend. I told her my clothes were too Japanese. She had an answer for that. She said she'd saved money with what she traded on the black market and could buy us new American clothes. She said she saw beautiful dresses in an American magazine and beautiful shoes. When I said I wouldn't go, she went straight to my dormitory window and threatened to throw herself to the ground. I had to believe her, so I agreed to go.

I didn't tell her that I too had gone to a palm reader who said that I wouldn't have to go back to America, my wish would come true, and that I would be able to stay with my boyfriend. But, there we were, all bundled up on the ship going to the United States. I couldn't eat, I couldn't sleep.

Suddenly, we felt the ship making a 180-degree turn. Over the loudspeaker, the captain was saying that Pearl Harbor had just been bombed, that we on the ship were considered the enemy of the United States and that we had to return to Japan! I jumped up and down, and yelled, "Oh, Mother! I'm so happy! I got my wish!" I started to hug my mother when she slapped me hard.

Back in Japan, it was so awful. There were American planes overhead bombing us. They flew so low that I could see the faces of the pilots. My mother made me stand next to a white fence and make myself as flat as possible. She told me I should wear white so that maybe they couldn't see me as well. I wanted to shout at them and say, "Please don't bomb us! We're American, just like you!"

Then I told her I missed eating fish. She just bowed her head and said nothing. And then we heard the American planes once again. I told my mother that I heard that the real Shirley Temple was in one of those planes. Her answer was, "That's impossible."

Years later, back in America, I was sitting with the husband my mother made me marry. He was a useless man. I worked 6 days a week, 12 hours a day in a department store while he sat at home with a ridiculous strawberry patch, tending to our children. All he cared about was Chinese philosophy. I told him I wished he'd never found me. He named our sons with kings' names. I told him he should have given them paupers' names because they would never be rich. He had the nerve to say that being rich isn't everything, that he was growing strawberries. And then he said that I liked working because I was learning proper English. He was insufferable. He had been interned in a camp in America during the war. I told him he learned to be lazy there. He had three meals a day, a place to sleep and he didn't have to work. I told him it must have been heaven for him. His response? "For the rich, it was hell."

Oh, how I wish I had saved that Shirley Temple doll. It would be worth so much money today. I would be rich!

I am an American-born Japanese woman. I am 84 years old.

ARRESTED DEVELOPMENT

These stories are indicative of the need of children to anthropomorphize their dolls. Dolls may be the only thing over which children have control and the only thing for which they can make the rules.

This is another story told to me by Alexis, my friend who is Chinese American and legally blind. This story is about his sister.

Angela

I've had a Christmas-edition Macy's Snoopy since I was one year old. I'm now 22 and still have Snoopy. I recently took Snoopy on a road trip while I was a carrier for the Museum of Art in Los Angeles, traveling in a semi from LA to New York. The semi had two drivers and two beds.

Thinking about this, my brother imagined that Snoopy perhaps might have a taser inside of him to protect me. But he didn't. I would never want anything inside Snoopy. After all, my mother has been repairing Snoopy for 21 years, trying to match the material on his body and face.

I managed to find another holiday edition of Snoopy that lives in the room my brother stays in when he visits. My mother had suggested using the new one to fix up the old one, but that horrified me—it would be like taking body parts from a twin! Definitely unacceptable.

I met Suzanne in a Weight Watchers meeting. The men and women in these meetings often have stories to tell. I actually wrote a poem about Suzanne, her husband, and a cat. When I asked her about dolls, she shyly told me this story.

Suzanne

I was never allowed to have real Barbies or Kens because Barbie had boobs. I got to have Skippers and Scooters, the boob-less ones. My little sister would stick them in her slippers and pretend they were speedboats.

ASSIMILATION

I felt empathy when I heard the stories of Emilia and Isabel. Although we never moved to another country when I was a child, we did move seven times before I was 12 years old. The feeling of being the new kid—the one who doesn't know how to dress, what to say, how to say it—is very familiar to me. We were also one of the only Jewish families in the neighborhood I grew up in. I remember feeling at sea singing Christmas songs in school and seeing all the decorations. I didn't know who Jesus was. At that time, no Hannukah songs were ever sung in school, nor was there ever any mention of anything Jewish. I wanted a Christmas tree more than anything. The need to feel a part of, to fit in, to be like everyone else, is pulsating throughout these two stories. I wish that more people could understand how it feels to people, children especially, to come to the United States not knowing the language or the culture and what they do to survive.

I met Emilia through one of my nieces. She was in a Jewish sorority at the university, even though she had been brought up Catholic. She said she felt more welcomed by the women in this sorority than any of the others. When I told her about my book, she offered this poignant story from her childhood in Guatemala. It is a tribute to her mother.

Emilia

I was born in Guatemala and we weren't wealthy. I remember it was my sister who had all the Barbies. She would get them either as gifts from the family or from friends of my mom. She was the firstborn, so she always got the best gifts and I would always get the hand-me-downs. But, what I would do ... I guess I was a little jealous ... I would grab her Barbies and I would get a blue pen or a red pen and start drawing on them. I would fill out their lips with red and their eyes with blue. I would practically destroy her Barbies. We had this neighbor who also had Barbies and we would just grab everything. We had all the little dresses, shoes, and clothes my sister made herself for her Barbies and we would put them on the street pavement. The streets were really small and the houses were really compact. We would dress up each other's dolls with clothes and play with them.

Anytime we would go to this one store where they had walls of Barbies, I would always cry, "Mom, Mom... they're so pretty!" It was just the image of beauty and wealth, I guess. It really attracted me. She could never do it. She would always tell me, "Tomorrow." It's funny when parents say "tomorrow." I was a kid and I would smile and say, "Okay, tomorrow!" And I'd always have this smile of hope that my mom was going to get me that Barbie tomorrow. And the next day I would bug her and I'd say, "Mommy, Mommy, are you going to get me that Barbie today?" And she would again say, "Tomorrow." And I don't know how many times she would say that until I finally realized that she could not get me that Barbie. I would just have to learn to be happy with what I had. I learned that the Barbies I had destroyed were really valuable to my sister, and I was completely happy with that.

I didn't grow out of Barbies until I was in my teens; because when I came here to the United States, my mom had managed to buy us a lot of toys. I just couldn't believe it, and my siblings were so mesmerized by them. She had been here for about 2 or 3 years, and she had collected everything we would want. Toys, clothes, practically everything we ever wanted but could never have back in Guatemala.

When that happened, I left them in their boxes. I didn't open all of them. I have ten-year-old Barbies still in the packages at my sister's. I never finished playing with them. I'm 20 years old now and sometimes I start thinking about it and all I want to do is go home and open all those boxes and start playing with them. It's a part of my childhood I never want to let go of because the change from having nothing to everything taught me so much. In the United States, Barbies are pictured like the type of woman you can never be, but for me it was like the type of life I could never have where I would go home and have a Barbie house and a wall filled with Barbies and just *having*. She got me way too many Barbies. I love her so much. Here you can buy a Barbie for 10 or 15 dollars. Over there, it can take your whole paycheck to get a good Barbie. It was a great experience to see the value of a simple toy and not take things for granted. Every time we meet I find myself looking at that box thinking, "Why haven't I opened it?" It's because you don't want to let go of that little part of you that longed for them and once you have them, you're just like…you don't know what to do.

Should I finally open those boxes and allow myself to be consumed with the joy of having more than I ever needed? I realize that it's better to keep the anticipation and excitement alive within myself by leaving them in the boxes. That way, someday, I can give them to my own children and teach them the same lessons I learned, thanks to my mother and a few dolls.

Isabel was a student at the community college. She told me the story of her escape with her mother and siblings from a violent father to crossing the border to the United States to try and have a better life. Her doll story is similar to Veronica's.

Isabel

Isabel sat in the back of the 3rd grade classroom. She looked around at the walls not understanding what any of the words meant. She kept her head down, hoping the teacher would not call on her, would not notice her even. She was the only girl in the classroom with brown skin. No one looked like her.

Two weeks ago her mother and her three sisters were stuffed into the trunk of a car escaping to this new country, escaping from their father who when he was home—which wasn't often— would beat their mother after drinking two bottles of tequila and smashing them ceremoniously against the walls.

Her father had been gone for 3 months this last time. Her mother told her only 3 days before they left that she had been saving extra money from mending peoples' clothes, doing their washing, and cleaning their houses in the hopes that she and her daughters could have a better life. The last weekend, her mother put all their furniture out in front of their house to sell to their neighbors, praying that her husband would not suddenly return. She also put all their pots and pans and the painting of the Virgin de Guadalupe on the front porch. But what hurt Isabel the most was when her mother put out her doll to sell, the one her mother had hung on the wall, not allowing her to play with until she was big enough.

The rich lady Dona Gutierrez bought it for only 6 pesos. Isabel had looked up at that doll every day since her *tio* Javier had given it to her. Someday she thought she would be big enough, good enough, to play with her. She longed to hold her, to brush her blonde hair, and look into her big blue eyes. But now, here she was in the classroom, looking at all the blonde-haired girls with blue eyes, and feeling very much alone.

None of these girls ever had to ride in a trunk, not making any noise, feeling so hungry like their stomachs were eating away their insides, having to pee and not being able to go yet. Praying to *la Virgen* to keep them safe and let them cross without getting caught. Praying to *la Virgen* that their mother would never have to be beaten again and praying to *la Virgen* that their new life in *el norte* would be a better one, a safer one. No, none of these girls probably ever had to do that and she couldn't even tell them. Not ever.

BAD GIRLS

My mother used to sing, "When she was good, she was very, very good and when she was bad, she was horrid." I never really understood until I was much older that she was letting me know I did "bad" things. All kids do bad things, I believe; in most cases, they just don't know they are bad. It's just an in-the-moment "fun" thing to do. These stories demonstrate this. Naughty, naughty.

I met Charlotte while walking my dog past her house. She sat down on her front steps, and I recorded her doll story. When she told me the story, her movements and voice became just like a little girl. Charlotte was probably in her late 50s. This memory was vivid for her.

Charlotte

When I was a little girl, about 10 actually, I lived in Hagerstown, Maryland, and I had this big old doll. It had kind of rubbery skin. We lived in the upstairs level of a four-apartment house. One day I was sitting on the back porch in the middle of the day when I discovered a can of some kind of gasoline—not turpentine— something that's dangerous if you rub it, but I didn't know. I had steel wool, and this rubber doll had gotten all dirty so I was just pouring this stuff all over it and scrubbing like mad with the steel wool.

Unfortunately, nothing happened as far as cleaning the doll, but I did get a terrible spanking when my father came home and found out. It could have caught on fire and killed me, and the can was right beside me.

So I'm sitting there scrubbing this thing and I look up into the sky and I see this red ball moving, like turning and swirling, as it's going across the sky, pale pinkish and whitish and stuff. Much like these candy things they used to call black balls. They had a licorice coating and you could suck on them and go through many layers of color until you got to a tiny seed that was in the middle.

It was like a black ball that had several sucked-off layers. It was kind of pinkish and whitish and turning and turning, and I am just scrubbing this doll. And it was just the weirdest day sitting out there; it was very quiet and my sister was off somewhere. And then I read—my father read at the breakfast table the next morning—that there were sightings all over Washington, DC (we lived about 80 miles from Washington, DC), that there had been *flying saucer* sightings while I was scrubbing the doll with the steel wool and then got a terrible spanking because it nearly caught on fire.

I was told this story while waiting in a doctor's office. What struck me about Diana's story was my sudden understanding that a child's personality can be very strong. This little girl knew what she wanted and what she didn't. Stuffed animals were in, dolls were out.

Diana

My little girl—I had a feminine, sweet little daughter who seemed to be directed toward animals and stuffed animals, which she called "stuffed up." I bought her this beautiful doll for Christmas, absolutely gorgeous, and we all opened our Christmas gifts. Santa Claus had come and there was a candle burning on the table. My sweet little girl took the doll and burned the doll's hair off, totally off! When I confronted her, she said, "No. I didn't do it. The baby got in the fire." She was maybe 5 or 6 years old, old enough to know better. I don't think she would have done this with a "stuffed up" animal.

When I asked Joanne if she had any childhood doll stories, she immediately looked ashamed, her head down. She had felt this guilt for a good 30 years. She was one of the dog park regulars. I think she felt better after she unburdened this story.

Joanne

Once I had made some pajamas for my Tiny Tears doll, but they didn't fit. As hard as I tried to get her arms in the sleeves, it just didn't work. I was very frustrated and started shaking her. I must have shaken her very hard. Through my own tears of disappointment, I saw that her eyes had crossed! How many times had I been told to uncross my eyes, which was a fun pastime for me, with the warning that they might stay that way!

I guess I showed my Dad my shame and sadness, and he said he would send her to the doll hospital. It seemed like a long time that I had not seen her. I don't remember if I even asked about her. However, rifling about in the front closet one day, reason unknown, I saw her headless body up on the shelf. That was disturbing. Poor Tiny Tears with no head! I do not remember how the story was resolved or explained, but I never saw her head again.

I may have learned a lesson about my anger or strength after that, or at least my pattern making or sewing skills. Let's just say I don't remember shaking any other dolls after that!

This story was told to me by Roxie's brother, Steve, with whom I worked for 25 years at the community college. He has four sisters and no brothers. They were brought up Catholic in an upper middle-class neighborhood in Nebraska and later in New Jersey.

Roxie

We had a nun doll from one of the aunts in Omaha. Roxie took it to school and swung it around by the rosary belt. She got sent to the principal's office.

BARBIES

How can we live as little girls and not have Barbies? I never had one. I didn't even know what they were. This symbol of American lore represents excitement, repression, oppression, and unfulfilled desires. In the case of my mother-in-law, it was a way to make much needed money. It was through interviewing my mother-in-law, Josefina, that I decided to write this book. There are as many layers of the Barbie experience as there are stories. The having or not having a Barbie can be a deciding factor in a little girl's life, at least in this country.

I met Jane at the community college. She was one of my students. Her story was a survival story about growing up poor with many siblings. As in many of these stories, the dolls were both an escape and a grounding.

Jane

My dad passed when I was 2, so it was a financial hardship for my mother with seven kids. The first doll I had was big, and that sucker went with me wherever I went. She was a Holly Hobby, a country-style doll wearing a peasant cap and a prairie dress. She was soft with long brown hair. I played in the mud with that doll. Its eyes opened and closed. She was my imaginary friend. We talked. I had to find baby clothes to fit her. We played hide and seek together. I don't know quite how that worked, but it did. I would steal my sister's makeup and put it on the doll. I got in big trouble. My sister was 12 years older. She had better quality makeup than the sister who was 9 years older than me. I would steal her rollers for my Barbie. I would sit with my Barbie in my sister's old potty chair and go potty with her. I even made her wax fingernails with candle wax. I called her *Sissy*. I was left alone a lot, so my dolls were my buddies. We would make red berry pie together. I had to do things so my brothers couldn't blow them up with their Lady Fingers firecrackers. They used to put them in the butts of frogs. That's why I stuck to my dolls and protected them.

And then there was the neon turtle bean bag. He was hot pink and hot green. I sewed and repaired him all the time. He was always there for me when I had a bad day and was also made of soft material. The neon turtle reminds me of my childhood. I don't know what happened to him. I was very upset the day he got a hole in him. I was less than 10 years old. I don't remember his name. If I saw another one, I'd buy it.

I'm from Canadian, Texas, a small town. From the time I was 7 until 11 or 12, I had to rescue my Barbies from my brothers. They liked to cut their hair, amputate their fingers, and draw certain features on their bodies to make them more lifelike. I never understood at 7 or 8 what those features meant, so I always tried to clean them off. I didn't have a Ken doll.

One of the Barbies had her hair cut off, so she became the boy. She went from being "Lilly" to "Sam." I made them their own clothes with old socks and ties. It was easier to make skirts for the girls. The boys had flat feet and the girls had pretty toes, so it was harder. I cut little cardboard feet and would take pieces of socks and stitch them up tighter. Sometimes duct tape became a belt. My mother had an extensive flower garden, so rose petals made particularly good halter tops.

I met Jessica through a mutual friend. Her story showed me how compartmentalized a child can be.

Jessica

I always wanted to be a mom. I had 36 Barbies and one that was supposed to be her sister, but I pretended it was her baby. It was like a 2-inch tall Barbie, so I'd have the Barbies give birth to that doll. Then I had regular-sized dolls and I would pretend to give birth to them. My sister and I slept in the same room. I have a distinct memory of when I was probably 6 or 7. I'd put a blanket over me and spread my legs and pull out a doll.

I had a boy best friend at the time and we played sports, but we'd trade off. I was a tomboy, pretty athletic. I would say, "Okay, you can play my husband." I did lumberjack stuff. Like a pioneer woman, I always swaddled babies. I was probably playing house until I was ten or 11. He played the husband a lot of the times, and I played the wife and had a baby.

My mom has always been an occultist. She believes in things like spirits. I was acutely aware of her beliefs, which added to the fear I had at night. I guess I had that thing where I thought the dolls would come alive at night and that kind of scared me. Sometimes I'd sleep by the refrigerator in the kitchen, and I'd bring my sister with me because I was afraid to sleep in my room.

I also used to collect China dolls, the porcelain dolls. I had dolls that weren't for touching. I even had a Barbie doll that I never took out of the package. I kind of collected things: dolls, erasers, pencils, baseball cards, Hot Wheels. It wasn't always gender specific, which I kind of like about my childhood.

I have an American Girl doll. They're collectible. She is Samantha. They have books that go with them. She is a Victorian-era rich girl. According to the book, she was an orphan who found out she had this rich aunt, and then she went away to live with her. It's kind of like acting. I had a dollhouse that went with Samantha. There were scenes I could set up. There was cast iron on the side of the steps, and there were old-fashioned school desks. The desktop had drawers in it and a place to write on. That was her desk for school. I had a wardrobe that actually opened up. My sister had the Swedish immigrant doll. She had a ton of

Barbies as well. My mom says my doll's worth about $800 right now.

Joanna danced close to me in a Zumba class. She later became a Zumba teacher.

Joanna

We were traveling in Mallorca years ago and heard there was a flea market of sorts. When we got there, there was a boy, filthy, with equally filthy naked Barbies laid out on the ground.

It seemed to me he was pimping these naked Barbies. Who would ever want to buy them? I wondered if when he got older he would be pimping naked women.

Josefina was my mother-in-law — may she rest in peace. She was the inspiration for this book.

Josefina

Hoy (Today)

Looking out my kitchen window, I see Josefina sitting on the deck with her swollen legs sticking straight out as she combs the hair of one of her many Barbies. Soon she will make them dresses in happy colors of red and blue, and plain *calzones* (underpants) without lace. Her knees are swollen from bone on bone after walking for 15 years behind Juan without even a suitcase to hold her one dress, *un rebozo* (a shawl), a pillow, a little box of plates, and babies in her arms. She is smiling and singing with the radio to a romantic mariachi song. In the song, a husband is singing to his wife, reminiscing about their youth and reaffirming his devotion to her.

Niñez (Childhood)

Her first job, when she was only 13 years old, was in the *Nuestra Señora de Guadalupe* seminary, where she made tortillas, washed clothes, swept, cooked and cleaned for 30 people for one peso every month.

Josefina and I are in my kitchen now, sitting at the table and drinking herbal tea. She tells me that her mother died of dysentery when she was young. Her father gave her little sister away after that to a family who didn't want her. They made Marienne sleep in the corral with the pigs and the cows because she disgusted them. A tear leaks from Josefina's proud face as she tells me this. We drink more tea.

Hoy

Josefina is putting little pink ribbons in the hair she is carefully braiding on one of her Barbies. Josefina's face is rich with wrinkles from 79 years of laughter, tears, and *coraje* (courage). She has had her brown skin kissed by the hot Mexican sun, unlike Barbie, who has also never been surrounded by children, grandchildren, and great grandchildren, screaming, dancing, fighting, or crying.

El Marido (Her Husband)

I ask her about her wedding day. She looks at me directly with her sharp, brown eyes and tells me that she left her husband dancing at the party and went home with her father. Juan didn't come to get her. Eight days later, she went to find him. He was living in a tiny room, with only a *petate* (bedroll), a little corn, a *metate* (mortar), and a small container of petroleum. She told me she asked him why he didn't come for her. He turned his head to the wall and said he was waiting for her to come. They had ten children.

Hoy

Josefina swings Barbie's stiff arms up into the air while she slips on the latest carefully made pink gingham dress. She tells me about the stiffness in her own arms when she held out a blanket for hours in front of the lean-to by the side of the road where they were living, soaked from a storm, trying to protect her babies. Her arms were aching as they shook, but she had to hold the blanket up to protect her children from the rain. She had to wring out the blanket and hold it up again, *rezando a Dios* (praying to God) to keep them well. They had moved 40 times already because Juan was never satisfied with where they lived.

Sus Hijos (Her Children)

We are sitting at the kitchen table again looking through the window at the morning glories climbing the fence on the deck. She tells me that they often had no food at all when her children were babies. She barely had milk in her breasts to feed them. She shakes her head in disbelief and anger when she thinks of those times.

Josefina likes the tea I buy her because it has lots of different *hierbas* in it to calm her nerves.

I look at her kind, brown, wrinkled face across the table from me. She is telling me about her eldest son, Evodio, who surprised her one day with a present. "*Mira, Mama, lo que tengo para usted,*" (Look mama, what I have for you) he said. "A blonde baby with blue eyes. I found her at the orphanage, and no one wants her."

Carmen became Josefina's eleventh child. The word got out later that the child was Evodio's from an affair he was having and that the mother had threatened to abort. He wouldn't hear of it and promised her that his mother would bring up the baby as if it were her own.

Carmen suffered greatly. The women never accepted her. She was ostracized, ridiculed, and often ignored. Josefina was caught in the middle. She couldn't throw this little girl out into the street. She had promised Evodio to keep her, but her daughters hardly had enough to eat themselves, let alone share with someone not of their own blood. They resented her blonde hair, blue eyes and fair skin, and what they considered to be the doting of their mother. At age 18, Carmen tried to kill herself by swallowing too many pills. "She's just trying to get attention as usual," they said.

She tells me she is proud of her children because none of them are drug addicts or in jail. "They all know how to work," she says.

She smiles, recalling a story about her sons Antonio and Lorenzo when they were little. They would get up early because they were hungry and didn't want Josefina to have to stretch the food for all 11 children. So they would go from house to house asking for a little *taquito*. Antonio would do the talking. He had no shame.

Once, when he was 10 years old, his father, Juan, had a guest at the house named Sacramento. Antonio put his hands behind his back and began to dance and dance until Sacramento gave him 20 pesos. He took the money and ran. He bought *un burro de queso con un chilito* (cheese burrito with chili) and ate it, slowly.

I show her the mangos I just bought at the farmer's market. We sit together at the table, sipping tea again. She tells me about her son Agustín when he was 9 years old. His favorite fruit was mango. She said he and a friend walked down a steep cliff near their house because there was a mango orchard down there. When they got to the bottom, a storm came in and they couldn't get back. When her son didn't come back at night, Josefina went to the Red Cross, the Green Cross, and the jail to look for them. She finally called the firemen, who climbed down the cliff to look for them. A farmer had seen them and offered them a barn to sleep in. They slept face down on a bed of cornstalks with their little arms outspread. When they got up in the morning, they noticed that underneath the cornstalks were hundreds of scorpions. Awake all night and sick with worry, Josefina was beside herself. Then suddenly she saw Agustín walking toward her, smiling, carrying a boxful of mangos on his head.

We were laughing this morning when I reminded her about the leather suitcase she found in East L.A. a few years ago. Even though I've heard the story before, I ask her to tell me again. I can picture her looking out her kitchen window in the projects near Sears. The streets are filled with old cars, broken glass, graffiti, and mothers with their children. The smells emanating from the apartments are from *tamales, enchiladas, pozole, frijoles, salsa,* and *mole.* "So, you saw a suitcase on top of a car," I prompt her. She tells me that it was there all day. "And it wasn't on top of a car, it was in the flatbed of a truck." She said she waited until Carmen came home from school. She thought that if it were still there, then she would ask Carmen to grab it and bring it in. She counseled Carmen to touch it first to see if it didn't have a dead animal or something inside. Together they put the fine leather suitcase on the floor in the living room and opened it up. Josefina told me that Carmen and she looked at each other then, puzzled. "Mama, it's only grass!" Carmen said. Together they looked at the bricks of grass in amazement. "Why would anybody do this?" they said to each other. They decided to wait until Antonio came home. He would know what to do. After conferring with three of her sons, they decided it must be marijuana. Antonio sold the suitcase full of grass to a neighbor named Heito. Josefina told me Antonio gave her $200. But, what really made her happiest, she told me, was that she got to keep the leather suitcase.

Sus Hermanos (Her Brothers)

"What about your brothers," I ask her? She cries again. She tells me her brother Antonio came to visit her after 14 years of absence. When her husband Juan saw him in the kitchen, he said, "Who is this man? You don't have a brother Antonio. I will not permit him in my house." He told her that he had to leave. When she told her brother what her husband had said, he asked her to give him her *bendición* (blessing). He said he thought he might never see her again. And he didn't.

"Did you have another brother, Josefina?" I ask her. She looks out the kitchen window when I ask her that. Her jaw tightens. She tells me her brother Jose stayed with her and Juan when he was young. She said his job was feeding a neighbor's cows.

Josefina supports her weight with her hands on the kitchen table and slowly stands up, walks over to the kitchen sink, grabs a pot, and starts to scrub it hard as she tells me that Juan beat Jose with a thick rope because he came home late one day. She turns to me and with clenched teeth says, "I said to him, 'Hit him until you're tired, Juan! Beatings don't cost money. And you haven't even bought him one *camisa* (shirt). You aren't even worthy of a name. You are no one to us!'" She put the pot in the dish drainer and we walked back to the kitchen table. "Do you want me to make you a cup of tea?" I asked her. She nods her head. "Juan beat me after he beat Jose," she told me. "But my tears were for my brother's pain."

Ahora (Now)

Now, Josefina has seven houses where she can stay. Her children pay for her to travel to East Los Angeles, Santa Cruz, Denver, or Guadalajara. Her son Rito built her a house with three bedrooms, a kitchen, and a patio in the front where she keeps a dove that sings to her every morning.

We drink more tea. She teaches me how to make *pozole, tamales,* and *enchiladas* during the 6 weeks she stays with us. It has taken me 18 years to get up the nerve to ask her to show me how, and 18 years for her to get over her shyness around me to accept that she can teach me something. We laugh at the sink and the stove together. I am thinking I feel more comfortable with my mother-in-law than with my own mother.

Josefina is talking on the phone to her family in Guadalajara. She is telling them that I'm so good to her because I bring her tea. I also love to buy her presents. I bought her a white sweater today. She told me not to do that because her family will be jealous because they haven't bought her a sweater. Or worse yet, they will want the sweater. My kids say that she's my little doll. I like to dress her up. If I buy her a pair of shoes, she won't wear them. She's too embarrassed to wear something new. She keeps them in a special place in her closet in her house in Guadalajara. She tells me that that is where she has kept all the things I have given her. When my mother passed away, I gave Josefina her shoes. They wore the same size. Exasperated, I say, "But Josefina, guarding them in the closet doesn't make any sense. You're supposed to enjoy them." She laughs her easy laugh, covering her mouth with her hand and tells me that she doesn't want to get them dirty. She'll save them for a special occasion. "What special occasion? Josefina, you don't even like to go to *bodas* (weddings) or *quinceañeras* (birthday celebration for a young girl of 15) anymore." She sits back in her chair, laughs again and says, "It's true, isn't it?"

Josefina tells me that a house without children is a sad house. Josefina loves to hear the television blasting, the radio playing mariachi music and romantic love songs, children crying, screaming, dancing, playing *barajas* (cards) and sucking on *paletas* (popsicles) that are dripping down their square chins.

Barbie's black high *tacones* (heels) need adjusting. Josefina is tugging on them and remembering how she worried about her children walking *descalzos* (barefoot) in the wet dirt. They would always get fevers and sometimes get *anginas* (swollen glands). Josefina lifts up the blue dress with flowers on it that she just finished making for one of her Barbies.

She is angry when she thinks of the people in the market in Guadalajara where she will sell her Barbies. She tells me that they lift up the dresses and look to see if the Barbies are wearing the original *calzones* (underpants) with elastic and lace. She says that half the time they get smudge marks on the dresses and then just throw the Barbies down on the ground if the *calzones* aren't original. She told me she just sews normal panties. "Why does it matter if the underwear is fancy or not?" she asks me. Still, she has enough *tela* (cloth) now to make a thousand dresses for the 50 Barbies that her son Jorge found for her at the flea market. She can sell them for 45 pesos each.

Hoy

It's Sunday and I'm looking out my kitchen window at a big lump under a blanket on the swing. It is Josefina. She sleeps as long as my cats.

Now she hoists herself up to sitting, turns on the radio and begins to sing softly. She has a blue *rebozo* (shawl) wrapped around her shoulders and is wearing the sunhat I gave her yesterday. She will leave us today at 3 p.m. and take the Amtrak to Los Angeles.

She is surrounded by four suitcases, three of which are entirely full of Barbies.

Kim was a student in the community college. Her story made me smile.

Kim

So, I'm the youngest of seven, right? And my oldest sister is 7 years older than me. My mom bought us a Barbie doll to share. Can you imagine? I was like 3 maybe and my sister was 7 and we had to share this Barbie doll. I just remember fighting about this Barbie doll in the backseat of a taxicab. It was probably in Michigan or Maryland. I was an army brat, so we had to move a lot, going from one base to the next. So we were in the back of this old cab, fighting over this Barbie doll; and my mom grabbed the doll, grabbed the two of us, and beat the shit out of us because we were fighting over this doll.

It didn't turn me off to Barbies. After that I was determined and I bought as many Barbies as I possibly could with my allowance.

She wouldn't let me have a Ken doll. I used to take the Barbie dolls and I'd cut all their hair off so I'd have a guy and I'd put holes in the breasts and push them in because with the old Barbie dolls you could do that. They were softer. And then I would turn them into boys so they could have sex.

I met Nancy at the dog park. She had two pugs. She had (may she rest in peace) a terrific sense of humor and imagination.

Nancy

My nephew was having a birthday party. That year it was all the rage to hire someone dressed as a cartoon character to come to a birthday party. There were no male characters left to hire, so we hired a Barbie. There must have been about ten 4-year-olds at the park, eating cake and ice cream, and having a good time at this party. It was already 2:15 pm and the Barbie hadn't arrived yet. My sister began to worry. Then an old beat up Dodge pulled up and took a while trying to parallel park. Out came Barbie. Well, kind of. Barbie was walking a little slow. As she got closer, my sister and I realized that this Barbie must have been in her mid-sixties. She also had a cigarette dangling from her mouth.

"Hi kids!" she said in a rather raspy voice.

We looked at each other. My sister whispered,

"Did you see the wrinkles on her face!"

"Uh, yeah. How could you miss them!"

The kids were oblivious to the imperfections of Barbie the elder. They were delighted that she came to the party!

With a little difficulty, Barbie the elder sat down on the grass while the kids climbed over her. She graciously held her cigarette away from the kids. My sister and I looked on in amazement.

"Well, at least she didn't blow cigarette smoke in their faces."

"Yes, there are always things to be grateful for."

Later that night, I thought about Barbie the elder. Did the woman who was supposed to be Barbie flake? Get sick? Was this the owner of the company's mother? Next-door neighbor? Someone she grabbed off the street?

That's one great thing about kids and pets. They don't have any expectations, so no disappointments.

BLACK AND WHITE

Until fairly recently, not only did little girls have to have impossibly thin wasp waists, enormous breasts, and long slender legs like Barbie, they also had to be white. The stories told by women of color in this chapter portray harboring feelings of "other." Internalized racism was fostered by the media with the lack of variety of skin colors that we human beings have. I'm so relieved that it is finally changing. Nowadays it's not unusual to see a little girl with an African-American looking doll.

It brings me back to a childhood memory when we took our one and only vacation from New Jersey to Florida. We rode in my dad's Plymouth Plaza through the South. At one truck stop, we stopped to go to the bathroom. There were four. Two that said "colored." I headed straight for one of those because it had a women's sign on it as well. My mother admonished me in a harsh whisper telling me I couldn't go in that one. I didn't understand and she refused to give me an answer. I will never forget that.

Cheryl is a colleague as well as my dental hygienist. I always befriend my hygienists! Maybe this is because I insist on using nitrous oxide (just kidding). Cheryl gave me two stories that touched me deeply.

Cheryl's 1st Story

My daughter was in a toddler group. I observed her through the two-way mirror they had for parents. She would go every week and her goal was to get as many baby dolls in her arms as she could. As her mom, I was just mortified. She would go up to the older girls and grab the dolls right out of their arms. Pretty soon, they'd see her coming and hide. So her teacher, Janice, in the way that the Children's Center teachers were trained, would say, "You really want those dolls, don't you?" And I was like, "Oh my God!"

I don't know what to make about inborn prejudices, but I remember there were a couple of black baby dolls and the girls would give her the black ones. My daughter didn't care. She just wanted them. I thought that was interesting. Obviously, I couldn't talk to them about it. I did make sure my daughter had a black baby doll, which was one of her favorites.

And then there was the Barbie doll phase and I wouldn't let my daughter have one. So one day she came home from a friend's house and said, "Mom, Sally has some really old Barbies and they're *sturdy*." I think my daughter used that word to convince me it was ok for her to have one. Over the years, Barbies had become thinner. Somebody eventually gave her a Barbie. At that point, I thought *whatever*. She was kind of out of her doll phase by that time anyway.

I know Gina both as a student and a theatre artist. She's from Cuba. We share a similar sense of humor.

Gina

I collect black dolls. Not for the same reason other people I've met do it. I don't understand my fascination with them other than that I'm Cuban, and in my country, as a child, I really didn't like being this white. I have always felt mixed races are more charismatic. In Cuba, we have a kaleidoscope of colors, anywhere from onyx to milky white. I really think the most beautiful people I've ever seen are those with real dark skin who have almond-shaped aqua or emerald colored eyes. I went through a period in my life when I collected black dolls, preferably with light colored eyes, when I could find them. They were all over, taking over the house until I moved into a tiny apartment. Now I have only a couple left having given away most of them to my granddaughter. Perhaps I was so attached to them because when I was a child my mother used to buy these larger-than-life porcelain dolls that I was seldom allowed to play with lest they got dirty (talk about taking the "fun" out of dysfunctional). Maybe that's the reason I loved these black dolls so much.

The black dolls were the beauty of my island and I could actually play with them when I chose to. Or on some abstract level I thought totally erased from my subconscious mind, it could have been that I had been involved in Santería, the Afro-Caribbean religion. Their entities or *Orishas* were given characteristics and colors, and they were given priority in a house, a room with an altar, fruits, special flowers—believers have these dolls dressed up accordingly to represent the Orishas. What surprises me is that I never got that into the religion to get dolls. All I know is that when I started collecting, my black Santería Orisha dolls became part of my family. They were companions of many meals prepared in my tiny kitchen until I had to let them go. They were the only dolls I felt I could handle without worrying and felt were mine.

I met Jasmine when she was a student at the community college. She's a slam poet and performance artist. Her sense of social justice is on par with mine.

Jasmine

Michonne Barbie! Super Cool! I must admit that when my mother bought me baby dolls when I was younger she got me the white dolls with brown hair... because she figured that since I'm black and white that's what my babies would look like. (Maybe a slight bit of color consciousness there.) My real babies are rainbow —they range the spectrum! But the real truth of how I've grown to understand and appreciate blackness is that all black children, regardless of their complexion, need to be comfortable with the darkest of dark skins. Why? Because the world doesn't embrace darkness. And who should be the strongest supporters of being black? None other than us lighter skinned tribes. In fact, I will go a step further to say that in this day and age all people should be buying their children black dolls, blue dolls, green dolls. It really doesn't matter. I think embracing and being comfortable with our variety of colors is important in making a "one world connection."

Lara told me her story at a party. She swore me to secrecy about her identity.

Lara

I was born in the fifties to a Caucasian father and an African American mother. They were both therapists and feminists. All this was very unusual at that time in history. I never had a doll to speak of. I think it's because all the dolls at that time, including Barbies of course, were white. My parents bought me stuffed animals. I assume this was because they were gender- and race-neutral.

Laverne's my bestie. She conducts workshops about racism, and what makes her happy is doing for others. I met her when my then-husband and her boyfriend were playing doubles in a tennis match in Monterey, San Francisco. When we met, we couldn't stop talking to each other. We never saw the match.

Laverne

I am part African American and part Caucasian. I found out the truth of being adopted when my mother who brought me up died suddenly.

As a child, I had a Chatty Kathy and a doll that was a walking doll.

My sister Larise was adopted and had just come from Korea. She couldn't speak English. She was very good at sewing and making things, so our mother encouraged her every chance she got. She tried to make her feel welcome. I was supposed to make her feel welcome, too. I had twin sisters who were older and also adopted. I was led to believe that I was the only "natural" child.

I had a walking doll with a soft body from the knees and the elbows up. She had white and pink fabric with full length pants to hide the wires that made her walk.

Larise, encouraged by our mother to sew whenever possible, took the doll and made the long pants into shorts. With the extra material, she made little bows. When I saw my doll, I totally freaked out. It became a huge emotional memory for both of us.

BOYS WITH DOLLS

I was quite happy to hear the stories from men. Never having had brothers, I was unsure what stories I might hear. I did have two sons and soon found out it's not much different, if at all. They escape with dolls, they torture them, they learn from them. Therral's story was particularly touching because it seemed the doll was the window to a reality he needed to be in.

When I told Al about my book, he asked if I took stories from men. I assured him that I did.

Al

I have very strong memories of early childhood. I can remember wearing a diaper, having a bottle, etc. I have very clear but not complete, of course, memories, just certain moments. One of the earliest ones is being in my wooden crib, wearing a diaper and standing up in it, and being very, very angry because my mom had given me a rubber baby doll. It was kind of like an over-sized Kewpie doll. I can remember taking it by its leg—I can still remember the weight and the swing and the physics involved and taking that thing by the leg and being very, very angry that she had given me a doll. I had no interest in dolls whatsoever and I knew that I was a boy and I remember taking that thing and flinging it by its leg. I can still feel the muscle memory of flinging it out of the crib, out into the room.

If I was wearing diapers, I must have been around 2 years old. I can't remember being able to speak. I had two older sisters, quite a bit older.

I do remember later on, however, friends who had Major Matt Mason. He was an astronaut doll. He was part of the NASA program. I never had one, but I thought it was cool. I remember my friend, who was preoccupied with death, brought it to school; he had a metal index card box and he'd put the doll in the box and bury it in the sand all the time. But I thought Major Matt Mason was kinda cool.

I know Brian through the local theatre community. He is an actor, director, playwright, and short story writer. This is the first story he gave me.

Brian and the Fatties

When I was very young, just starting elementary school, my sister (who was a year older) and I used to play with little plastic and rubber baby dolls that we called "Fatties" because of their rather plump appearance. We had houses set up in which they lived and we had elaborate story lines going on. When we were ready to play, we'd say, "Let's go play fatties," and everyone would know what we were talking about. That, of course, was true at home. The phrase was pretty meaningless anywhere else.

One day the entire family was at a nursery so my parents could look at some new plants. My sister and I were on our own and spied some low, moss-like ground cover. We admired it and, as children will, commented in tones that carried throughout the nursery that the ground cover would make great "Fatty grass." It was perhaps unfortunate that standing very close to us at the time was a rather heavy-set couple. They were not amused. My parents were mortified and hustled us out of there quickly. (Explaining would probably have made the situation worse; "Why did you allow your children to call their dolls "Fatties"?!)

Of course, upon reflection and removed from the nursery, the story became irresistible and was told by my parents on many occasions, usually when either my sister or I were close enough to be thoroughly embarrassed!

Diego is my firstborn. He was a high-energy child.

Diego

When he was about 4 years old, maybe 5, for some reason he had a doll. It had a porcelain face, a frilly dress, and lovely blonde curls. In Spanish, the word for doll is *Mona*. He called the doll Moni. He was in the kitchen, holding Moni with both arms, making her dance, singing, "Moni, Moni, Moni." And then suddenly without warning or change in attitude, he threw Moni as hard as he could against the kitchen floor. Moni's face shattered into many pieces. His father and I, watching this, burst out laughing. While it was quite shocking, it was wickedly funny. He then took Moni without her head, held her to his little chest, and said, "Poor Moni, poor Moni."

*I met Lucien through the local theatre community. He is a brilliant actor.
He works with children with disabilities.*

Lucien

In 1992 I graduated high school. My mother worked in the pharmacy department at the hospital in Monterey. My graduation present was purchased from the hospital gift shop, a plastic Batman doll. It was maybe 16 inches. A big one.

I showed my friends Adam, Sean, Jessica, the trio of siblings who I grew up with—am best friends with to this day still—and they thought it was the best graduation gift ever.

We just called him Giant Batman. I think maybe this was because we grew up with comics and action figures and a standard action figure was 3 or 4 inches, unlike his 16. He was christened Giant Batman spontaneously.

What I remember about that day is that I had just graduated so we were unemployed or some of us had the day off or whatever and we just spent the day at the beach with this doll, joking around, talking to it like it was a real person in front of people, taking it grocery shopping, to bars. And then the next thing I knew we were on a trip to Yosemite with Giant Batman. Sometimes we would try to catch one another off guard. While someone was doing something, we would hear someone talking and we would look around and see someone off somewhere having an intimate conversation with Giant Batman. Then, shortly thereafter, we all moved into a house together, which post-high school it kind of turned into a youth hostel-type environment. Giant Batman was there. He tended to get in a lot of fights and then people would point him out like, *What's with the doll?* And then Giant Batman, with the aid of his controller, would get aggressive with people. His controller was usually someone's hand.

Giant Batman started to earn a reputation, as well as some of his controllers, as having kind of a volatile personality. And then from there he went to England with me, Wales, one summer—I have a bunch of pictures of him there.

He moved to Texas with my friend for a while and we shipped him back and forth through the mail. When my friend got married, Giant Batman went on a honeymoon with him. There are pictures of him in Paris, Mexico, the Coliseum in Rome. He recently was in Costa Rica with one of the siblings (another honeymoon). He became part of our gang. We would just talk to him and he would listen.

It was kind of a good way of measuring people's worth. Some people would just go with it. Really like it. Other people would feel instantly alienated. Get angry.

They would say that it's just a doll. And then Giant Batman of course would get aggressive. Or one of his controllers would, and then it would just kind of escalate.

My friend Sean bought him a little suitcase like the kind for a Ken doll. So when we took him overseas there are photos of him waiting in international airports among travelers with a little suitcase. Alas, he doesn't have a passport. He just recently got a Facebook account. Again, it just started off friending people we knew. But then it just started interacting with these other phony accounts I was making. He became the antagonist who would fake celebrity accounts who had thousands of followers who thought they were the real thing. They were getting into these weird battles with the doll on Facebook depending on whether it would be Jeff Foxworthy, Sam Elliott, or Antonio Banderas, to the point of sending death threats, then requesting to be friends with Giant Batman. Giant Batman was very elitist and wouldn't accept friend requests from people he didn't know, which then led to more death threats. All kinds of stuff happened like people really pleading to be friends. There exists a video somewhere at my house of the Giant Batman show, which is kind of like the Johnny Carson show. Giant Batman is a talk show host.

My mother and then my friends' parents, they just relate to Giant Batman like he is a real person, too. So he's just been accepted. People talk about him. Spouses are fine with him. There's never any question about him being a part of everything. We sort of pass him along, too, like when someone is going through a hard time or is off on a journey, we're like, *Okay, take Giant Batman with you for protection.*

There was a time when my friend and I had Giant Batman with us out at 3 o'clock in the morning. We were wandering the streets and the police stopped us to see what we were doing and why we were out because we were young. This was in Pacific Grove. And I remember holding Giant Batman with us. It just became second nature to us after a while, even as a joke, *Oh, we're going out, let's take Giant Batman*. And then we would converse about real things we were going through and the ever-present doll would be there. This was where it kind of became like a painting that had the same painting in the painting and the painting in the painting, to infinity.

I remember sitting in my friend's living room watching the video of the Giant Batman show, kind of like the Johnny Carson show, and that everyone was laughing. I was sitting watching everyone laughing at this and one friend made the comment, like "I would like to see what a therapist would have to say about you guys in this video." Then I looked around and I realized that Giant Batman was sitting on the couch. It's been 10 years since the video's been made and people are laughing at this video, how absurd they think it is, and everyone is taking it for granted that Giant Batman is sitting on the couch with us, just like one of the boys. This is so normal to me. And it has been going on for 20 years now so it just seems part of my normal life. He lives with my friend now, who's a responsible person, got an important job, three kids. I've seen my friend have a near meltdown before when he couldn't find the Giant Batman doll. Like when I helped him move for instance, he was afraid he'd lost him. And it's great to hear like spouses say, "Oh, honey, you've got everything packed? Honey, did you remember to pack Giant Batman?"

There's a giant cat woman now. Just recently found a giant cat woman. Never had a giant Robin.

Giant Batman is different from Bruce Wayne. He was more like an entity. A lot of the posts are down now because people used to comment and I would end up deleting and blocking them. I'm looking through the mail now. This one might be one.

I wish he were here.

Steve was introduced in an earlier story he told me about his sister Roxie.

Steve's 1ˢᵗ Story

Growing up with four sisters, I had a lot of experience with dolls. Coming from an upper middle-class background, my sisters had many dolls. They had the requisite Barbies and they had collector Little Women dolls. They only had three of the four. The fourth somehow never appeared. They were supposed to sit prettily on their dressers. Each dresser would have a doll on it that no one could touch. But, of course, they were always playing with them and, as a result, one of them was missing its perfect shoes. It had a torn, frilly petticoat. It was kind of pretty, as those things go. When our mother stormed into the girls' room one day and saw the disheveled Little Women doll, she swept everything off the dresser in a furious rage.

One day, my sisters put Midge's head down the toilet and then they cut off her hair. They must have been angry at Midge for something or angry at someone else and taking it out on Midge. When our mother noticed that Midge, Barbie's best friend, had her hair completely cut off, she went downstairs and poured herself a stiff one: either a martini or a Manhattan or a Tom Collins.

Right before dinner, our parents would have their awful-tasting cocktails. I could tell they looked forward to their one, two, or three before-dinner drinks. It was bizarre.

I met Therral in an improv class in Santa Cruz. His connection to dolls and his awakening about personal freedom touched me.

Therral

I was about 4 or 5 when this happened. We had been playing down the crick and were all wet and muddy. My mom came to pick us up driving this big old LTD. It was big and black and we could all pile in there on the vinyl seats in the back. I have 65 siblings. This is true. So, we're riding along and my mom just reaches around and says, "Here, Therral, I got you something." She'd just been to the thrift store. She hands me this doll. It was a boy doll. I was surprised at how big it was. I mean, I'd seen the little dolls, but this was a doll that I could really go for and develop a relationship with. I remember it had these skimpy clothes on, which I thought was really cute, because we had to wear long sleeves and long pants and all that kind of stuff so we wouldn't get jiggers. The best thing about this doll was two things: One, when you laid it down, it went to sleep. Its eyes closed. I loved that! And I would wake it up. And two, if you fed it a bottle, it would pee. I was so into this doll. It was really, really special.

I look back now and I think it was the beginning of my own awareness of my own body. So, I was very close to this doll for years. Charlie. It's everybody's first pet name, huh? Charlie or Jimmy. It was a used doll, but I didn't know that at the time. She bought it at the thrift store and I look back and *huh*? It was new to me from the far-off land. We didn't have a lot of dolls. The dolls that a couple of my siblings had were homemade, kind of rag dolls, quilted and such. This was real plastic. The beginning of the plastic movement. I mean, it wasn't Barbie time yet. This kind of had firm substance to it, much better than those rag dolls. I couldn't get into those.

Having this doll was the first time I realized there was a world out there away from my reality and it was very exciting.

COLLECTORS' ITEMS

While the history of a collection held my attention, what was more telling was the reason behind the collection, the reactions of the children to whom the dolls were given, and the emotional weight of it all. Never having had dolls as a child and hearing about this abundance, I was surprised in the same way as when I went to my best friend's Christmas celebration and saw a similar abundance.

I met Dana through the theatre community. She's a playwright and a feminist. I was an actor in a play she wrote. She had two stories about dolls.

Dana

I was more of what you might call a doll collector. I never played with dolls. Even as a child I don't remember playing with them. Except for one time I remember I had this one doll. I think I was probably about 6 years old and she was a very pretty doll. I took her to visit family friends—not from my neighborhood—but my parents took me there to play with their daughter. And I left my doll there. When I came back to get my doll, she had cut off its hair. And I remember saying, "Well, why did you do that? How could you cut off my doll's hair?" And she said, "Well, it was messy so I just cut it off and she looks a lot better." I was outraged.

And then the next doll I got was a Tony doll. And that one had long blonde hair. I think you could style it and curl it and give it a perm or something, but I don't ever remember doing that.

And then by the time I was in the sixth grade, I started getting these foreign dolls from a great aunt that I never saw. She would go on these trips and although she didn't have any children or grandchildren, she would give these dolls to her sister, my grandmother, and my grandmother would give them to me.

I had dolls from all the European countries, basically. I could tell you a little story about each one of the dolls, just what was told to me. But as far as my relationship to those dolls, it wasn't there.

What was popular in those days was Storybook dolls. There was a series and I had the bride and the groom and a bridesmaid, and there was one called the Queen of Hearts and another one called Sugar and Spice. They all kind of looked alike, but they had different costumes. Those are real collector's items now, but my mother gave those away. She thought the foreign dolls were more valuable than the Storybook dolls, which was a mistake.

I remember going on TV in the 50s—I was in Fort Smith, Arkansas, which is the town I grew up in. They had a local TV station and I got asked to come on TV to show my doll collection. I only know this from it being quoted back to me. I don't remember it, but apparently he said, "Dana, which one of the dolls do you play with?" And I said, "Oh, I don't play with my dolls. I collect dolls." Also I had allergies and an itchy nose and I was rubbing my nose the whole time on TV. My mother was mortified.

And then there was the doll from Japan. My father went back into the service for the Korean War. He volunteered and went to Japan. He sent me back a beautiful Japanese doll of silk. I think today they are made more out of plastic. They still make them in the long kimonos, but this one had a hand-painted silk face and she is very lovely.

My mom, when my dad was away, had a boyfriend—a young soldier who got sent away to Germany and sent me dolls from Germany. So the collection just kind of grew and grew. So when I moved from California to England, I couldn't take it with me.

There was one doll that I was attached to and it was not my doll. It belonged to my step-grandmother in Oklahoma. The doll's name was Violet and she was life-sized, about 4 feet. She was like a ragdoll, just really huggable. Whenever I went to visit my grandparents, Violet would be sitting there and I would just grab her and sit with her in my lap. She was almost as big as me.

When my step-grandmother died, she left me the doll. She didn't have any children of her own. She had lots of nieces and nephews, but I got the doll and I was really, really pleased. I passed her on to my daughter as well. She's taken real good care of the dolls. She even has the one that had her hair chopped off. She had someone make a dress, almost a replica of the original dress, and got it a wig. But the wig was not blonde. The original one was blonde, but she made her a brunette and she's beautiful. And then there was the Tony doll. She got the costume made for that, a replica costume for that as well, because the original was falling apart. She has taken really good care of Violet and has gotten her new clothes. Because her head flopped around, she started wearing out just right under her neck. I sort of darned it and stitched it and tried to keep it from disintegrating—but she's kind of fragile that way.

Then there is just the head of a doll. When my mother was very young, she had smallpox, and something happened to her doll. It broke or something. So her father took the doll's head and used plaster of Paris to fix it. I don't know whether he used the doll as a mold or took a cast from the doll and then made the mold, but it's just the head of the doll that he made for her when she had smallpox. And written on it is "Given to Lisa May when she had smallpox." Each little doll has its own story.

The doll that was from Portugal is like a stuffed doll, a soft doll. She's not a raggedy doll, just soft. She has on a headscarf and on top of that a hat and two aprons, one tied in the back and another one on top. And she's carrying a little bag. The story was that she was making bread and she ran out of flour so she just put her hat on her scarf and tied back her kitchen apron and put her best apron on top and went off to town without putting her shoes on to get some flour.

I also had a Greek guard doll. I remember my delight in looking in the old Colliers magazine and there was a picture of Richard Nixon in there holding a doll just like mine when he went to Greece. I think it was when he was Vice President under Eisenhower. And he went there as an ambassador and they gave him this doll and there's a picture of him holding it. That's my doll!

I've given my daughter nearly 100 dolls. Most of them are about 6 inches, 6 or 7 inches. I do have one collection that's really nice of American Indians. An Indian chief who has a hand carved face, a very sculpted Indian looking face, and a squaw, and two little ones. The two little ones look more like the Storybook dolls looked. They look kind of plastic. But the Indian chief looks very impressive and the squaw is pretty nice, too. So I remember being very proud of that family of Indians. It was part of my heritage that there was American Indian on both sides of the family. I was always taught to be proud of my Indian heritage.

I think because I grew up in Arkansas, which is such an insulated part of the country, I never even saw the ocean until I was 19 years old. And having these dolls from foreign countries just sort of opened up my vision of the world really and—when I got the chance, I did a lot of traveling to other countries. I went to Russia and I got a doll from Russia. If I went to a country that was different, then I would bring my daughter back a doll. And then when my younger brother went into the Navy, he bought this big doll about 4 feet tall of this East Indian woman in a very exotic costume and beautiful face. She had a bare midriff and was in a sari. He brought her back onto the ship in the Navy and took a lot of whistling and catcalls from all his mates in the Navy. He brought it back for my daughter. He had a lot of fun bringing that doll back. And he said she became sort of the mascot for all the lads in the Navy while they were on the ship until he got back.

There are some dolls that my mother bought, some lovely bisque dolls (bisque is a kind of China) and she made costumes for them: Romeo and Juliet, for instance.

I bought an antique doll once in Arkansas that was supposed to have been 100 years old when I bought it, so that would make it more like 150 years old now or more. It had a broken foot, but I think it was from the Civil War time. It was china. Its head, feet, and hands were made out of china. The rest of it was cloth.

I didn't like Barbie dolls. I couldn't understand Barbie dolls in the middle of the feminist movement. It just drove me crazy. Of course, these days they have slimmed them down, the Barbie dolls, I think. They are not as exaggerated in their figures as they were in those days.

Looking back on it now, one thing I did love and that I did play with were paper dolls. I saw something just recently online that made me remember that. In McCall's magazine, I used to cut out the doll and then design dresses and then cut out my own designs. I loved cutting. And I think, in a way, Barbie dolls took the place of paper dolls, because they had all those outfits you could put on them. But I didn't see that—all I saw was that horrible exaggerated figure on the Barbie dolls.

I met Dar in the dog park. Dog park people become friends. We tell each other everything. Dar's childhood story about dolls is indicative of who she was then and who she is now.

Dar

This is about my grandmother owning a children's store. It had high-class clothes and toys and bears and dolls. Every year she'd give me a new doll. One of the classics ... I don't remember what they're called now. They're very popular. People collect them and they're worth a lot of money. She was in Longview, Washington. A nice little store in a nice little town. Because I did not like dolls, it was a little odd, but she always wanted me to be a little girl, so I got little dresses, little hats, little shoes that looked just like my dolls. If I could be a doll ... if only I could be the girl she wanted me to be ... She also used me as a model. She would take photographs and have them in the paper, have me all dressed up like the dolls. I would be in little patent leather shoes and a hat and little white gloves. I was about 4.

My mom was not part of my life a whole lot. We lived together, but we didn't have a very good relationship. I had a brother who was younger and a sister who was the youngest. After many years of my collecting these dolls from my grandmother, my mother would also buy me dolls. Every year it was, "Here's a new Barbie and a new Ken and a new box." My sister got dolls also, but she liked them.

I was made to play with this girl up the street. Her name was Debbie Jones and she was very fem. She was adopted. She was really a big brat, but she wanted to play with dolls and we were forced to play together. So we would play dolls. And I would say, "OK, I'll play dolls with you for this amount of time if you'll come outside and play ball with me. She'd always lie and trick me. We'd play dolls underneath the dining room table and I hated it. It was just about the hardest thing for me to do, to be fantasizing about Ken and Barbie. It just didn't work for me at all. I'd say, okay, now it's time to go outside and play ball and she would always have some excuse. But one day I did get her to go outside and I was trying to show her how to throw a ball and she so much didn't want to play ball that she threw the ball through a neighbor's window. Even after this my mom kept making me go to her house and play. We did that for a long time.

These dolls that my grandmother kept giving me turned out to be a really beautiful collection. Because I wasn't using them and kept them in a box, my mom put them on display in her house. That was nice, but I always knew they were mine. Well, one day they weren't in the case and I said, "Where are my dolls?" And she said, "Well, you don't play with them." And I said, "No, I don't play with them. I'm saving them. Where are they?" And she said, "I gave them to your niece." My niece was not a very responsible person and at that age—she was probably about twelve—the dolls started deteriorating until I finally took them back. Their original boxes were now mostly crushed, but I had them.

Years later, after I had taken the dolls back, I was laid off from my job. I was a grownup now. I had my son. It was summertime and I wanted to take a trip, so I decided I was going to sell the dolls. I started going around town calling people, researching and finding people who knew something about these dolls, and everybody I called—most of them were older women—was really excited to see this big collection of dolls. I met all these great old ladies who had grown up making clothes for these dolls and they knew how to repair them. They wanted to show me how. I didn't find that necessary, but I met all these wonderful old people and none of them had money to buy them. They just loved them. So they had some suggestions and I went to a store in Los Gatos that dealt with dolls primarily; the woman was really impressed with the collection and she offered me $3,000. I figured that since she was the only person I had gotten an appraisal from, if she right off the bat said $3,000, they must be worth more than that. So I started trying to find more money... and nobody would top that. Meanwhile I made arrangements for my son and me to go on a camping trip to Montana. I went back to the woman in Los Gatos. As soon as I walked back in, she gave me a look that I knew meant I was going to be screwed, and she asked, "You want to sell your dolls?" And I said, "Yes." And she said, "Well, I'll give you $1,500. And I said, "Oh, no. No more?" And she said, "No." And that's the end of my story. I got $1,500, and my son and I went on a fishing trip. That's it.

I moved into Diane's apartment in Santa Cruz when she moved to Baltimore. I used to model with her sister Celeste when she and I were in the San Francisco Models' Guild in the 1970s. Diane is a ceramicist and painter.

Diane M's 1st Story

There's a doll that my mother made when she was at Agnew's. That's the state mental institution. And, in my memory, I was 7 years old, 6 or 7 years old. It seemed she was there a long time. I finally got to visit her—we lived next door to my grandparents in a duplex so they took care of my sister and me. So I went to visit her and she gave me this doll that she made me that was like a jester doll. She had embroidered the face on it and put a jester's cap on. The doll was made out of these little round scrap pieces of fabric that were, I guess, put on like a pipe cleaner or something. The doll was probably close to 12 inches long. It was so colorful and it was in all these stacked circles of fabric. I don't remember if she made my older sister one too. She wasn't as obsessed with dolls as I was.

At the American Visionary Art Museum in Baltimore, they have this incredible thing in their permanent collection that someone who is mentally ill did: intricate embroidery and words, you know, very compulsive stuff. And she made it all out of thread from scraps of towels. She must have begged for the needles. But it's so intricate. And it is kind of interesting how the sewing arts, the crafts, can really be something that can envelop one when you are in that state. It's just like so textured and I think it has buttons on it. So it's very crazy quiltish, but it's full of this incredible embroidery that has words.

I have a feeling that what my mom got for the pieces of material was a pretty standard project back then. It had kind like a sock puppet head. It was probably something that everybody did I bet.

There was a doll that my Aunt Jane gave me on her deathbed. It was a China porcelain doll, probably from the mid-to-late 1800s. It was wearing a brown striped suit that had a blonde painted shorthair texture. I was very proud of this doll and I loved my Aunt Jane. She was very smart. She was a teacher in Santa Cruz. In fact, she lived next door to Santa Cruz High. I believe the house is torn down now. I was so happy with this doll, and wanting to show it off, that I had it in a baby carriage. It was also antique, a hand-me-down from the family. It was all wicker. I was only about 5 or 6 at the time. And the doll, the China doll, fell out of the baby carriage and the head smashed, I guess I was wheeling it really fast, showing it off or it went over a bump, who knows what? Kids don't really believe that things are going to break. And also one of the legs broke so severely, the pieces couldn't be found, so it almost looks like a peg leg today. It's a very sharp shard and the other side is a little black boot. This doll is a good-sized doll, I would say 16 inches. So I was very upset and my dad valiantly glued it back together, except for a couple of little pieces. I always admired how he put it back together. And of course, it was precious, and I never treated my dolls, or that doll anyway, like that again.

Steve's 2nd Story

I got a teddy bear for Christmas from my aunt in Omaha. When you bent it over, it made a growling sound. So I would chase my sisters around with it. I grew up and moved out of the house and never knew what happened to that teddy bear. Then I found out that my Aunt Helen in Omaha, who collects dolls, had gotten it again and was going to sell it to a collector, so I raised a stink and got it back. I have it in my room on a little table in a corner. I also have a small beanie baby teddy bear sitting on the big teddy bear's lap. I am 60 years old.

Even though I have a degree in theatre arts, I divorced myself from all things theatre for 20 years. Wilma, a fellow colleague and theatre artist, knew I had been an actor. She convinced me to do a show for the faculty at the community college. I was once again hooked and have continued acting, directing, and writing plays ever since.

Wilma's 1st Story

I remember another story about dolls. When I was 9 or 10, I started collecting (I don't even know if they have them anymore) Dolls of the World. Do they have them now? They were about an inch shorter than a Barbie.

Anyway, my doll was about an inch shorter than Barbie and a little chubbier, so she wasn't a Hollywood model type, she was a normal little girl. And you would start a collection of these things and you would get a doll from England and she would have a little British outfit on or a doll from Spain and she would have a little mantilla and castanets. Or a girl from Hawaii would have a grass skirt. The whole thing was to get as many of these as you could. And there was a competition in school, in the third or fourth grade, about who had the most dolls from around the world. We also had this competition about who could get the biggest collection of Dolls of the World.

My father was in the toy business. He was a toy salesman and he kept bringing me another doll from around the world for every holiday or every anything—Hanukkah, whatever. He built me these shelves in the bedroom I shared with my sister. The shelves were exactly the right height for the dolls from around the world.

And so my dream goal was to fill every shelf (there were three shelves). My dream was to get all these dolls. But at some point, they stopped buying me these dolls, so I had about ten of them from different countries, weird countries like Portugal, Albania and Bolivia with their little native outfits. I adored them, but I kept wanting more.

I remember the apex of this craving was when I went to my friend Myrna Hershon's house. Myrna was rich and she lived in Hewlett, which was one of the five towns that were really rich. I lived in Long Beach, which was not rich. I went to Myrna's house and she had every doll from the whole collection. She also had a cupboard in her bedroom and every shelf in that cupboard was filled with these Dolls of the World.

She had at least 25 or 30 of them. I remember feeling such envy and such anger that I was kind of immobilized. I went home and I gave all my dolls away. End of story.

I hadn't thought of that story until I started thinking about Raggedy Andy, because I remembered that was real love. But the around the world dolls were about greed or lust or competition or one-upping. When I realized that I would never win, because we were poorer than Myrna Hershon, I gave up. I just gave them all away.

Myrna used to live in our town and then they moved to the five towns. Myrna had a dress for every day of the school year. A different dress. She was sort of the talk of the school, but that part didn't bother me as much. I mean, I liked all her different dresses, but I didn't need all of them. But the dolls really cinched the deal for me.

I thought I had an upper edge because my dad would go to the annual toy fair in Manhattan and get samples of all these new games and things. He would get everything as samples. I remember my parents had a coat closet where they would put all these samples. At Hanukkah and Christmas all these samples would come out and they would be our presents. We loved them. Trains and puzzles and dolls, everything. Balls and boomerangs, all kinds of stuff.

I didn't like what was happening to me, even at that age, like 9 or 10 at the most. I didn't like how I felt having such envy. Not just jealousy, but envy, of somebody else's life that I could never have.

COMPANIONS

Something these stories have in common with others in the book is the comfort of a companion. The dolls are someone to talk to, someone who can be trusted.

These stories are not all about children. The senior in an assisted living facility found a way to combat her loneliness through her human-sized doll. It more than likely cost her about $20,000. After the woman passed, her children didn't want the doll. It now resides as a mascot in the nursing home. As a practical joke, one of my friends got permission to take him out and bring him to a birthday lunch for me. When I arrived, there he was, seated at the table. A camera crew was there coincidentally to do a photo shoot as an advertisement for the restaurant. They took one look at our "companion" and avoided us completely.

The woman who told me Beatrice's story wishes to remain anonymous. When she told me about this full-sized lifelike "companion," I was intrigued. When I saw a photo of him and then met him in person, it pretty much blew my mind. He is apparently now (after her death) a mascot of the assisted living home where she resided.

Beatrice

We have this business where we help people move from houses to assisted living and from bigger apartments in assisted living to small rooms in nursing homes—downsizing they call it. So, there was this woman, Beatrice, a very angry woman, who was moving from an apartment at Palisades Retirement Assisted Living into a studio there. She seemed confused. She had gotten our name and she needed help moving.

She groused, "People are charging me too much money. I just need to move a couple of things from two rooms into one room." First she told us her children were going to help and she didn't need us, and then her children abandoned her, so she called us and said she needed us again and this went on for a couple of weeks until it was finally moving day and no one showed up to move her. We felt bad and went down to help her.

We got to the place she was moving from. It was just your normal one-bedroom apartment. Beatrice told us that Fred was already there waiting for us. We didn't know who Fred was. We just took her word for it.

When we walked in, she was kind of rambling and we thought maybe Fred was the orderly or the physical therapist. You know, there was a lot going on. She finally said, "Here's Fred." And we were just … He looked about 65 or older. She said, "This is my companion. Fred, meet Robin and Chris." She smiled at him and said, "Of course, Fred gets the good chair." And here's this guy. Very lifelike. He looked so real, completely life-sized, sitting in the only chair. He looked quite comfortable. He was wearing glasses and had a book in his lap. Beatrice chose to sit on the edge of the bed to watch TV with Fred, because there was only so much space. You can't fit that much into these rooms.

We honestly thought he was real at first. He was just sitting there so relaxed. He scared us. It just took a few seconds to realize he was a doll. He had wispy grey hair. He looked like an elderly pre-teen, with weird boobs.

They didn't allow dogs in assisted living, so she had Fred. She was about 88, I think. And she'd had Fred for about 5 years. He was quite something. Who knows what Fred was capable of? There he was in his khakis and red sweater, wearing a watch. I wonder what time he thought it was?

In her mind, she had obviously gotten screwed over by her husband and her daughters, so she was all alone, except for Fred.

I wonder what's going to happen to Fred when she dies? He probably gets everything! She probably even has him listed as an in-patient at Palisades Retirement and has to pay for him!

I met Dana through the theatre community. She's a playwright and a feminist. I was an actor in a play she wrote. This is her 2nd story.

Dana Talking About Tina

What I just thought of is not my story, but it's one of the sweetest, most wonderful stories I've ever heard. Her name is Tina and she lives in San Jose. Her mother died when she was quite young. She had two brothers and the father was all of a sudden a single father.

He ended up sending the two boys away to a residence school—what do you call it? Boarding school. She remembers going on her birthday. They went to the boarding school to see her brothers who had gotten together—it was a Catholic boarding school—and bought their little sister a statue of the Virgin Mary, a glow-in-the-dark statue. She took that home with her. It meant so much to her. She spent many hours in her closet with her glow-in-the-dark statue of Mary.

I met Francine through the theatre community. Her story about giving away her most precious doll to a boy who was less fortunate than she touched me deeply.

Francine

I have memories of the dolls I loved as a child. But one doll remains a part of me to this day. When I turned eleven—in 1959 —my paternal grandparents gave me the best birthday present of my young life. No one else in the family had ever given me anything other than practical things like underwear, socks, second-hand toys, or clothes too big so that I would grow into them. I unwrapped the large package and saw that it was a cardboard suitcase. The writing on the box said some things on it I don't recall but indicated what was inside. My father was filming me unwrapping my gifts. He was an amateur filmmaker. In the 50s, he used 8mm film. I have it somewhere in the stack of old home movies. He caught my joy and awe as I brought out Jerry Mahoney from his case. Packed in with him was a handmade pair of pajamas and another outfit made by my grandmother.

I learned to throw my voice spending happy hours alone with my new best friend. I wondered if someday I might upgrade to a Jerry with eyes that moved, like the one on the Paul Winchell Show. But for now, I could not have been happier.

One time I planned a puppet show for the little kids on the block. But at the last minute I bailed. I was too shy to be a ventriloquist in public. The kids' moms were mad because I had disappointed their children.

I made a bed for Jerry and put it next to mine. I became accustomed to the feel of him on my lap, my hand in his back holding the dowel and pulling the string that made his mouth move. He became animated, a part of me and at the same time a separate being.

We would have long conversations. About what, I don't remember. It was safer than writing in a diary. My mother once told me that writing things down was dangerous because someone could find it. I tore up what I wrote when I left my room. I didn't trust my mother. I felt safe with Jerry. He was my best friend.

When I was 20, I went apartment hunting with two friends. We were about to settle on an old house in Palo Alto near where we all worked. The landlady was a single mom with a young son. He must have been about 8 or 9. He had webbed fingers on his hand. I felt sorry for him. I thought about all the stuff I'd have to move and wondered *Did I want to take Jerry Mahoney with me for the rest of my life? Every time I moved?* He had been shelved for several years at that time. On impulse (a regrettable trait I have), I offered the boy my Jerry Mahoney doll. I told him how special he had been to me and that my grandmother had made the extra clothes for him. In the end, my friends and I decided not to take the house, but I don't remember why.

Years later I began to regret having given my puppet away. I had fantasies of finding him in an antique shop, my own long-lost Jerry, along with Grandma's hand sewn clothes. One day in an antique store, I did find a puppet like Jerry. His name was Danny O'Day. He was in good condition and the asking price was so reasonable I could not resist. It felt so good to hold him on my lap like I did Jerry all those childhood years ago.

Soon afterward, I stumbled upon a Charlie McCarthy. I was developing a collection. After five dolls of different sizes and no Jerry, I realized that there had to be some Jerrys out there. I went onto eBay and, to my delight, there were several original Jerry Mahoneys for sale. The prices and conditions varied. I bid on one that looked to be in good condition, while some did not. The cost was affordable as well, and soon I had Jerry back in my life and the hole in my heart and soul filled.

I know Melissa as a fellow colleague in the community college. She is like a sister to me. She's down-to-earth with the kind of laughter that lights up the room.

Melissa

My first doll had bright orange hair and a gingham orange dress and plastic pull string. She said something. I can't remember her name.

A story I remember was when I was going over to my grandmother's house for Christmas and all the godchildren were getting presents from their godparents. I didn't get one because my godparents were on my mother's side, so all my cousins were getting all these extra presents and I was just sitting there. My very favorite uncle, Lorenzo, who later died of AIDS must have noticed that I looked sad. He came out with a cheap doll that was supposed to look like a Barbie in plastic cellophane with a paper label on the top. I remember thinking she was a cheap Barbie, but it didn't matter, because of his kindness. He happened to have an extra doll. It was the fact that he even noticed that mattered so much to me, even though it was a cheap Helen or Sally, it wasn't even a Midge or whatever the Barbie names were. It was a "Betty," but I loved it just the same.

One thing I used to do was use my mother's high-heeled shoes to be Barbie's cars. I also used to (weird part of our psyche) have the male Barbies have the female Barbies in bondage, that sort of helpless Barbie. They wouldn't ever have sex or anything because I didn't know what that meant, but there was always that submissiveness, the male dominance.

I guess it's a pretty vivid image I always carry in mind. My parents had little money, and with three kids and one salary, buying toys was not a priority. But my Mom always improvised things for us to play with. However, when I turned 9 and later 10, I got my two dolls that I loved very much. Funny enough, as I think of this now, I realized that I never gave my dolls a name; they were just my dolls.

My first doll was blond-haired with blue eyes. She had a white blouse and pants, a cognac, light-chocolate hooded jacket with a zipper in front and white shoes. For some reason, I always thought of her as my Eskimo doll, even though she did not look like one. But her hooded jacket with the fur around the hood made me think of that.

The second doll was brunette with green eyes and had a lovely light lime green dress in a see-through material imprinted with flowers. It had a solid white camisole and underskirt. She also had an elegant hat with large bows all made from the same green material and white shoes. That was my elegant doll and I always imagined that I would be getting dressed like that when I grew up.

Very seldom would I play with the dolls because I didn't want to break them or tear their clothing (made from not-too-resilient fabric), but every so often I would comb their hair and give them a manicure and pedicure (without using a hair brush or nail polish—just pretending). I would take their clothes off and pretend to iron them and then get them dressed again. But most of the time I would talk to them from a distance. My bed had a bookshelf right next to and above it (it was a double pull-out bed that had part of it hidden under the bookshelf.) So my dolls would sit on top of the bookshelves and I could see them both from any part of my room. Most of the time I would talk to my dolls in the morning, at night (before going to bed), or when I came home from school.

Unfortunately, my dolls did not have a very long life. I was about 16 years old when one day I came from school and did not see them. I knew there was only one person who would take them. I went to my little brother and I asked him where my dolls were. He said he didn't know anything about them. Later on, I found out that he took them and gave them to one of my next-door neighbor's daughters who tore them apart, clothes and all, in less than 10 minutes. I was very upset and I cried when I heard that. They were very precious to me; they were my little friends.

The only other dolls I remember were when I was very little (around 5 to 6 years old); my mother used to use the back of an old wooden spoon to make dolls (she did that for my sister too when she was little); she would put a piece of cloth on the front part of the spoon and tie it at the base of the spoon (beginning of the handle) to make the scarf and the dress; then she would draw a few dots for the eyes and nose, a line for the mouth and a few lines at the top part for a little bit of hair (bangs). So we used to hold the dolls/spoons by the handle (which was covered by the piece of cloth) and treat them like real dolls.

But any time somebody talks about dolls, the image of my two little dolls pops in my mind right away. They were my most precious dolls and friends.

DEAD AND GONE

Both of these poignant stories stayed with me for a long time. Daraj, one of the few men I interviewed, had an opportunity to speak about death to a little girl, much to the relief of her mother. He has many years as a theatre artist and was the Santa in a department store. I'm pretty sure this encounter was deeply moving for him as well. The second story left me wondering just how much good it was doing to tell this little girl that when people die, they turn into dolls.

Daraj is a fellow actor. He's also a playwright and works with children. This Santa Claus story is very sweet.

Daraj

I had a job being Santa one year. It was at a local community center. Most of the children got on my lap and asked for the latest doll that was advertised on TV. I would sneak a look at their parent to see if buying that was even remotely possible before I would reassure them that it just might happen. If I saw a worried look on the face of the adult who brought them there, I would tell the child that Santa had to buy a lot of toys and dolls for lots of children and sometimes he didn't have enough even if they had been very good all year.

One afternoon, a little girl shyly got up on my lap and looked directly at me, how children do, with her bright blue and trusting eyes. When I asked her what she wanted for Christmas, after we had gone through the preliminary questions about being good, she simply said, "I want a picture of my brother."

I wasn't sure what to say to that and glanced over at her mother who looked distraught.

"You want a picture of your brother? Is that all?"

She nodded her head in agreement, looking deeply into my eyes with total faith that I would comply.

I couldn't help but ask her, "Where is your brother?"

"He's in heaven."

I looked over at her mother whose head was bowed. What happened next was a spur of the moment discussion about death. I owed it to the little girl and to her mother. I'm not totally sure what I said, but whatever it was seemed to satisfy the little girl. She hopped off my knee and took her mother's hand. The mother smiled at her little girl and then lifted her head until our eyes met. There was no mistaking that.

I met Kenzie at a party. When I talked to her about my book, she offered this story. Very sad and loving.

Kenzie

A friend of mine died recently. He left two young daughters, one who is 4 years old. My daughter, good friends with their family, was cuddling with the four-year-old after her father died. She said to my daughter, "My daddy died." My daughter replied, "I know." She then said, "My mommy told me that when people die they turn into dolls." My daughter replied, "Oh."

When my daughter told me this story, we both looked at each other and said, "How creepy!" First of all, is she going to think now that all of her dolls are dead people? Or is she going to spend the rest of her life looking for her daddy in a doll? We are hoping that she probably misunderstood something that her mom had said. Maybe it was something about your spirit leaving your body. Let's hope so.

DOLLS AND THE STAGE

When I was 11½, I was thrust into the culture of another state by my parents' moving from New Jersey to Los Angeles. I had to find a way to somehow fit in. Having curly hair, uncool clothes, and a thick New Jersey accent assured me of having no friends. Watching our school play, The Diary of Anne Frank, gave me the idea that maybe I could pretend I was someone else by wearing costumes and speaking in unusual ways to help hide my shyness. It worked. Luckily for me, my parents were not against this newfound interest. These two stories are glimpses into the fantasy world of theatre. They depict how loving parents can support their children and bring them into the magical world of make-believe.

Brian's 2nd Story

My mother had done a lot of knitting and sewing. She soon started making dolls. Generally, she would just find a doll. It wasn't a matter of buying a doll. It would be found at a garage sale or something in some grubby state or whatever.

When I directed *Ten Little Indians*, my mother made the Indian dolls that were on the mantle and were one by one slowly disappearing. She made those using apple heads, the dried apple heads. She made a different Indian doll for each of the *Ten Little Indians*. We gave them away at the end to cast members. And, of course, I kept one. I still have it. The apple has gone completely black, but it still works.

My father never saw the dolls my mother made for me. My mother first started making me dolls after my dad died. I think it was basically a way to kind of be connected to what I was doing. I was in my late 40s.

Both my parents were really kind of behind me doing theatre, although when I got out of grad school and told them that I just wanted to go and find a theater company or something like that, both of them sort of raised their eyebrows like, *and how are you going to support yourself?* type of thing. Absolutely true. No way to support yourself doing that, and I didn't do it.

I had friends who ran away to New York and that type of thing and, as is typical, they are not making it. But my parents were both supportive. My dad's support was what I called kind of quieter than my mother's. My dad did posters for some of the shows. He did the poster for *Ten Little Indians*. He did the poster for *The Importance of Being Earnest*. He did the poster for *Playboy of the Western World* when I did that at Cabrillo College. Things like that. So he kept his hand in that way. My mother wanted to be supportive. If there was a costume that needed to be made, she would work on it.

For instance, she made the costume for a friend named Sue for *The Importance of Being Earnest*, when I directed that. She didn't make a lot of costumes, but she did make that one. And then she made a doll with that specific costume.

Sue didn't know she was going to get the doll. I think my mother surprised her with that one. And then, of course, Sue wanted to keep the dress that my mother had made specifically for her. And the theater company was saying, no, that's our property. It was made for us. Eventually a friend of Sue's went to the theater company and bought it for her. So Sue does have the dress and the doll.

That was something that she did—the dolls for me. The first one that she did was for *A Christmas Carol*. And that one came as a surprise to me. I don't believe that I knew she was making it. She came to see the show first because, of course, she didn't really know anything about what the costume was.

She saw the play and she gave it to me after—it might have been before the run was over, I'm not really sure. She created the doll from that. That was just kind of a standard Victorian men's costume. It wasn't a big sort of to-do type of thing it was just—she had it, she did it, she brought it, and that was that. I don't think she came to opening night. I can't remember exactly when she saw the show or how she developed the doll. But then after that, it wasn't a matter that she was going to do dolls for every show that I was in, because she didn't. But for the ones that kind of struck her fancy, then she would busy about and do a doll out of it. It was a loving gesture to her son. And, as I say, it was also a way of keeping involved with what I was doing. Not that she didn't have involvement with her church groups and stuff like that, but to keep some involvement with me, this was a way of doing that.

My mother basically made just character dolls. And sometimes, like with the character in *Times Square Angel*, she didn't even really try to do a doll that looked like the character that I was playing. In fact, on that one, I'm not sure whether she saw the show because I told her it was such a dreadful show that she probably didn't want to see it. I told her that one of the characters I played had some magic stuff, so she took it from there and did this kind of swami-looking doll from that. But it had nothing to do with the character I was playing in the show. The show was terrible and the production was terrible, but the doll was wonderful.

Generally speaking, I didn't have the dolls during the show. It was usually either close to the end of the run or after the show was over. I did show them to people. I showed them to the cast.

I can't remember what Sue's Lady Bracknell dress looked like, because that one—I know my mother spent a lot of time on that one because she was trying to duplicate the dress that she'd made. And she really did. I mean she really duplicated it. That one and the Major General from the *Pirates of Penzance* are the two that are the closest to what people were actually wearing in the show. Those were ones that she spent extra time on.

Of course, I've got them now. I don't have them out. I don't have a place to really display them. Although having taken them out now and looked at them, I thought, okay, I do have a place where I could put one out and rotate the others in. But I'm the only one who's really going to see it because there are not many people who drop by and come into the house. At least for me they would be there. They are not something that goes to a specific theater so I couldn't give them to a specific theater and have them displayed. And it wouldn't really mean anything to the theater because it only means something to me.

Wilma's 2nd Story

My daughters, Valerie and Johnna, knew Tommy Marquez. Tommy, Johnna's best friend, did costumes for Cabrillo stage and he also worked in Hollywood a lot. He still does.

The three of them were actively involved in collecting as many Barbies as they could. We would go to Goodwill and find Barbies, find them just everywhere, for presents. Tommy would make costumes for them, and I would make little outfits out of old socks and little spandex dresses and stuff like that. We had an active Barbie life going on.

One of the things Valerie did as a little girl, which she told me other people did a lot, was that she would behead them. But then they would put them back on.

The ultimate Barbie story is that when my kids were little I was in a production of the *Bacchai* at Cabrillo. Because I was a single mom at the time, I would bring my kids to rehearsal. They would sit in the theater and we would do the *Bacchai* rehearsal, which was about Bacchus, the God, and his mother whom I played (whose name I can't remember), and whom evidently, he beheads at the end. No, she beheads him. I don't remember. Anyway, she beheads him and she eats his head or something and there's blood all over the place. There's wild dancing.

I remember Judy Slattum, the director, wanted us to be with one breast exposed so we all did that. It was the 70s. So, okay, they would come with me to rehearsal. And then one rainy weekend, after the show was well over, the kids were out in the living room with all of the Barbies spread out and I hear: *Oh Dionysus, king of this, king of wine* or something. I go in and they have all the Barbies dressed in togas with one breast exposed and they have Dionysus. They have the mother with blood all over her hands and they have all the Barbies dressed for the production.

They had memorized every line of the production, and they were reenacting the Bacchai with Barbies. They probably used ketchup for blood. They had the whole thing set up. And they were little. So that was a wonderful experience with Barbies, that they became Greek tragedians.

126

DOLLS' DEMISE

The reactions to the death of their dolls in this chapter range from utter despair to amusement. When our mother threw out the paper sack that contained our rabbit puppets, I felt a deep sense of betrayal. Sometimes dolls are the only material possession that a child feels is truly their own.

Carmela was a student at the community college. She should be a poet.

Carmela

I am now 33 years old and thinking about all the ups and downs I've been through on this road called life. When I was 8 years old, the same age as my son is now, my grandma gave me a porcelain doll for my birthday. I was filled with so much joy. As I got older, I gave all my dolls away.

Recently I was in a thrift store and came across the same doll my grandmother had given me when I was 8 years old. The doll had been through hell and back, just like me. The face had been cracked and glued back together—just like my heart; the clothes had been ripped and sewn back together—just like my pride; the pants were full of holes—just like my soul. Was it God's way of telling me I'm still the beautiful porcelain doll inside that still survived through faith?

I met Diane in an improv class. She's a brilliant monologist, comedienne, humanitarian, and artist.

Diane G's 1ˢᵗ Story

When I was about 7 years old, I had one of those dolls that was the same size as me. It was stuffed and had little elastic feet so that you could put it on your feet and dance with it. I really loved that doll and, honestly, I don't think I ever gave it a name, but I really liked her. This is a simple story really.

This is Cleveland, Ohio, the Midwest, and the homes, including mine, had basements—and in the winter and any time of the year, actually, our basements would quite often flood. I will never forget this one day when I came home from school and my mother hadn't been home yet. We both came in at the same time. It was really raining hard and I was about to go down into our basement where my father had put up a stage for me. It wasn't a raised stage. It was on the floor where he had created a curtain that opened and closed. I was going to go down there and play with my doll, but I couldn't get past maybe the third step. The entire basement was completely flooded. Our cat was missing also. It was just awful. So finally, it subsided a bit and I went down to the basement with my mom (we both wore boots). The cat was fine. He was sitting on top of the washing machine. But there was my doll floating face down in this yucky water. I just remember my mother saying, "We can't keep this. It's full of...possibly...it's unhealthy." It was very traumatic.

I remember it was a time in my life when I felt like I had something I was attached to and I loved and I felt like I hadn't even gotten time to enjoy it that much and she drowned. It was just misery. I don't know. A little kid seeing a basement completely flooded. It was bizarre. And there were a lot of things floating. Anything that had been on the floor was floating. So there she was, my poor doll.

Kari is a visual artist. I loved her story of Agatha the Cleaning Lady.

Kari

My mom made soft sculpture dolls and sold them at art shows. One doll didn't sell, a cleaning lady character. She became mine and lived happily in a bucket on top of a shelf in my room. She was named Agatha (I was heavily into reading Christie then). She met her demise when a bat flew into our window and roosted with Agatha before my dad caught and killed it. Sadly, Agatha the Cleaning Lady was deemed unsanitary and tossed into the trash.

I met Katie through a writing group. The strength of love between siblings rings through this story.

Katie

My brother, a troubled person who eventually committed suicide, acted out against the cranky, snoopy old lady across the alley, ironically named Mrs. Good, by dismembering all my dolls and throwing them, limb by limb, heads last, into her back yard. I always liked his sense of humor, and rather than becoming angry —which I think he also would have enjoyed—I found this delightful. My mother did not.

Pat's 2nd Story

I grew up in Los Angeles and I had a wonderful rag doll. It was very special. I was 5 or 6, and I was a little girl with brothers who were 12 and 13 years older than me. They liked to shoot pellet guns. Brothers.

They took my doll and hung her by her neck. Are these the kind of stories you wanted? This story makes my husband cry. They hung her by her neck and shot her full of pellets. It was horrible. Now I think it's kind of funny.

You know, you learn to live with this. These are bad doll stories.

DON'T BE CRUEL

Larise is a good friend of mine. Her story about mending a broken doll and secretly keeping it for herself in an orphanage is fraught with fear, violence, and the need for survival. I performed this story as a monologue. To this day, Larise makes handmade dolls and has been responsible for many children feeling loved and safe.

Larise is my best friend's sister. There were four young women in this family, all adopted. She was born to a Korean mother and an African American soldier. She still makes dolls and is a survivor of sexual abuse. I wrote this story as a monologue and performed it using movement and masques in an Artists in Residence community group.

Larise

Do you want to be happy?

Gone are the days when my heart was young and gay
Gone are my friends from the cotton fields away
Gone from the earth to a better land I know
I hear their gentle voices calling, Old Black Joe

I'm coming, I'm coming, for my head is bending low
I hear their gentle voices calling, Old Black Joe

Why do I weep, when my heart should feel no pain
Why do I sigh when my friends come not again
Grieving for forms now departed long ago
I hear their gentle voices calling, Old Black Joe

I'm coming, I'm coming, for my head is bending low
I hear their gentle voices calling, Old Black Joe

Where are the hearts once so happy and so free
The children so dear that I held upon my knee
Gone to the shore where my soul has longed to go
I hear their gentle voices calling, Old Black Joe

—lyrics of "Old Black Joe"

First Home

I am Amerasian. My Korean name is Yung Su. I am half black and half Korean. This is what I remember when I was five and a half years old. I had three brothers, Yung Giree, Su Yong Yee, and Myong Myongani, and one sister, Chun Su, and my parents, who were very kind to me. Our house was a restaurant with four rooms. I learned later that our house was a house of ill repute.

Sometimes the police came on a raid and we ran for our lives out the back door. Often I saw girls dressed up in traditional Korean clothes wearing make up, sitting with men and serving them on the coffee table in the restaurant.

Sometimes my siblings and I played a fun game of running into the marketplace to see what we could grab.

One night a man spent the night at our house. He slept in the communal room in which our whole family slept, next to me. He pulled me into him. This was not a good memory.

On the playground, an older teenage boy pulled me against him too.

Even though monks came to our house and we said Buddhist prayers, the restaurant also celebrated Christmas. We knew it was a holiday and that we had to behave and be good or we wouldn't get something from Santa. We didn't know who Santa was, but we knew he put nuts in our shoes if we put them outside the night before near the chimney. It is dark outside and we have to go behind the house to put our shoes on the chimney. I am afraid to think of a stranger on our chimney, so I never do it. I put my shoes out, but I never go to get them back in the dark. My father always asks for the head of a horse or a cow. He never gets that.

My father has a job wallpapering and also making paper lanterns. He drinks a lot of alcohol. He beats my mother and that scares us. One time he threw a table and beat her. He was always kind to the children, though.

My mother makes rice wine there although it is illegal. She tried to commit suicide three times in front of me and sometimes she pretends she is dead.

One time when she was trying to jump into our well, she fell down and hit her head. When I saw her, she had a gash on her head and was lying down on a cot.

My mother has a hard time with me. My mother also never takes me with her on trips. She gets very angry and spanks me or beats me and then she cries. If I wet the bed, I have to put a basket that is used for grains on my head and run through the village with no clothes on. The people in the village can beat the back of the basket with a stick if they want to. It doesn't hurt if they do that. The basket almost covers me.

My sister sometimes repeats what other children say about me. They call me a name that means "nigger" in Korean. It's *kam dung ee*. That word hurts my feelings. My sister tells me that they say I am African. I understand that it is bad to be African.

My mother goes away now for two days. When she comes back, she asks me if I want to be happy. I know she wants me to say yes. She gives me the choice. I understand that if I go to live somewhere else, I will be happy. So, the next day I say goodbye to everyone in my family. My mother takes me to an agency and someone from the agency takes me to the orphanage. I wear my best clothes: a red jumper and a white blouse.

The Orphanage

In the orphanage, there are three groups of children: the babies, the 4–5-year-olds, and the 6–12-year-olds. After 12 or 13, they say you won't be adopted. The younger children sleep in cribs of bamboo. The older ones sleep on cots of bamboo or on the floor. When I get there, they think I've had pneumonia, so they make me sleep with my head against the door, not facing the other children so I won't contaminate them. That is lucky for me because when I wet the bed, the heater nearby dries me off so I don't get in trouble for that.

I am 7 years old, so I'm in the group with the oldest children. There are about 24 of us. We are all Amerasian. Half of us are part white and half are part black. This is because of the American soldiers, I find out. There is one 100% Korean girl. She has a disability, and no one thinks she will ever get adopted. She is mute.

They tell us we are going to get to go to America or Hawaii, so they are trying to get us used to using English. They have us call some of the workers "Sister" and the others "Mommy."

It's Christmas time and we're going to go to the army base to see the soldiers. One little boy, who has the lightest skin color, is chosen to wear red pants, a red sweater, and a red hat. He doesn't want to. So "Sister," as we were taught to call her (a girl of about 16 or 17), shoves him to the ground so hard that his face starts to bleed. When he gets up, he has big bruises on his forehead and cheek that are swelling up. After that, he puts on the clothes.

All of us are physically and emotionally abused in the orphanage. There are dolls that the American soldiers have given to the orphanage on the walls. We aren't allowed to touch them or play with them. There is a toilet brush that is used as a decoration on the wall, too. If the worker called Sister doesn't think we are asleep, she hits all of us on the head with it, except her favorites. There is also a wooden stool that she beats us with. Sometimes as punishment we have to put our hands above our heads until they tell us we can put them down again.

We take baths together in a huge tub that looks like a swimming pool. Yesterday the little mute girl wasn't moving fast enough, so Sister hit her on the head with a cup that we use to wash ourselves with. She hit her so hard that her head busted open. The blood was all over. She was fired today.

The children who look the most white are treated better than the ones who are half black. The teachers have their favorites. I am never one of them.

We are at the army base today. I look at the long tables with white tablecloths on them filled with plates of hard candies. Some have jelly inside and some have chocolate. They sparkle like jewelry. There is a huge Christmas tree there, too. They make us eat American food—turkey, mashed potatoes, gravy, and cranberry sauce. We aren't used to it, but we have to eat it in order to get our Christmas stockings from Santa. We have to sit on his lap and then he will give us a red plastic stocking filled with an orange, an apple, one pair of socks, and candy.

The soldiers come and visit, especially during Christmas. They bring candies and dolls. The nuns hang the dolls up high on the walls because we can't be trusted to play with them. The dolls are not to be touched.

Now I will tell you the doll part: The house next door to the orphanage has a barbed wire fence with a hole in it. I like to play in the field next to the hole. I peek through the hole imagining what the world might be like outside. One day, I see the body of a doll lying close to the hole. The doll—with one arm, two legs, and no head—had been tossed aside. For days, I squeeze my skinny arm through the hole desperately trying to reach the doll. It is just beyond my reach. Finally, I find a stick, poke the doll closer and get the doll to the hole, grab it, and pull it out. I hide the doll under my arm, in my armpit, so the nuns won't find it and throw it away. Because I am very, very good and not likely to get adopted, there are hours when no one pays much attention to me during the day. During this time, I wash the doll and use some fabric to make her a molded head, an arm, and a pretty dress. I tell her all my secrets. She knows everything.

I hear there is another orphanage. That one has all Koreans. They never get adopted.

Last summer in the woods, Sister taught us some American songs. She hit us with a long willow stick if we sang the wrong words. We didn't know what they meant. The songs were "Old Black Joe" and "Onward Christian Soldiers."

Yesterday, "Teacher" pulled me out of the line in dance class. I was ushered into the cafeteria and a black man was sitting in the dining room. I had to sing "Old Black Joe" to him. I didn't know why. That man took me out to lunch. I didn't know what to say to him. All I knew was "sister" and "mommy" so I said nothing.

I imagine that all Americans are either black or white. At the orphanage, they said if dark people adopted you, it would be better because they were nicer than white people and we would get fewer beatings.

Today a social worker told me I was going to be adopted. I was going to get to go to the United States. She said another social worker would take me there. I can't believe how lucky I am!

The United States

I don't recognize my new father as the man who I sang to in the cafeteria and who took me out to lunch. He isn't in his uniform. When I see my new mother, I am worried. She has on red nail polish and makeup on her face. Only prostitutes like those in our restaurant did that where I came from. I am hoping that she will beat me soon; then I'll know that I won't be sent away.

My sisters have light skin. They aren't dark like the soldiers. The oldest are twins. My younger sister is three years younger than me. They are sweet and wonderful. They told me they wrote me letters and sent them to Korea, but I never received any. We all have names that start with the letter "L." My father taught the sister closest to my age how to say two things in Korean: *Ahpple*, which means hurt, and *Benzo*, which means bathroom. She says those two words all the time to me. She is becoming annoying very fast.

My first Christmas with my new family is at the Ford Ord military base. There is a lot of commotion. There is a Santa Claus, decorations, a tree, and lights. My sister LaVerne made cookies for Santa. I know we have to behave and go to bed early. I am still afraid of Santa Claus because he is a stranger.

It is morning and there are presents everywhere. There are even presents for me. I got a bowling set, lots of clothes, and a stuffed dog that I saw in a store and told my new mother I liked. I still have that stuffed dog my new mother gave me for me my first Christmas. I named it after an uncle. Its name is Bok Don Ye.

There are many new customs I am learning in my new home in the United States. Everything is different. I try hard to be good. I especially want to please my new father because I am afraid if I am bad, I will be taken away from my family and then I won't be happy.

Last night, my sister was sick. My new father is giving her a rubdown to get rid of the fever. Now he is doing the same to me although I'm not sick.

My sister is still sick so she crawled into bed with my mom. My dad crawls into my bed and is doing bad things to me. He tells me not to tell anybody.

It took me 20 years to tell. He is a decorated sergeant in the army. He is famous now for his bravery in the war. I confront him after my mother dies. He admits that he did it, but doesn't apologize.

I will never forgive my father, but I love the United States and am very proud to be a citizen. Every 4th of July, I lead a group of friends and family on a march around the neighborhood. We sing American songs, bang pots and pans, and carry the American flag. At the end of the march, I dance in a circle around a big firecracker that we light in the middle of the street, and that starts our 4th of July festivities.

"Onward, Christian Soldiers"

Onward, Christian soldiers, marching as to war,
With the cross of Jesus, going on before!
Christ, the royal Master, leads against the foe;
Forward into battle see His banners go!

Onward, Christian soldiers, marching as to war,
With the cross of Jesus going on before!

At the sign of triumph Satan's host doth flee;
On, then, Christian soldiers, on to victory!

Hell's foundations quiver at the shout of praise;
Brothers, lift your voices, loud your anthems raise!

Like a mighty army moves the Church of God;
Brothers, we are treading where the saints have trod.
We are not divided, all one body we;
One in hope and doctrine, one in charity.

Onward, then, ye people, join our happy throng;
Blend with ours your voices in the triumph song.
Glory, laud and honor unto Christ the King;
This through countless ages men and angels sing.

Larise is 60 years old now and still makes dolls.

DON'T TOUCH

Hearing these stories about teasing the children with beautiful dolls that they were forbidden to touch was surprising and sad to me. I was first going to call this book Up High on the Walls because of that. Children have so many rules as it is that not being allowed to touch their dolls seemed cruel.

Geraldine's 2nd Story

When I was a kid, about 5 or 6, my mother sent me this beautiful elephant from America. It was all yellow and pink, all very velvety with big, long ears, and my grandmother wouldn't let me play with it. She wrapped it in a white cotton sheet and kept it in the bottom of a wardrobe and whenever she went out shopping, I would sneak into the bedroom and I would take the elephant out of the sheet and play with it and then I would quickly wrap it up in the sheet before she came home and put it back in the wardrobe.

My mother sent it from America. But my grandmother wouldn't let me play with it because she was frightened it was going to get dirty.

Johnny was a student at the community college. It's always interesting to hear about dolls from a male point of view.

Johnny

My grandma had Barbie dolls I thought were porcelain in a big glass and mirrored display case. When I was really young, I went and opened it up and reached for one. My mom grabbed my hand just in time and then I heard my grandma hollering from the other room. I don't remember exactly what she said, but it was something like, "Oh, no, you can't play with that." My grandma was a big, overweight lady and she was braying, "Johnny, you don't play with the dolls... they're not toys, they're really important. This one is Miss So-and-So from 19-whatever." I don't know ... she gave me a date and a name. She started telling me about all of them. They freaked me out. They were like a bunch of porcelain dolls who were staring at me. They were always creepy because it was at the end of this hallway and it was always really dark. All you could see was their eyes twinkling at you, about 100 of them. This was around the time that Chuckie was coming out, so it really freaked me out. I was not happy. It scared me. I was pretty little. I must have been about 4 or 5 years old.

Laura Laura is a librarian at the community college where I work. She is also a visual artist. When you read her poignant story, try to imagine it with a southern accent.

Laura Laura

I have dolls. Being a girl in the South, you grew up with dolls and there were some that you played with and some that you just looked at. My mom has some china porcelain dolls that her grandmother brought over from Germany when she came and those were the "look at" dolls. They lived in the cedar chest. My mother is 94, and they're still in the cedar chest at her home and she brings them out any time one of the three girls visit her. It's like "the bringing out of the dolls," but you can't really touch them, you can only look at them. I had the obligatory Barbies and those were "play with" dolls and then there were just the rag dolls, the Raggedy Ann dolls. I had an Aunt Esther who made Raggedy Anns. Until I was 20-something I thought she had invented them. So Raggedy Anns you got to cuddle when you were sick.

So there have always been all different kinds, and they always had unspoken rules about them. Now what I do is I "liberate them." I find dolls in second-hand stores. People give me their dolls. If they're the ones that come in that plastic thing and they have the long, curly hair and flippy eyelashes and impossible dresses and stuff, the first thing I do is cut all their hair off until it's like *Schindler's List* short and then I take their eyelashes off and take their little clothes off. They're just liberated. They have more personality than they ever did when they were first put in those little boxes. And then I take their arms off. I rearrange their legs. I take one leg from another doll and then put it on somebody else. Or replace the leg completely with a piece of furniture: a furniture leg or a wheel. Sometimes I take their arms apart with a cloth body and insert teeth or barbed wire or something and then put a coat hanger on the back, a wooden coat hanger or whatever, and those are the angels. It's funny because a lot of times people think I'm referring to Christ when they see these dolls that are obviously angels. Their arms are spread out and their feet kind of just go together naturally. Mostly it's atheists who think that. It's kind of funny.

When people ask me what I do with art, I tell them I rip the heads off of baby dolls and then they either want to talk to me or they don't. People are either drawn to them or repulsed by them (dolls in general—the scary-eyed dolls). Someone always has a story like, "That used to terrify me when my sister played with this doll and it would just stare at me." I've had people give me dolls that had bad memories for them and they don't want to throw them away but they just don't want to bury them. They've heard that I make art with dolls so they give them to me. The dolls have their own personalities. It's a good starting point for me with my artwork. I do found object art, so it's a departure.

It's all relative now but I think it was a few years ago, maybe a decade ago, that I had just come back from an unusually painful trip back home. I'm from Alabama. I'm almost 56, so I was in my mid-forties. A lot of memories had been stirred up. I was saying to myself, *I'm an adult now. I'm ok. I'm an adult. I have distance. I have all my healing powers and healing tools and it's up to me if I incorporate this back in my life.*

So I took this doll that I have and I took her hair and cut all of it off. I took her clothes off. I took her eyelashes off and I started manipulating her so she would be just an angel and I hadn't yet taken her body apart—I had puppies at the time and one of the puppies got her when I was gone to get iced tea and "helped me" with my artwork and tore her little leg off. At first, I thought it was a horrible accident, but it ended up being a happy accident because as I was putting it back together, I thought well... the porcelain part of her foot had been broken so I had a jawbone from some kind of animal that I put that in there instead. Then I was sewing it together with wire and I had some beads and buttons with it. The other leg I ended up tearing completely off and putting in a wheel with a piece of wood. I don't remember what it's called. It goes with furniture normally. And then at the heart, I had a little heart that I had found that was rusted and I opened up her breast where her heart would be and I put it in there, then sewed around that and put an army man on top of it to protect her. I had some acupuncture needles so I just started armoring her up so that she could choose where her tender parts still were, but she could also choose to protect her heart. And then the coat hanger thing happened. And I put her up on the wall. I did it in a kind of frenzy because I didn't think I was going to keep it. It probably took 3 or 4 hours and then I put her up on the wall. My family really liked it a lot and encouraged me to keep doing these dolls hanging on the wall. On her body was the word "fly." The reason for that is because I found these little cards from the first grade or kindergarten where you trace over the words and I pinned that to her and she was "Fly" and I had another one that was named "Dream." She had some of my wedding dress on her.

It was surprisingly therapeutic. Thank goodness for therapy or we would all be artists. I had this one counselor/therapist who had us tear up phone books while we were telling our story of rape, rage, insecurity, or nightmares; I filled up a big room with torn up telephone books. I was in Florida at the time and those are good-sized telephone books. It's that tearing up thing and telling the story at the same time that worked the magic because then after you do that, you can walk away from it. I feel that especially when I'm working with the dolls—it's funny because if I'm in a good part of my life, it's not that easy. It's not that immediate. I incorporate doll heads and whimsical things with kind of a sense of humor, but it's not as edgy.

I have one doll that's called "Look Homeward Angel," and she's bound up. She has wings from the Bali dolls and her whole body and the wings are wrapped up in bubble wrap and then barbed wire and then silk thread and the poem that goes with her is: *Look homeward angel, though none will know your name there.* It's not where we can really reinvent ourselves, just represent ourselves to our past in a more protected and wise way.

Dolls are not animated, but they can be witness to what goes on in our lives whether we're children or adults or in a room where nothing else is supposed to be going on. There are so many dolls that I get from people that you can see the tear stains on them or that someone's cut their hair or that it's matted. Just a different kind of care that they've been through. They may have been left out in the yard. They have their own life. They mirror what the child's gone through and they survive. I mean, the plastic can break or the porcelain can shatter, but there is still that essence. At what point is that no longer a doll? At what point did that child lose her childhood? It's such an interpretive part of them. And then when people give them to me, they tell me their story. It's like they can lay it to rest. They can tear up that phone book and leave it in that room and go on.

*****

This is what my mother is like: My mom is always doing something nice for other people. In Arkansas, we drove quite a while to get to the school where she was a librarian. We'd go down these country roads on the way and there was this one house that was totally ramshackle, but my mom would go in and take the woman food to eat even though my mom is a horrible cook. She hates to cook. So I always felt sorry for that lady. I would just sit out in the car because my mother would say, "You know, you don't go in." But now I know that the woman was a hoarder, kind of like I am. So you go up these rickety stairs and this huge porch where a couple of dogs are and you go in. It's one of those shotgun houses. In the parlor looking up she had all these baby dolls hanging like they were hanging with a noose kind of thing from their necks all along the crown molding and it was baby doll after baby doll after baby doll after baby doll. Before I walked in my mother looked in and said, "She has a lot of dolls and it would be impolite to comment on them." That was all the preparation I had. I think I was in 6th grade. I walked in and it was amazing. I couldn't take my eyes off them, and this big woman comes out and says, "Oh, you like my baby dolls!" And I said, "Yes, ma'am." And she started telling me about, "This one I had before and this one I got from the trailer." They were all hanging and their little necks were crooked and they were looking down. But then you had to be careful where you stepped because there was so much stuff on the floor, so it was a challenge to keep walking around with her and listening to the story of these hanging baby dolls and then not stepping on whatever was on the floor. Meanwhile my mother was just acting like it was all very normal and it would be rude to comment on them. So, I didn't.

The first time I got married, my parents disowned me. They were afraid I wasn't going to graduate from college. So they took everything back, anything that I had gotten from my home. I was living alone at the time. I put it all in a U-Haul and met them at a motel, and they took all the stuff back. I proved them wrong though because I got married in February and I graduated in May. And so there was a lot of resentment until a couple of years ago, even though my mom and I get along famously now. She always says she's "lived long enough to be a nice person."

When she gave me my grandmother's doll she said, "I'll give it to you on one condition. That you don't make any artwork out it. You just need to appreciate her for what she is."

My great grandmother had a general store so it was one of those cloth dolls, but she also had a porcelain head and real hair, wispy, red hair and a cloth body. My grandmother had drawn a little heart on her.

Unfortunately, my mother had someone make her new clothes, so now our conversation—my mom is still in Alabama—goes like, "Hi. How're you doing? How's the weather?"

"It's good."

"Do you have that doll under glass yet?"

"No, I don't."

"Well, you know, that's really an heirloom. I wouldn't have sent it out there if I would've thought you weren't going to take care of it."

"It's on a bed in a bedroom that we don't use and it's fine."

That's where my sewing room is. So the next phone call is,

"Hi. How are you doing? Do you have that doll under glass yet?"

So now, it's, "Hi. I don't have that doll under glass. How're you doing?"

It's like she's saying, "Okay, I give this to you free and clear," but not. "You have to take care of it the way I want you to take care of it."

*****

Someone gave me a stuffed cougar, like a "Charlie the Cougar." It's up high. On a high shelf. The doll my mother gave me, my grandmother's doll, is sitting on the lap of Charlie Cougar. And she's very happy. How protected can you get? A taxidermy cougar!

*****

But back to the Barbie dolls: It's kind of funny because when you think about Barbie dolls you think about the Barbie bathroom. The Barbie bathroom is the employee men's bathroom in the library at the community college where I work. People have such a reaction. When we started it, people said, "Oh, no one really looks like that." You know, a normal reaction to Barbie in

153

general. And it's a sex symbol. That really destroyed me when I was younger. I thought I had to be blonde and skinny. So in this bathroom, which is filled with Barbies and images of Barbies, people are always adding to it. I mean, after all, most of us are librarians and we work in the "information" field. We have a couple of Barbies who are getting down lesbian types by the toilet paper. We have all these newspaper articles and stuff about Barbies that are up on the walls in there. And every once in a while, there will be a librarian or two who say, "Okay, we've had enough of the Barbie bathroom. We're going to get rid of it." But no, I have students I tell about it because they are researching that era or about the company Mattel or about Barbies. And I say, "Oh, would you like to see our Barbie bathroom?" It's a good thing to have. It's a good relief. Sometimes it goes over "appropriate" workplace décor. But there's only one man here, so now it's the Barbie bathroom. Shorthand for "I have to go to the bathroom" is "I need to go see Barbie," and you can say that in front of any student or to your coworkers and they know where you are or you can say, "I need to go talk to Barbie."

Sometimes we all need to talk to Barbie.

I first met Robin in a yoga class. We had a very serious teacher who smelled like strawberry lotion, lit strawberry incense, and had no sense of humor. She and I became fast friends.

Robin's Sister Nina

My sister Nina had a doll with Marge Simpson blue hair that stood straight up. As the little sister, I was never allowed to play with it, even though Nina never did. It was porcelain and had beautiful clothes made out of corduroy with a matching hat, fur collar, and rubber shoes. It lived in a small flowered shoebox. To touch it would have been certain death for me. So I would wait until my sister wasn't there and then scale the shelves to get the box down. I would lovingly touch its clothes and change them, then put it all back very carefully, exactly how I found it.

FAKE DOLLS

Dolls that are a comfort make sense to me. The story about the dolls on Brazilian TV with the working genitals gave me pause. However, the story I was told by my son about a bachelor party he went to was so bizarre that I decided to fictionalize it from the doll's point of view. When he first told me the story, I thought it was funny. But then it got more and more frightening as the details came out, reminding me of "The Lord of the Flies." This is the only fictionalized story in the book, although many of the details are true.

I asked Cecilia, a student at the community college, what she might know about dolls in Brazil. She told me this story about Brazilian TV.

Brazilian TV

On Brazilian TV, there was a program about people having mannequins custom made to sit around the house as companions. The people went on about them and how it made them feel good. They are able to do amazing things. They are replicas of people with working genitalia.

My eldest son told me this story about a bachelor party. I felt the need to tell it from the blowup doll's point of view. This is the only story in the book that is partly fiction.

Guys and Doll

My name is Jessica. I'm sexy. I'm also pretty. I make people happy. Last night a woman named Barbara held me next to her in a tent. I think I made her happy.

Yesterday my life was different. I was flat and tucked inside a box on a shelf in a store. I could hear people talking when they came in. Sometimes they laughed, sometimes they whispered, and sometimes they were very loud. Although they walked down my aisle, they didn't pick me. There's a lot of us here, but it seems like the ones in the other aisles get picked first. I don't know why I don't get picked. Maybe it's because I don't have any hands or feet.

I'm not sure what I look like exactly, but I remember hearing voices talking before I was put into the box by the people who made me.

She'll do. Just put a little red on her lips and her nipples and she'll be sexy enough.

So, I guess I have red lips and nipples and I'm sexy.

Just for fun, let's try an experiment and give her a few emotions and some physical sensations.

—How can you do that?

I'm a genius.

—Oh, I forgot. What if it doesn't work?

So what?

—Maybe she'll get returned.

So what?

—What about her hands and feet?

Nobody cares about hands and feet. This is a cheap version. Stumps will do. As long as she has a vagina, an asshole, and a mouth, that's all she needs.

So, I have everything I need. And then this morning, my life changed.

Oh my God, Hon, look at this one! Jessica Simpson! She's perfect!

—But she doesn't have any hands or feet.

So what? He'll love it!

I was taken off the shelf and packed into the back seat of a car. And then after that, I was transferred to another car. In the back seat, a man blew air into a plug in my lower back. I felt myself getting bigger and bigger. My arms and legs were unfolding and expanding. Whoopee! This was a great feeling. My breasts were popping out and my stomach was getting round and puffy. My face was filling with air.

Everyone in the car seemed to be enjoying my bigness. The man in the back seat was holding me out of the window. I was being blown about by the wind. This felt very different than being flat inside the box. People were honking horns as they passed by us. They were smiling and making signals with their thumbs up. I felt so popular!

The car finally stopped and we got out. I was being held under the arm of the guy in the backseat. This was a new sensation for me. I could feel the heat of his arm. I liked that. I was suddenly aware of smells that were different from the store. As we walked, I noticed there were lots of tall trees that smelled very good.

You guys looking for the bachelor party?

—How'd you guess?

Fifth campsite on the left. That's where the river rafting guides will be waiting for you. You and your rubber lady friend have a good time now.

The guys were being very quiet now. They snuck up behind someone and put my legs around the back of his neck. He screamed, grabbed my legs and peeled me off of him. Then he turned me around, held me out in front of him and laughed.

I was now being shown to a group of people who were called guides.

Can we tie her to the front of our raft?

—Sure, why not?

Jessica the masthead!

Most of the guides were laughing, except one. She was the only woman. She didn't look at me.

What's up with Barbara?

—Who knows? She has no sense of humor.

Whatever. This is a first, isn't it?

—For sure.

I was tied to the front of a raft, and they put a t-shirt on me. One of the older guys said they had to. I don't know why. Everyone was drinking beer and laughing. Being in the water was so much fun! I loved this. Whenever we went up and down too fast, my t-shirt would go up and my legs would stick out. They would all laugh when this happened and a guy named Jonathan would pull my t-shirt back down again. I got dislodged under the next big wave and fell into the water. I was floating. I liked this new feeling, bobbing up and down in the water, but Jonathan jumped into the water and grabbed me. He grabbed me too hard with his powerful arms and *pow!* I suddenly felt myself getting smaller and flatter. My arms and legs were limp. My face was getting smaller. My breasts were receding into my body.

Look at Jessica! She's deflated!

I was now drooping in Jonathan's arms. I didn't like the feeling of having no air in my body. He put me down on a towel and put some kind of glue on the slit in my stomach. He blew on it, concentrating very hard, and checked to see if it was dry. Then he turned me over. I felt hot air being blown into the plug in my back again. Oh yes! My breasts popped out, my face filled up, my arms and legs, my whole body got big again. He fixed me!

I wanted to be in the front of the raft again. People on other rafts had admired me when they passed by. I was special. No other raft had someone like me on it, although there was a group of people on one raft who looked away when they saw me. They all had crosses hanging around their necks. One of them tried to sneak a look at me, but someone else on his raft turned him around to face the other direction.

Look at her face. Doesn't she look frightened?

—Oh, they all look like that. Don't pay any attention.

But why?

—Never mind.

Other campers came by to admire me. They were smiling and drinking beer.

Let's put a little lube on Jessica.

A man began putting an oily liquid into the holes on my lower body.

Hey, guys, wait! It's getting dark out here. Let's put this glow stick to work!

And now, another guy stuck a glow stick into the hole behind me on my bottom. There was light coming through my body.

Other guys came by and stuck their fingers into my holes. They were laughing and having a good time.

I think what Jessica needs is this shot glass.

He stuck a glass into that same hole in my bottom, which made the glow stick go up higher. The guys enjoyed sticking things into me. I felt very popular.

Hey look! The lubricant dried up. I'd say that looks like sperm, don't you think?

Almost everyone laughed except Jonathan. He was quiet and he wasn't the only one. Barbara, the quiet guide, wasn't laughing either.

The guys then started packing up their camp gear and checking to see if they brought everything so they could put it back into the car.

Hey guys, let's leave the guides a tip. Why don't we give Jessica to the guides and put a tip inside her.

The hole I had at the bottom in the front was now being stuffed with paper money. And now one of the guys was presenting me to the guides who were all standing around waiting to say goodbye.

Here's a gift for all of you. Enjoy! She's got a little something inside for you.

One of the guides took me, held me upside down and took the shot glass out. Then he started taking money out of the hole. He started passing it around and then he put the shot glass back in. He left the glow stick in there.

Hey, Barbara. Stop looking so glum. Here's your 20. Maybe that will perk you up.

—I don't want the money. I want the doll.

What? You a pervert or something?

—Just give me the fucking doll.

Barbara held me very close to her and took me into her tent. She got a wet cloth and carefully cleaned off all the stuff that the guys had put on me and in me. She took out the shot glass and the glow stick and held me as she went through her clothes and took out a pair of socks, gloves and a sweater.

She put the socks and gloves on the ends of my stumps. And then she put a sweater on me. She caressed my face and looked into my eyes.

I won't ever let anyone do this to you again. I promise.

I didn't know why she said this. I had fun! She kept trying to close my mouth, but she couldn't do it. Then she held me and took me into her cot with her. She fell asleep with her arms around me. I liked how warm her body felt and how I could feel her heart beating. I spent that night looking at the top of her tent and thinking about my first day out of the box. I liked being appreciated by so many people. And Jonathan fixed me! I had a new feeling. It was hope. Maybe tomorrow I will make people happy again.

FIX WHAT'S BROKEN

What does one do as a teacher when confronted with this kind of thing? She tried to help him with an anecdote about how her father helped her, which was kind. But who knows what happened to that little boy?

Diane M's 2nd Story

I've always liked to repair things that my students break. Kind of a strange story is that I brought up this doll subject with a student of mine who I found out was only 5 years old. He seemed younger, but I was told he was 6 and later I found out he was 5. I caught him very openly underneath the table in my art class—and he looked very adult doing this— putting his mouth on another kindergartner's penis. In reflection, I don't think it was the first time, but at the time I tried to tell myself, well, kids fool around, everybody plays "doctor," but it was pretty disturbing because when I saw what they were doing, I screamed and picked him up and he said, "Are we going to get punished for this?" And I said, "We love you and we just want you to do the right thing and we've got to talk about this."

The parents were called. I had to talk with the parents and everything. So his mother came and the boy had been crying. She left the room for a moment and I was in there alone with him. I just said, "Oh, do you want a sucker?" I would give them suckers when they helped me clean up and things like that. He took it and he immediately calmed down. I said, "I've got to tell you, I had this doll once that broke into all these pieces and it was just so amazing how my dad glued it back together. Has your mom ever helped you put something back together?" He told me a little story about something that broke and how his mother had helped him with that. I said, "You know your mom can really help you. She can really help you." He didn't want to tell her what had happened. He did tell another adult after he had calmed down. He told one of the male teachers. I never found out what happened.

GET ME OUTTA HERE

This little girl just needed out. Child sexual abuse is unforgivable. These poor little girls used their dolls as their only escape from the horrific tragedy they were experiencing in real life.

I met Ashley in a doctor's waiting room. We had a long wait, so I told her about my doll book. Her face appeared ashen when she recounted this story of her childhood.

Ashley

My grandmother always gave me weird porcelain dolls for every Christmas and for every birthday. They were (kind of) creepy.

My dad built a shelf all around the top of my room, a shelf that bordered the ceiling. The dolls were up there on the shelf, so it was like these creepy dolls watching me sleep.

When I was 9, I found out that my dad's mother had died and that "Nanna" was a step-grandmother. When I found that out, my grandpa gave me my real grandma's doll. My dad is 63 now. His mother died when he was 14. This was a doll that she had when she was a child. It was homemade and was made out of porcelain. It had my great grandmother's real hair on it. It was very creepy looking. She made all the doll clothes for it and stuffed it with some kind of buckwheat husk. After that doll went up on the shelves, it only lasted for about a month or two. They all came down and got put in boxes. I haven't opened them for 12 years. It was so creepy because I felt like that doll was watching me. Anywhere I was sitting in the room, I felt like the doll was staring at me. It was too much.

Magdalena was a student at the community college. While she told me this story, I found myself holding my breath.

Magdalena

The name of my doll was Tommy. He was the likeness of a young boy with freckles and red hair, wearing overalls, and sat about 8 inches tall. His home was on a night table, between the two beds in the bedroom shared by my sister and me. I'm not sure what it was about the doll I loved so much. Perhaps it was because the other toys were animals like bears and puppy dogs, but Tommy was like a person, only better—someone I could trust, someone who wouldn't hurt or betray me.

Tommy bore silent witness to everything that went on in that room. The doll was there while my sister and I played games or talked when we were supposed to be sleeping, or in the morning when we were getting ready for school, putting on the uniforms we had laid out so carefully the night before: plaid jumpers and blue knee-high socks and blue vests and loafers. And the doll was there at night when I turned my head to the wall and tried to will myself from my body when my father entered my bed and touched me inappropriately. After my dad went back to his own bed, Tommy would still be there with me.

No matter how bad things got, I knew that if I could use that doll as an anchor point, I would be able to stay alive, that things would be all right, that I could be just a little girl playing with her toys.

Marylou is the partner of a woman I know. She told me the stories on the condition that I keep it entirely anonymous. I changed names of people and places. There are two of her stories in this book, the second one being the one I have given a warning about. She warned me that her stories were gut-wrenching and horrifying. I had no idea just how terrifying they would be. A big part of me hopes they aren't true. I am also warning you, dear reader.

Marylou's 1ˢᵗ Story

Speculation

I held my rag doll and rocked back and forth on the floor. As I looked down, there was a spider, a brown one, crawling under the newspaper that might have been from 2 weeks ago, or maybe a month ago. I didn't know. I was alone once more. Well, not really alone. I had Jacqueline. Jacqueline with the bright red braids and the green ribbons, Jacqueline with the plaid green dress and the soft yellow shoes, Jacqueline with the black button eyes and the embroidered black eyelashes looking so trusting, so at peace. I stroked Jacqueline's braids and patted her dress down. I tried to pull it down further than it would go as if to hide the genitals that Jacqueline didn't have. I knew that Jacqueline didn't have what I had down there, but I wanted to make sure she would be safe.

Looking out the window and hearing the traffic in the street was always reassuring to me. Even hearing the constant police sirens, the ambulances, and the gunshots were something I was used to hearing. It was okay. It was outside and I was used to being inside.

The one sound I didn't want to hear was the sound of my drunk father coming home. I could hear him coming up the steps. I could hear him fumbling for his keys. I could hear his heavy breathing. It was then that I would clutch Jacqueline even closer to me and rock back and forth furiously, hoping he wouldn't come in my room again.

When he would start with me, I would think about Mindy who sat in front of me in school. Mindy who had black patent leather shoes and pink socks with little flowers on them. I would think about Mindy whose mother picked her up in a powder blue Lincoln Continental. Mindy always had very clean hair, trimmed just so, neatly falling just below her shoulders. Mindy probably lived on the other side of town where they had big houses and big yards. I heard Mindy talking one time about her maid and her cook. Mindy's room probably was filled with all kinds of dolls, fancier than Jacqueline. Mindy's mother was probably never called in to the principal's office, either.

When my father would leave, huffing and puffing, I would look at Jacqueline, and stroke her braids and pull down her dress, and say, "It's over now. We're okay."

HAVES AND HAVE NOTS

I can feel the wanting of the dolls and the needing to suppress that desire. Sy's story about a father's wish that he could get his little girl the doll she wanted and the extent to which he went to get it for her reminded me of the love I felt from my father. Oddly enough, even though I never really had a doll per se, I can't remember ever wanting one, except the one time when I so desperately wanted to impress a popular girl in my elementary school.

Cheryl's 2nd Story

I was in the second grade when we wrote letters to Santa. In my letter to Santa, besides asking for a doll that had a baby carriage, I had to write what else I wanted. I asked for a warm winter coat for my mother because she was always cold. She was a single mom, and although I wasn't aware of all the hardships she was experiencing, I did know she was cold.

One thing I didn't know is that the letters were sent to the Chamber of Commerce. Out of all the letters that were sent, they chose mine.

One day, close to Christmas, my mother and grandmother were pretty excited. They said a visitor was coming. I didn't understand why they were so excited, but I could tell something unusual was going on. Pretty soon there was a knock on the front door and Santa Claus came in. He had the doll I had requested as well as a warm winter coat for my mother.

I knew I was supposed to be very grateful and I tried as hard as any seven-year-old could. What was devastating for me was that I could tell it wasn't really Santa. His beard coming off was the first thing I couldn't help but notice. He also had on fake plastic boots that showed his real shoes underneath. I had so many conflicting thoughts going on in my head. If this really wasn't Santa, was there really a Santa? Why were my mom and grandma pretending he was Santa? How did that man know about my letter?

I was happy that my mom got a warm coat, but I did have conflicting feelings about me getting my doll and her baby carriage.

I met Chris in the dog park. What I liked so much about her story was the laugh she had when she told it. She literally turned into a little girl and giggled. She kept apologizing because the story was sad.

Chris

I think I was probably in the second or third grade and I loved dolls, but we were very poor. I had no dolls. I did have one that came with a cereal box or something, but I never had a real doll and every birthday or Christmas I always wanted a doll.

My mother actually did give me a "dance-me" doll once. You know the kind that you put on your feet, with the yellow yarn hair, like a Raggedy Ann type doll, only it was life-size. So that was a good doll memory. My dad was a student the whole time I was growing up and my mother always typed until she became a librarian. But we were so poor. Three kids. No money.

So the story is I went to a birthday party for a girl named Jackie who was in my class—and she was, you know, kind of your middle-class girl, but by comparison she had everything.

I don't think she got this doll at the party. I think she got this doll given to her for her birthday, but before the party. Her mother gave it to her, and it was a really special doll. It was the kind that looks exactly like a baby. This was in 1960. I was just so knocked out by this doll. It might have peed when you gave it a bottle and all that stuff. But I just remember being so impressed with this doll because it was a very expensive doll. I was blown away by it. I was playing with it at the party—I kept touching it and Jackie asked me if I wanted to borrow it. So I said, "Yeah." My mom came and took me home, and I took the doll with me. And so from that point on in my mind it was my doll. I forgot that Jackie had loaned it to me. It was my doll.

I probably had her for a few months, and I just loved her. I probably played with her a little too rough. I might have given her a name, but I don't remember. But that doll went with me everywhere, and I probably wasn't as careful as I could have been. So, at one point, I was doing gymnastics and I threw her up in the air, and she fell on the floor and her face completely cracked, like you could have pulled it off. She had a porcelain face and a white dressing gown. Her face cracked really badly. Like completely. So a couple of things happened. I kind of lost interest in her. I'm not proud of this. I kind of tucked her away because I think I was freaked out thinking *this isn't my doll* even though I'd had her for a few months.

So, of course, Jackie started saying right after that, "I need my doll back, I need my doll back, I need my doll back." I just kept putting her off, you know. I mean there was no way we could have ever replaced that doll for her. We didn't have any money. And I just remember putting her off and trying to dodge her at school and it got to be a really big deal and one morning, early in the morning, there was a knock on the door.

When they came to our house (we lived in a very exclusive neighborhood in the Berkeley hills)... there were five of us in it and, you know, again my dad was a student and we didn't have any money. Even though all the houses up there were real mansion-like, I'm sure the mother understood as soon as she was standing on the front porch that there was no money there. So there was Jackie's mother and Jackie saying, "We want our doll back *now*." So I said, "Oh, sure," and I ran into my bedroom and got it with her face cracked like it was, kind of like at the hairline, so I tried to cover it up. "Here's your doll."

They probably didn't notice right away. They just left. I had combed her hair over and you couldn't tell. I mean, you wouldn't be looking for it. You couldn't tell. But the next day at school, Jackie came up to me and said, "Hey," using her hands to indicate where the doll's face was cracked off. I'll always remember that. And I just said, "I'm sorry." And that was it really. That was it. I kind of got off the hook.

I never played with dolls again. I was probably 10 and I never ever wanted a doll again after that. I didn't want to play with them. That was it. Jackie and her mother never did anything about it. They probably had many conversations about it. I'm sure Jackie got in trouble for lending me the doll in the first place. The mother was really angry when she was standing at the door, and I'm sure she was angry with Jackie because *why did you lend her this doll?* She had bought the doll for her daughter who probably had it only one day before I came along and broke it, and that was that. It was expensive and I always felt bad about it.

We weren't friends after that. End of the friendship. End of my doll experience. That was it. Never spoke to me again and we were in the same class. Probably neither one of us knew how to deal with it.

I wish I had a happy doll story. I want to have a happy one. This brings up a lot about my childhood. The fact that we really didn't have money. The fact that I really did love dolls. The fact that I was deceptive. I don't feel good about it. It made me feel so bad about myself, but then I got over it. I was 9 or 10 or whatever. But thinking about it, I thought dolls should be happy.

This story was actually told to me by Elsa's daughter, Emilia. The struggles of mothers everywhere are often similar.

Elsa (Emilia's Mom)

Elsa lived a very rough life in Guatemala. Her parents were separated, and for a while, she lived with my grandma. She was passed around a lot. So, she would have to work for her food each day. When she was little, she never got any toys, so she would make her own toys. She would grab the corn leaves when they were dry and grab the little hairs that come with them and stuff them. She would tie them and make little heads with the leaves flowing out like a dress. Those were her Barbies. She would draw little eyes on them. She would make them every day because they would disassemble. She never got to experience a childhood because she got pregnant really early in life. She was 17. I think that's one of the reasons she was so determined to give us a better life and to give us whatever we wanted. She gave us as much as we needed, sometimes more, and that's because she lacked so much in her own childhood.

She was very crafty. She had to make money for herself and she would get these hair scrunchies, the big fat ones, and unthread them. She would make smaller scrunchies, and she would put them on the dolls and sell those dolls with the scrunchies. What she wanted to sell was the scrunchies. For anything she wanted, she would have to make it herself or work for it. And one of the things she told me was that she would make her own little dolls and she would play with them. She really taught me that when you want something in life, you have to work for it.

I know Joan as a fellow theatre artist. Her keen observation of people is what makes her a good director. This story exemplifies this quality of hers.

Joan

I remember going to the beach in Marin County because it was so beautiful there. I lived in San Francisco at the time. One day I was there when a family appeared. There were two lovely little girls around 4 years old. Each had her fancy doll with her, full of lace and ribbons. They played for a while as I watched them. They had the dolls talking to each other, just like little girls will do. And then, as if out of nowhere, they simultaneously threw their fancy dolls into the surf and watched them bob around on the waves, their mothers frantically running after the dolls to retrieve them. The girls were just as content to watch their dolls bobbing in the sea as they were to have them talking to each other.

Robin

I came from a family that didn't have a lot of money. I learned early on never to ask for things. My first doll was from Goodwill. It was a cloth rag doll made out of white sheets with a painted face and black shoes. It was shaped like a slender gingerbread boy. It was housed in my pocket most of the time. When it got grubby, I would wash it and iron it, including the hands and feet. The face faded after a few years, so I painted nail polish cheeks on it and took a pen and darkened the eyes. I named it Ally.

Christmas was always a hard time for my mother. She felt bad because she couldn't afford to get much for her daughters. I remember an old five-and-dime store called Ben Franklin's that had a 2-ft. tall doll with a blue dress sitting on a shelf. It had the kind of eyes that opened and closed when you laid it on its back and the kind of hair you could comb. I would stare at it whenever I went with my mother into the store. One day, when I went into the store, the doll was gone. That Christmas, the doll from the store was under the tree for me. The odd thing about it was that even though I had pined for it, it didn't compare with Ally. Ally was not so high stakes, but thoroughly mine.

I am 60 years old and I still have Ally.

It was my great honor to hear a doll story from the editor of my favorite literary journal, The Sun. If we signed up at the writing conference at Esalen, we could have 15 minutes with him. I signed up right away. I doubt if he expected me to ask him for a doll story.

Sy

When my daughter was young and I was just starting the magazine, we didn't have a lot of money. There was a store nearby that had an unusual mix of things, and it had a beautiful porcelain doll in it. At the time, it was too expensive for me to buy for my daughter, even though I knew she really wanted it. One of the unusual things the store had in it besides the doll was sheet music. My father had passed away that year, and while I was in the attic clearing out his house, I'd found sheets and sheets of music, collections of years. I gathered up the sheets of music and brought them to the owner of the store offering them up in a plea for a trade: the sheets of music my father had collected for most of his life for the porcelain doll my daughter wanted so very much. He agreed.

I DON'T LIKE DOLLS

Not many people expect to hear these kinds of stories when they hear the title of the book.

Bonnie is a theatre artist extraordinaire. She is the backbone of many stage productions, multitasking and putting out fires in her indomitable way. Her story, as all the others in this book, touched me.

Bonnie

I had a younger sister. She was 3 years younger than me. She was about probably 4 or 5 when she fell in love with Barbie dolls. Maybe she was even younger than that. She played with Barbie dolls. All her friends played with Barbie dolls. I just thought it was the dumbest thing ever. I mean, I didn't like the way the Barbie doll looked. I thought to myself, "Girls don't look like that and it makes me uncomfortable. I don't like it and I'm never going to be that way, so where does that leave me?"

My parents put a lot of pressure on me because they said, "You have to play with dolls." What I wanted for Christmas was a red tractor, and they gave me that and I loved it. I rode it all around the block. I just loved that tractor. We lived in Rhode Island at the time. I was definitely a little tomboy, but finally one day they said you have to get a doll. And I said, "Why?" And they said, "Because it's not natural." We're Catholic and Italian.

So my mom drove me all over and I just kept looking at the dolls and there wasn't one that spoke to me at all. And I just said, "I'm sorry." And she said, "You have to pick one out. If we don't go home with one today, your father is really gonna get mad." And I just looked at her like, "What?" So finally, we go into this one last place and up at the very top, top shelf, all covered with dust, I kid you not, I spot this little doll, she had really short hair and a pair of overall dungarees. She was like a little farmer doll. And I went, "Ok, that one." And the guy said, "What? You want that one? I can't sell that one." I said, "That's the one I want." And he looked at my mom and my mom looked at me and I said, "It's a <u>doll</u>." So the guy went up a ladder and took it down and cleaned it all off and I said, "Yep, that's the one."

The guy didn't want to sell it because it was too "plain Jane." I mean girls don't like dolls like that. They like them with little dresses. I named her Jane. Jane had blue eyes and she had a little round face and blonde hair that was all kinky, like an Afro, really tight to her head. I never really saw a doll look like that so I don't know where they came up with it. She was plastic. This was 1958.

But the look on the guy's face when I said that was the doll I wanted! I was embarrassed—he embarrassed me. My mother was kind of nervous and looked at me and looked at him, back and forth, and he said, "Well, we have a lot of other nice dolls." And I said, "No. That's the one I want. That's the only one I want."

So, I brought it home and I actually liked the little doll. She was sweet. I kept her for years. My parents were so happy that I picked out a doll, you know. I used to take her on the tractor with me because she had blue jeans on and she was like a little farmer's girl.

At a very young age, I just knew how... what that whole thing was about. There was no doubt in my mind that I was not ever going to be a conventional person, live that life, or live the life of that kind of woman, and I haven't. This story is about identity and the importance of other people wanting you to be normal, to fit in. They began to worry that I wouldn't fit in and be normal. They probably even thought they might have done something wrong. And I knew all this. I was 8 or 9 years old at the most and I figured it all out. My brothers always made me play their football games and I always played better than most of the little guys and they loved playing with me and one day I looked down at myself and saw my breasts and I said, "That's it for me. Nobody is tackling me anymore."

I don't remember what happened to the doll. We moved around so much and I never played dolls with other girls. It just sat in my room. That was my doll.

I met Heidi in a local improv class. She is also a painter. I bought one of her paintings of birds for my sister. Her story, as most of them, delved into the psyche of little girls.

Heidi

When I was a kid, I wasn't that into dolls. Partly I think because I had a sister 7 years younger. She was all the doll I needed. But anyway, my best friend was 2 years older than I was and didn't live too close so we only saw each other on overnights and weekends. She had a doll. I can't remember the name, but you could turn this plastic pom-pom on the top of her hat and she had three different faces. It was really weird, so of course I wanted one. And then I got one and I just never played with it.

My friend came over one time and I told her to bring her doll because I thought we should play with them. We played with each face and we went down the stairs and back up the stairs and finally threw the dolls out the window. It didn't really smash the faces because they were plastic. It was like a ritual that we decided to do. I don't know how they got the idea of three faces, except I think one of them was a sad face. I remember one had the measles (at least I decided it did) and the other was a happy face. So maybe it was like, "Let's see if it has a sad face now! Boom!" It was really cruel. I guess it was our ritual for getting rid of the dolls. It wasn't about smashing them to smithereens, it was more about being "over" dolls.

Marcy is a counselor at the community college. Marcy's story is a breath of fresh air in that it's one of the only humorous ones. It's also a commentary on human nature at a young age.

Marcy

My main situation with dolls is that I never wanted to play with them when I was a little girl. They were not realistic enough for me, and that pretty much summarizes my whole personality to this day. And I kind of really didn't get it. Why did anybody want to play with dolls? They're not realistic in any way, and I have no imagination. I really had no interest ever in playing with dolls.

So one time when I was in nursery school in the synagogue, the theme of the day was for everybody to bring in their dolls or their stuffed animals. I had a doll, but I never played with it. I remember during recess or whatever, some girl was really covetous of my doll and just out of nowhere while I'm like carrying it around, she just punches me. It was the first time I was ever hit, ever. I had no attachment to the doll. I don't even remember what it looked like. So, she punched me in the face and took it. Stole it. It was a big enough punch so that when my mom saw me I had a bruise and was swollen. I remember that my mom called that girl's mom. The result was that the girl had to apologize to me. She was weeping and crying because she also had to give me her favorite doll. I remember feeling totally guilty. I was really pissed that she hit me, but I remember feeling really guilty because not only did I have no attachment to my doll, but I saw that she was super attached to her doll and I felt guilty that she had to give me her doll. She had to apologize and give me her favorite doll. And I could give a shit about her doll.

Yeah, it was wrong that she hit me and I didn't want her to hit me, but I felt shitty because she really cared about her doll. I just ended up putting her doll in the bottom of my closet.

IN SICKNESS

What happens to a parent or a child when they are very ill? Can a doll or many dolls make up for the sadness?

Aaron was a student at the community college. He had lived a very lonely childhood because of his physical disabilities. He, like many others, used his doll for escape and comfort.

Aaron

My name is Aaron and I'm 37 years old. I spent a good part of my childhood indoors with poor health. I was teased mercilessly in school for being different.

I think dolls are beautiful—the art, the representation going into the faces, the designs.

Lorrie was a big doll that didn't talk. She was my "little sister," as I wasn't going to have a real one. She still lives at my grandmother's and apparently has "friends" now, which freaks me out horrifically. One of them is a little sailor boy complete with sailor suit and Brylcreem hairdo.

The first doll I had was Chrissie. My dad made my mother give the doll to my grandmother because he didn't like me having dolls. I have her back now. I live with my mother and Chrissie.

Jill is my hair stylist. She has a big following and is active in the LGBTQ community. She is compassionate, with a wicked sense of humor. Because of her charisma and outgoing personality, she is often asked to emcee events. Her story is unique because of her mother using dolls as compensation for her heart condition.

Jill

When I was born, I had a serious heart condition. I had a brother who had died from that condition, so my parents bought me any doll I wanted. I had a dangerous operation when I was 5 years old, and I remember taking my Raggedy Ann doll with me to the hospital. Now I have hundreds of dolls ... Tiny Tears, Betsy Wetsy, Storybook Dolls (little ones made out of clay—a collection of those, but not a complete collection like my sister). I had Ginny, Jill, Saucy Walker (it had braids, supposedly you would hold its hands and the joints would move so you could walk with her). I had Raggedy Ann. My mother once made me a lovely doll, probably about 3 feet tall. It's the only thing I remember her making me. I don't know what the deal was or what she was called.

I had a Terri Lee doll. She's very interesting. She might have been part black. She had a molded plastic face with full lips, brown painted-on eyes, and dark wavy hair glued to her head. She had lots of great clothes, was kind of chubby, more full figured than the dolls of today. Mom said there was some mystery around Terri Lee, like she might have been part black. I don't know what her name was, but she looked like Jacqueline Kennedy, a very sophisticated girl.

I had lesser dolls, too. I also had a Gerber baby doll that my mom sent away for with baby food or something. I had Patty Play Pal—she was "life size." She wore kid's clothes, maybe a size 3, which of course I loved. Betsy McCall—she was 8 inches and she was really fun. Her knees bent and she had dark hair with tiny little clips, a painted-on little mouth, and little rosy cheeks. She was one of my favorites. Betsy McCall paper dolls I collected from McCall's Magazine. I also had a dachshund named Nosey. Nosey was a stuffed dog, it was small. The last dolls were Barbies, around 1958 and 1959. The whole Barbie family.

In my adult life, I have collected hundreds if not thousands of dolls. I've started selling them on eBay. It's a sore subject at our house. I just figure... at this point, do my granddaughters really want all that crap? I mean, they've got so much. I have a basket with handles that has hundreds of nude dolls, to be used for art projects—Christmas, for instance. I guess you can say dolls have been a big part of my life.

IT DOESN'T LOOK LIKE ME

My little sister Sherry wanted a doll that looked exactly like her. I saved up my allowance and the labels on Heinz Ketchup bottles to get her a doll with her likeness. Of course, I couldn't keep it a secret, so I told her I had sent in a photo of her and pretty soon in the mail she would get a doll that looked just like her. It never came. My littlest sister, Josie, got a doll that she promptly named Baby Josie. The women telling the stories in this chapter wished the dolls looked like them. All dolls at that time were white-skinned with straight hair. I'm so glad times have changed.

I met Elena through my best friend. She is a political activist and a gentle soul. Her story is a mother/daughter trust story. It reminds me of other stories I heard where the disappointment of a little girl turns into a reflection of sympathy as a more mature adult.

Elena

I had my best friend's old Barbie; blonde, perky ponytail; because my friend had upgraded to Bubble Barbie, a platinum blonde à la Marilyn. I also had my Madame Alexander doll, Kitten, a blonde baby doll. Oh, I loved Kitten. I mothered her like a real baby, but there was that white blonde hair and button nose, so she couldn't really be my baby, me being brown-haired and Jewish. I longed for a brown-haired, brown-eyed baby doll.

When I was almost ten we moved to England for a year. Barbie and Kitten came with me. For Christmas vacation, we rented a Villa called the *Casa Mancini en Positano* before it had become the playground of the rich. It was an amazing place, an old run-down villa with tangerine trees everywhere and a long winding staircase down to the beach.

To get there we drove in our VW Van from London. We hit a little town at *siesta* time. We parked and as luck would have it there was a toy store. In the front window were lots of dolls of all shapes and sizes but I immediately locked eyes on a particular doll, a beautiful sweet-faced brown-eyed, brown-haired baby doll. She was perfect and would be the best Christmas present ever. (*Good* Jews that we were, we always got presents for Christmas). But our wise knowing parents said we had to eat first. After a delicious lunch, we went to the toy store, but it had closed for *siesta* and there was no waiting for it to open. We had to get to Positano that night. My mom assured me they'd find another doll that would be just as good.

We got to Positano late that night after driving on the narrow Amalfi Drive through the scariest rainstorm; I was sure we'd go off a cliff, but we made it. We settled in to life in Italy—good food, the beach, Italian friends. I waited anxiously for Christmas and my new doll to arrive. My parents did go on a shopping trip, so I was sure to get my doll.

Christmas arrived. We went to church with my new friend Nunzia. I had never been to church, so I was quite impressed with all the ceremony. Somehow, I figured out that I should not take communion though Nunzia encouraged me do so.

Then it was time for presents. My brother got a castle with soldiers, knights, and horses. I got a model garden and my sister a model farm set. But there was still one more gift each. I was so hopeful as I opened my last gift. It was the right size and shape for a baby doll. Slowly, I unwrapped the gift, opened the box, removed the tissue and there she was: a brown-haired, brown-eyed doll. But she was not *my* doll. No, this one had a hard plastic body and face and her hair looked more like a teenager's. I honestly don't know how I reacted. I am sure I looked disappointed, but we played dolls anyway (my sister got the same doll but with blonde hair).

It was one of those moments that teaches you not to trust even your mother. Later my distrust continued when I found out my birthdate had been changed, but that's another story.

A few years later, when we were back in Stockton, I begged my mom to take me to see the Beatles in San Francisco. She said, "Don't worry, they'll come to Stockton!" Of course, they never did. Fast forward to August 2014. I saw Paul McCartney at Candlestick Park. My mom asked if I'd forgive her now. I said, "NO and I don't forgive you for the doll either."

Of course, now that I have my own daughters, I'm sure I have not always lived up to their expectations, so I understand that my mom didn't mean to be misleading. Who knows, maybe the doll was way too expensive, as were tickets to see the Beatles. So, I guess I do forgive my mom, but I'd still like to have that doll and be able to say I saw the Beatles!

I met Jacqueline in a Jazzercise class. She had Barbies in the days when they were all blonde with white skin. She couldn't relate and did something about it.

Jacqueline

I grew up in the 60s. I had all the Barbies: Midge, Ken, Barbie, etc., and even though I knew I was beautiful, the dolls didn't look like me.

My father had his own closet. In the closet on the floor way in the back were two bottles of shoe polish. One was brown and one black. I would sneak into the closet when my dad wasn't home, drag all my Barbies in there, and carefully color my dolls to look more like me.

I knew Kelly as a student at the community college. Her relief at finally having a doll that looked like her is not unlike other stories I heard from people of color.

Kelly

I always had to play with little white dolls, being born in the '70s. They didn't have black dolls then. Growing up with little white dolls, I thought white dolls were prettier and more acceptable, but when they started making little brown dolls, I was excited because I felt we were being accepted. Now I buy my own daughter little brown dolls.

I had a Raggedy Ann when I was little. It had the closest to my hair type and the economical value of the clothing felt closer to home. I threw out my white dolls because when I had a black doll, I suddenly felt like, "This is me!" I finally felt that I was just as beautiful. The feeling that I was just as pretty as those white dolls walking around happened to me finally when I became an adult.

LOVE ME, LOVE MY DOLL

This is about the only doll I almost had. I was hoping that if I could impress a popular girl in my school with the promise of a fancy doll from a carnival, she would accept me. Neither of those two things happened.

This is me. A few writer friends told me I should put in my own story. So I did.

Helene

I never had dolls. I am told I had a teddy bear named Foo Foo although I don't remember him. But I once almost had a doll.

Always being the new kid in town was very hard. I never knew what I was supposed to act like to fit in. Each time—and there were 4 before I was 8—was a painful experience. Whatever I did wasn't exactly right.

One time I was the only girl in the 5th grade not to be invited to Marcie Tarzine's birthday party. My mother unfortunately got wind of it, and suddenly I *was* invited to Marcie Tarzine's house. I was petrified. She was the most popular girl in the school. She was rich. She was pretty. I knew that she didn't really invite me. I knew that this happened because my mother called her mother and she had been forced to invite the creepy new girl over and be "nice."

I was invited to her house on a Sunday at 2 p.m. I bit all my fingernails down to the quick. I couldn't eat. I couldn't sleep. What could I say to her? How could I impress her? She probably had everything any girl could ever want. What did I have? Nothing.

But on that Saturday, the day before the dreaded day, my uncle Sammy, the carnie, the one I adored, the one my mother said had a girl in every port (whatever that meant), the one who married a "floozy" (another word I didn't understand), paid us a surprise visit.

Uncle Sammy came walking in the side door, the one that opened to where we kept our washing machine, the one near the kitchen where I just happened to be standing. In his arms, Uncle Sammy had a big box covered in cellophane. Inside that box was a beautiful doll. A doll with a blue lacy cap, a blue lacy dress, white shoes with white socks, and eyes that had long curly eyelashes. Her lashes looked like they might even move up and down. Uncle Sammy handed me the doll.

"Here, *dahlink, shayna madela*, this is for you."

I grabbed the box and twirled it around, staring at this doll.

"Mommy! Look what Uncle Sammy brought me!"

The look on my mother's face was hard to read. She wasn't happy.

"That's nice dear," she said through gritted teeth.

Confused, I took the box to my room. I didn't dare open it. This doll, this fancy, beautiful doll was going to be my ticket, my way of showing Marcie Tarzine that I was worth something, that I wasn't just the creepy girl who didn't have cool clothes or whatever you were supposed to have to be popular. I knew my hair was wrong. Curly hair wasn't okay. I was too young to know how to fix that problem. But this doll, she would fix everything. When Marcie Tarzine saw that doll she might even want one. I could tell her I had an uncle who might just give me another one and if he did, I would give it to her, to Marcie Tarzine, my new friend.

Later that night after Uncle Sammy left, my mother came into my room.

"You can't keep that doll."

I looked up at my mother in disbelief.

"Why, Mommy? Why?"

She screwed up her face in disdain.

"Because he probably stole it."

I blinked and handed her the doll. My only hope.

The next day I wouldn't look at my mother as she drove me up the hill to the very top where Marcie Tarzine lived. I silently opened the car door and heard my mother sing out, "Be good! Have a good time!"

Marcie's mother greeted me at the door, but not before scrutinizing my clothes and my hair, and smiling in a placating way.

"Let me just show you to Marcie's room."

As she opened the door, I saw not only Marcie but a wall full of dolls. Every imaginable doll in the universe. On her bed were about another 20 stuffed animals.

I heard myself blurt out, "I could maybe get my uncle to give you a doll."

Marcie was not impressed.

NOT A DOLL

These stories have teddy bears and a ventriloquist's dummy. Erica's story about her cousin's teddy bear is rooted in the Holocaust. The teddy bear has survived 60-some years.

Janine is a fellow theatre artist, blues singer, and hair stylist. She grew up in New Orleans. Gee Whiskey is her sweet bear.

Janine

I had a stuffed animal. Gee Whiskey's nickname was Geetle. I still have him. He's been packed away for a while. He was just like a bear. He was fuzzy—he was all pink with these square legs that came out of his bottom and elephant tusks on the sides. He had a big round face and two ears. My sister found him in the garbage when I was one and she brought him home. My mother sewed on chest buttons and eyes and a nose and a mouth and I've had him ever since. Just recently I put him away because I thought I shouldn't sleep with him anymore. He was falling apart and I was trying to preserve him. He had only one ear and it just came off. I probably slept with him until I was 40.

It used to be that when I was little and I would play with him, I'd forget where he was and I couldn't go to bed without him. So my father would pay $1 to whoever could find him. I think my sister Jackie used to hide him just so she could get a dollar! She was 5 years older than me. This was in Tacoma Park, Maryland, right outside of D.C.

When my father died, I was 10. One day, I took Gee Whiskey and this other little animal that didn't mean as much to me to school because I was going to spend the night out. Somebody stole Gee Whiskey and I had a panic attack in the school. This guy, John Gensor I think was his name, had to finally fess up that he took him. I had that panic attack because my father had just died and Gee Whiskey was my connection. So Geetle (Gee Whiskey) means a lot to me and I know I should pull him out and clean him up, but he's got holes where his legs bend now. He's in a trunk. I'll never throw him out.

I met Ron through my father. I was pleasantly surprised to get this story. He sent it to me, unlike most of the stories where I interviewed the person.

Ron

Charlie McCarthy: Fiend or Fable

I'm taken when I remember my youth and what possessions and antics are most prominent and treasured. One prime example is the Charlie McCarthy puppet given to me at roughly age 10. Surprising because of the attachment and wonderment I felt about the then well known if not notorious doll. I was a sports-minded, gifted athlete who participated in all the typical games of the day. Charlie was out of sync with the fabric of my existence but compelling nevertheless. I was drawn to how life could be breathed into this mannequin, realizing the skill necessary to imbue him with lifelike qualities. At the risk of grandiosity, I suppose my love of Charlie had to do with an early penchant for an eclectic, diverse worldview. My interest was fueled by the TV show, which was popular at the time. My attempts at duplicating the ventriloquists' magic drew a humored but not gratuitous response from friends and family. Though my skills were notably lacking, I was not dissuaded. Rather I remained mesmerized by Charlie's potential.

Charlie was beautiful. I felt he was an artistic creation and had style. He was full of sassy confidence, self-assurance, and a cockiness that didn't detract.

He also was possessed of a sordid quality. Perhaps due to a prescience of the themes associated with dolls to come in movies and books, I felt Charlie had an ominous character capable of machinations and even acts within the realm of the sensory plane that were worthy of foreboding.

In retrospect, some 50 odd years later, I believe what singularly drew me to Charlie was his surreal nature. How could the so obviously inanimate essence of him also comprise such enlivening attributes?

He was a mystery. That is what drew me to Charlie and later to other forms of surreal existence. Jails and prisons, the Vietnam War, Nevada's legal brothels. All of which possess a netherworld quality.

As the complexities of adolescence inevitably took over my consciousness, I bid Charlie farewell and consigned him to a shelf, albeit not without regret. But I still think of him. He is not forgotten through the years amid other recollections long receded from memory.

RAGGEDY ANN

I wonder if Raggedy Ann and Raggedy Andy were precursors to Barbie and Ken. I believe it was frowned upon for boys to have dolls, but girls could have boy dolls or Raggedy Andys. The fact that they were made of cloth and often handmade made them all the more precious.

I met Marthann through theatre and music friends. Her story is much like other stories in which the doll is used to not only escape reality but to play-act what is happening in real life. The doll becomes a symbol of themselves, a confidante, and a most-loved friend.

Marthann

My Raggedy Ann

As a girl, I suppose it was typical that I liked and had many dolls. I had many Barbie dolls over the years, but no particular one stands out to me. However, the doll that stands out for me is my Raggedy Ann.

Raggedy Ann was created soon before my birth in 1959. My grandmother Muzzie made her just for me. Growing up, I did not think much about where she came from or even how much I enjoyed her presence. She wore little white ruffled knickers and a crisp white linen apron over a long-sleeved blue cotton dress. Her legs were striped with red and white and her hair was brownish-red looped yarn … but more brown than red, not like the ones you see in stores. I do remember comparing my Raggedy Ann to my friends' and there was no comparison. Mine was much more unique and personal. I clearly felt that then.

At some point during my childhood, my father gave me his old button up shoes that he wore as a kid in the early 1920s—they fit Ann perfectly!

Over the years her once white "skin" turned brown with age and oil and dirt from years of being handled. I even tried to wash her face, to no avail, until I began liking her with that weathered, worn look.

She was my pal when my parents would have parties downstairs or outside (while I would lie in bed and cry because I could not sleep). I took her on trips when we would go out of town. I had a small baby carriage with wheels and I would take her around the neighborhood. I put small diapers on her sometimes, too.

One of the memories I have is dropkicking her down the stairs, making her cry, then running down to pick her up and comfort her. I suppose I was playing the good guy-bad guy. Thinking back on my youth and how alone I was with my dad's heavy drinking, I'm not sure if this was an acting out of perhaps an inner rage that I was not even aware of at the time.

I would put her on floating devices in the pool ... and hear her call out to me, "Help ... don't leave me!" I never put her directly in the water, though.

Sometimes Lucy, our black cat, would sleep next to or on her, in my room.

She would often ride on our Dalmatian (Lily)'s back. Make-believe Ann was riding a large horse. Sometimes I would take her up in a tree that I would climb and pretend she was afraid. I would then encourage her and comfort her as we climbed higher. I'd put her in the blue and white woven bike basket so she would have a great view as I peddled through our neighborhood. My brother would let me take her with us when we passed out newspapers in the early mornings. Jay would pull me (and Ann) in the wooden wagon as we handed him a paper at each house.

At one point, one of Ann's button eyes fell off and was lost. My mother replaced both her eyes. It took me a very long time to play with her again because her appearance was so different. The first eyes were small black, round, bead-like buttons, but these replacements were larger and flat, round, black disk buttons. I had a difficult time believing that my mother could not find a matching button! Heck, she sewed all the time and had a large drawer filled to the brim with buttons. She suggested that I look for two I would prefer, but I could not find ones that I liked. The whole thing was overwhelming for me at the time. I just did not like the idea that she would look different. It seemed to change her whole personality. I did, however, later succumb to loving her again. It was not her fault that she lost an eye, for heaven's sake! In retrospect, the larger eyes made her look more alive and happier. Later, as a teenager, I used to laugh and say she was tripping, as they looked like enlarged pupils.

I also painted a vagina line on her front and a butt crack line on her backside with nail polish. I wonder what age I was ... my guess is around 5 or 6.

I have never shared this with anyone.

I took her to college and I kept her in the closet. Even though many college students brought their Teddys and other stuffed toys, I, for some reason, did not feel right about it. I mean, there I was away from home, I was not a kid any more. I did have her with me, though, like a secret friend. Just knowing she was there with me was comforting.

Over the years, even during my naval career, Ann followed me. She'd sit up against pillows in either the guest bedroom or on a rocking chair in my living room. When I deployed to Okinawa and then moved on to Cuba, I did not have her, as she was stowed in a bin in long-term storage.

Today, she resides in an attic in my house that I rent in Newport, Rhode Island. One of these days we will be reunited again and catch up on old times, perhaps remembering even more.

I met Rebecca through the theatre community. Her story portrays the rollercoaster life of a small child filled with wonder, joy, regret, and resignation.

Rebecca

My natural mother had a great sense of humor. Her name was Nolberta. One morning my mother told my older brother and me that we were going to visit a television station. It must have been 1961 or 1962, because I was 7 or 8 years old. She took only my older brother, Stephen, and me. My younger brother and my sisters did not go with us. Maybe she favored Stephen and me. We were both born in 1954; Stephen was born in January, I was born in December, in case you're wondering.

We rode in my mother's car, a 1959 Buick, on our way to the television station. She liked Buicks and every few years would trade hers in for a newer model. I liked her car because the back seat felt like I was sitting on a couch in the living room. It was so comfortable.

We arrived at the television station and to my surprise we were going to be on the "Bozo the Clown" children's television show! I was excited and fearful at the same time because I had never been to a television station and there were so many people I felt embarrassed. The next thing I knew, some man comes out and ushers my brother and me into a big room that had benches and other children. Then he escorted my mother to her seat nearby. Before leaving, my mother reassured us that we were going to have fun. She made me feel more at ease with her big smile and encouragement.

Then a big clown with a brightly colored costume and bouncing red hair came walking out into the studio. His costume had polka dots with many colors on it and a big red collar that looked like a six-pointed star. All the children started yelling and clapping their hands. My brother and I started laughing and clapping our hands, too. Then Bozo the Clown walked over to the benches where we were sitting. He started the show by asking some children different questions. Then he asked some of the children word games and the children yelled back the answers.

Bozo the Clown started saying things to make all the children start laughing more and more. He told the children we were going to play more games. Then he walked over to this big brown closet and pointed to the big doors. He asked the children if we knew what was behind the doors and we all screamed out, "NO!" He then told us he was going to play some games with us. He walked over to the children sitting on the benches and started searching our faces as if he was looking for the right candidate to pick.

He looked at me and asked, "What is your name?" I pointed to myself because I couldn't believe he picked me and I said, "Who, me?" Bozo the Clown replied, "Yes, you. What is your name?" I shyly said, "Rebecca." He said something like, "Well, Rebecca, it's your lucky day! Why don't you come up here and stand by me!" I got up from the bench and walked down to the television studio set. I saw gigantic cameras on the television studio set. He took me by the hand and I stood near him. Then he picked several other children who were sitting on the benches. When he finally picked four or five children, he stopped.

Bozo the Clown told the other children in the audience that he was going to take us to the big brown closet. Then he was going to ask us one question each and if we picked the right answer then we would be able to pick out a "PRIZE" from the big brown closet! I can't remember the question he asked me, but I got it right. Bozo the Clown said, "She got it RIGHT!" All the children started yelling. I was so excited! He walked me over to the big closet and swung the doors open. Then he told me, "Rebecca, you can pick out any prize you want!" I looked at him and then looked at all the toys and prizes in the big closet and my eyes popped open. It was overwhelming and I didn't know what toy to pick out. Bozo the Clown smiled at me and told me I could pick out just one prize so I should pick out the toy I wanted most. My eyes scanned the shelves and that's when I saw it!

I saw the Raggedy Ann doll sitting next to the Raggedy Andy doll. They were both sitting there, one right next to the other, and they looked so cute together. I walked up to the big brown closet and reached my little hand up on the shelf and grabbed the Raggedy Ann doll and took her off the shelf. I looked at Bozo the Clown and told him, "This is the prize I want. I want this doll!" Bozo the Clown acknowledged my prize and made some comments, and all I could hear were the children yelling and screaming. All I remember is walking back to the bench where my big brother was sitting and I sat down next to him. He was happy that I won a prize. I remember one boy, who didn't answer Bozo's question right, started to cry, but Bozo calmed him down and gave him a small gift from a bag and after that the boy was happy.

The television show ended and some people walked all the children off the set to meet their parents. They gave every child a small token or gift to take home. When I saw my mother, I was so excited I ran to her and gave her a great big hug. My brother and I left the television station with our mother and never forgot our trip to the Bozo the Clown children's television show.

When my father got home that night, I told him what had happened and how I won the Raggedy Ann doll at the Bozo the Clown children's television show. He was happy for me. But as the years passed, my parents did not have a perfect marriage. We lived in San Francisco at this time. There were many fights between my father and mother. It was horrible to be a child growing up in this type of environment. The day came when my parents were going to get a divorce. By this time, I was 14 years old and my parents had moved to South San Francisco.

When my mother and father got a divorce, I lost my Raggedy Ann doll. My mother had to move all our property to the San Joaquin Valley, where my Aunt Beatrice lived with my cousins. She packed away most of my belongings and my brothers' and sisters' belongings and had to store them temporarily at her sister's home in the valley. My Aunt Bea, as we called her, lived near Visalia, California, out in the country, as I knew it. It wasn't the city, that's for sure. My cousins used to call us "city slickers" and make us laugh. We would tease them about being "country hicks."

My cousins had no respect for our property and must have gone through our belongings, because the next thing I knew—after my mother had retrieved our belongings, there were some things missing that belonged to us. I was just a young teenager and couldn't do anything about it. I do remember getting upset with my cousins and letting them know how I felt. As time went by and I got older, I eventually forgot about my beautiful Raggedy Ann doll that I had won at the Bozo the Clown children's television show when I was 7 or 8 years old. It's nice to remember it now.

Wilma's 3rd Story

When I was 3 or 4, I received two birthday gifts in these beautiful long boxes, like flower boxes. And inside each one was a Raggedy Ann doll. One was Raggedy Ann and the other was Raggedy Andy. And I had all the books, so I knew who they were.

I liked Raggedy Ann, but she was in a little dress with a little apron and I didn't like carrying her around. So I stuck her up on a shelf just to look at her. But Andy had on a sailor suit. It was during the Second World War and my cousin was in the Navy. I took Raggedy Andy everywhere with me.

We didn't have day care back then, but people would babysit for me and I would take him along. I took him in the car. I took him to the bathroom with me. He helped me eat dinner. He was with me every second. I have really fond memories of that. I slept with him, of course. And I just wore him out. Completely. I remember my mom made a new red sailor tie because the old tie got lost somewhere. So she made a new sailor tie for him. And he was just my cherished thing.

Years later I found a picture—I never found a real one, but I found a picture of a Raggedy Andy doll and the whole feeling of love and security all just came flooding back to me when I saw the picture. I would love to find one. I would love to find the set actually, but I would probably just stick them on a shelf somewhere and look at them.

THAT WAS THEN

These stories are about having dolls during the Depression, how much they cost, and how they were purchased. The third one, however, depicts the terror with which little children can be tortured with creepy dolls. In this case, clowns.

Mae is a neighbor I greeted every day as I passed her house on the way to the dog park. What struck me about her story is that her family allowed the children to play with the good dolls only for the week of Christmas.

Mae

What I remember is that we had really nice dolls. After Christmas, we put them away and brought them out the next year. They weren't dolls that we played with. It was our present in a way. Not for a year, only for Christmas. We got to play with them for a week or so, and then we put them away with the trains. The good stuff we put away till next year. Each year we always got another doll, but not the same kind. One we sort of played with during the year. The good ones that had a China face we put away. It was a big Christmas.

When I met Muriel, she was elderly and blind. She had a terrific sense of humor. I met her in an improv class. It was quite brave of her to attend and participate in this class, although she couldn't do everything. She has gone to the other side, as it were, and I'm sure she's entertaining whomever with her dry sense of humor.

Muriel

In my day, if you sent in the box top from the package of Aunt Jemima's pancakes, you could get a doll sent back to you in the mail. A black doll with a checkered apron with a white *shmata* on her hair and a big broad smile. It cost 25 cents. This was during the Depression. All you had to do was fill it with cotton batting and you had a doll. Of course, you needed to baste it.

I also had a Raggedy Ann doll. The dolls that most girls had in those times—celluloid dolls—I never took to. You could buy them for 2 cents at the corner grocery store. They were about 3 inches tall. It came with a little cardboard house. It had little arms and legs and a strip of elastic for the arm socket ... the face was painted ... you could buy these at the candy store. My mother wouldn't let me go to certain candy stores. I never knew why.

UNFATHOMABLE—GRAPHIC CONTENT:
BE WARNED

Before the woman told me this story, she warned me that it would be graphic and horrifying. I thought to myself, how bad can it be? I never go to scary movies on purpose. I don't even go to war movies. I'm easily frightened. As this woman was telling me her story, I found myself feeling both terror and wanting to disbelieve it. When I left, she made me promise to change names and places, which I did. I also tried to push the story out of my mind, hoping that it wasn't true in some way, that maybe it was just a nightmare that she had and now believed to be true. Unfortunately, I don't think so.

This is from the woman whose stories I have warned you about: graphic, horrific, and unfathomable.

Marylou's 2ⁿᵈ Story

I think the first doll I ever got that I loved was when I was about 7, maybe 8. This was in San Mateo. I named her Frances, my little doll.

She's in pretty good shape too. I didn't do too much damage to her. And I had her when there was an earthquake in 1957. I was about 9 when it happened. Then when the earthquake in 1989 hit, I immediately went back to being 9 years old and the first thing I thought was, where is my doll? So she was the only thing I took from the house.

After this last earthquake, we had a broken gas main right next to our house over on Banderly Way, so we couldn't go home for three days. It was interesting to see that right away the thought of my doll came back to me and I wondered where I had put her. You'd think after 50 years she might be a little further away, but not really.

I have an older brother and then I have a much, much older brother, a half-brother, who actually lived with us for a few years when I was maybe 5 to 7 and he was in his 20s, so I never saw too much of him. He was always working or going to school.

I think my mother bought me Frances when I was really small, 4 or 5 years old. We lived in this tiny little apartment downstairs from a house. The house had two daughters in it. The father was a lawyer, the mother was a librarian, and my dad worked in a factory. We had one tiny little bedroom where I slept in a crib until I was 5 because they couldn't get a bed in there. And then my brother had a little twin bed. My parents were all crammed in there with us. The girls upstairs had all these things I wanted— they had shoes, oh my God. I never got the pair of saddle oxfords that I wanted so badly. The girls would polish their shoes white every week, and I would go out and moon over them, look at them and want them because, of course, their lives were a lot better than ours in many ways. My dad was an alcoholic and a pedophile.

I also wanted these little Ginny dolls they had—or maybe they were even Madame Alexander dolls. I don't know what they were, but they were the little ones with costumes from different countries and stuff. I just wanted one so bad. I was just so longing as a little girl and then when I was five we moved away from there.

Two or 3 years later, finally, their mother bought me one because she saw how I was still, after all these years, like 4 years, was still wanting one of these dolls. She took me to the toy store in Westlake in San Francisco. I still remember how it smelled there. It smelled like wood and plastic, just this wonderful smell.

I remember there was a toy store in San Mateo, too, that I would go to and look longingly at things. My mother did buy me a little bride doll when I was 10, for my birthday. She took me down there so I could pick it out for my birthday, which I thought was really sweet of her because, well, she knew I had really wanted things I never had. By this time, she was doing ironing and taking care of kids and stuff so she had some disposable income.

My dad was still in the picture when I was 10, but he would take all the money. My mom had caught him doing stuff to me when I was about 4, I think. I think she threatened him with his life. She was so upset I remember running over to her and putting my arms around her leg because she was shaking so much. Her legs were shaking. He would wake me up around midnight when he got home from work. He was on the swing shift I guess it was called, and then do stuff. When I confronted him 20 years ago before he died, he really didn't remember. But when you drink all the time you don't sometimes. But then he kind of looked like he maybe remembered.

He had had a lot of abuse himself and so he became pretty dissociative. He would go kind of in and out of whatever was happening. He did admit something. He said, "Well, maybe I would molest other kids, but I wouldn't molest you." This was 20 years ago when I was an adult. I was 40 years old or something. And I said, "Oh, that's reassuring." So it was validating, let's put it that way. It was really validating that he at least admitted that. He didn't say he was sorry. I had left the state by this time, but then I came back to California and a week later there was the 1989 earthquake. We were displaced for some time, so he couldn't reach us because the phone lines were down. When I finally got back in touch with him, he did say he was sorry because he thought maybe I was dead. He said, "Whatever happened, I'm sorry that happened." I was so impressed. I wasn't even thinking about him anymore. But I'd asked him when I was back there, "Dad, did you love us kids when we were little?" He sat there, looked out the window and said, "I don't know."

I was so impressed that he told me the truth. He said he didn't know.

God knows what I talked to my doll Frances about. Frances says I never talked to her about my dad. She says, "Nope, we only had a good time. We did fun things, we didn't talk about anything bad." I don't think so. But I did have these dreams that—one of the things that happened was, well, it's a long story, but people would kind of change character, like they would go from being somebody I thought I knew to being really different, like some of the people in my family would do these switcheroo things. So I had dreams of where there would be a doll, usually a baby doll, like baby-sized, and in the dream I would be very sure that it was a baby doll. And then I would turn around and it would become a real baby. It would be really scary. Then the real baby would turn into a doll. So I never knew what was alive and what was a doll and it was like—it was scary, really scary.

My aunts were part of ritual abuse stuff. It was just weird superstitious stuff that they would do that was really violent and mean, really mean to me and my brother and my cousins.

The adults I knew would turn into other people, basically. And I had a recurring dream when I was 5 that went on—I dreamt it over and over and over again. I mean, I still remember it. I would get in the car with my folks and my brother. We would drive downtown and we'd park in a parking place at an angle and then my mother would go in and buy something in the store and I would beg for a penny and I would put a penny in the gum machine and get my piece of gum. I would jump in the car and start chewing my gum, and we would pull out and all of a sudden, I'd look around and everybody would be different. Nobody looks like they are supposed to look. And I'm with these complete strangers who are going to hurt me in a big way.

I've had a few recurring dreams for sure. And I kind of switch dreaming and waking. I would dream and I would wake up and then I'd dream and I'd go back to sleep again so that I could compartmentalize things. I had a very active dream life. But I would dream that this Billy Goat Gruff would come out of the trunk at the end of my bed and kind of slay me with all these spokes and kill me. It's not too subtle. And then when I was 13, I had a dream that I was a soldier and I was alone and I'd been separated from my unit or whatever and I was underneath the floor in a basement in a barn and I knew that either the good guys or the bad guys were going to show up and they were going to find me because you could see the hatch thing. When you close it and open it, there's no way to cover it. In the dream, I hear boots up there from under the hatch at the bottom of the stairs and I go, okay, I've got to be ready for whatever. And I look up and I go up three or four steps and they open the hatch and I'm so relieved it's my mom and my dad and my brothers and God knows who, other family members, and then they all bring out these guns and shoot me and kill me. So little hints like that made me later go, *I wonder what that was about?* Now I know, but it took me so many years to have a clue. I remember after that dream I'd wake up and was just so upset, I was just crying my eyes out saying, "Mom, why would I dream that? Why would I dream that about you? I love you more than anybody in the world." Why would she be there? But I think even if she wasn't involved in that stuff, all adults were just suspect. She didn't protect me. She wasn't able to.

My dad's sisters would do these things like they would put suggestions into our minds to replace what really happened. One morning in Arizona (I was visiting back there) we got up and I said, "Jamie, look! (My cousin Jamie is a girl) Look, the sun is coming up on the wrong side of the sky! And we were thinking, *oh my God, that can't be happening.* So we walked around and walked downtown and I found a quarter on the sidewalk. I picked it up, thinking, *this will prove we were really here, right?* I put it in my pocket and went back and lay down and woke up an hour later. It was 8 o'clock. Of course, the sun rises on the right side of the sky and I find the quarter in my pocket and I see it really happened. So until we were around 40 we believed this because we were both there. *But of course, we weren't both there. It didn't happen.* And so, finally, at 40 I said, "Jamie, you know the sun couldn't have come up on the wrong side of the sky." What would discredit us more than if we said something happened, if we did remember something? Our aunts would say, "Yeah, and these girls think the sun rises in the West." And we would say, "Yeah, it did." So we would completely lose any credibility. As I said, our aunts put suggestions into our minds to be evil.

I've had some flashbacks... they had these bright lights, flashlights in our eyes and they would hypnotize us and describe this thing happening, what was going to happen and how it was going to play out, like where we should walk, that it was all in our minds. It didn't ever happen of course, we never went out and we never saw the sun on the wrong side of the sky.

They hypnotized us. And we believed it because we both collaborated it. It's like we both collaborated that the flowers were talking to us and saying the same things. We would write it down and of course it would match because they did it to both of us.

And then I had a memory of going to this Beatles concert, it was only about a year ago. I found out that Roy Orbison and the Beatles never played in San Francisco together. So again, it had been a memory that couldn't have happened. They only played together in England. And I remember seeing them. I mean we were in the car and my cousin's mom was driving—she was one of these people—and we see Roy Orbison's car and I said, "Look, it's like all these details of being close to this." And then I saw something on YouTube of the same concert and it wasn't anything like I remembered. And I went, *uh-oh.* So I tried to look it up and I found out that it was a complete fantasy. This time I was 13 years old. In my memory, the aunts would get girls pregnant as soon as they could and abort them at about six months. The baby would live for a little while and then they would kill it, this kind of stuff.

This happened to my cousin Jamie, too. But they gave her a C-section so she was able to have children. When she got pregnant with her first child and the doctor says, "Oh, I see you've had a baby before." She said, "No, I've never had a baby before." And he said, "Well, yeah you have. This scar couldn't be anything else. It's a C-section scar." And she went home and said to her mother, "What is this about?" And her mother just brushed it off, "Oh, the doctor is wrong, that's nothing." So Jamie just repressed it again.

They never got in trouble. Even when I was an adult and having memories and stuff, one little girl who was my cousin's daughter, and also her son were still being abused. I went to my cousin and I said, "You've got to protect your kids whether you remember this stuff or not. He still can't watch anything on TV that's new because it might entail death. He can't listen to any new music because it might talk about death or violence. I mean—his whole world is shut down because he's so terrified of these topics. I know that feeling. My cousin remembered. He said he would do what he could do to protect his kids. The mother was trying to protect the kids because she would say their grandmother (my evil aunt) had this power over them and she didn't understand what was going on. She was worried about her kids. But then all of a sudden the mom just disappeared out of the picture. Why did the mom disappear? And the little girl's best friend coincidentally ends up dead out in the desert 100 miles from where they live. How creepy is that? It *could've* been a coincidence, but it seemed like a really creepy coincidence.

When things happen like that, you become dissociative. I mean you have to compartmentalize, you do all kinds of mental tricks I think. Survival instinct is strong. My brother, when he was 23, became psychotic and schizophrenic and started remembering stuff. And of course, I thought that it meant he was really crazy because he was remembering about the people with the top half of them looking like goats and wearing masks. It was our relatives and the people that they knew. It was a larger group of people.

So after all that I've been through, my doll Frances was a good girl. She was innocent and sweet and safe and I could protect her. She didn't go through any of this. So I kind of became her on some level. It was something like that going on. When I got her, she was in one of these suitcases with a little place to hang up the clothes and her stuff. It had a little drawer. I thought I had died and gone to heaven. I mean, I remember not sleeping the whole night being just thrilled by this. Thrilled. I mean I was so excited. It was more than I could have dreamt in my wildest imagination. Way more. It must've been really cool to be my mom and see me just be so happy because I was an odd little child as you might guess. I was peeing the bed, had nightmares all the time, quit talking for a year at home, quit eating anything but white food for quite some time until I became really, really skinny. So then she'd force these vitamins down me. In fact, when my brother had his mental breakdown she said, "Well, God, if I thought anybody was going to go crazy, it would have been you. And I said, "What do you mean?"

They noticed I was different at school. I was very quiet, very shy of course, very withdrawn. And they saw that I was really thin. But I didn't do anything. I talked when I had to at school, but I wouldn't talk at home. I talked to my friends when I was on the street, but when I was at home I was silent. I think I was trying to give my mother clues each time. I don't know. I remember eating a lot of weeds outside, different things, trying them and chewing on them. I figured out all the edible things. We lived right next to the freeway, so everything was covered in grime, but I still ate it. And I climbed billboards to get berries and stuff, because I wouldn't eat at home. It wasn't safe to eat at home.

I would eat white food: mashed potatoes, a banana, a white piece of bread. We never ate rice, so I think that was about it. White bread, bananas, potatoes. If it was mashed potatoes, I would look carefully to make sure nothing was in it. But I would never eat jelly. I would never eat tomatoes, even afterwards. I had so many limitations about what I would eat that it was kind of a joke. It's like I would never put anything on a sandwich. If my mother made me a sandwich, it would be one piece of baloney and that would be it, with two pieces of bread. Nothing else. But I would eat store-bought things. So for a while she bought me these two cupcakes, you know, Hostess cupcakes, and put them in my lunch because they were prepackaged. If they were all packaged, I would eat those. She kept trying to get me to eat more calories, but she never forced me to eat. I thank her to this day for not forcing me to eat because that would've just been hell. It would've been just so bad. I had another doll that I had forgotten about until just maybe 10 years ago when my aunt returned it to me. This was a different aunt, my mother's sister, not the evil aunt.

My mother died in 1977, so in the '70s after my parents moved to Arizona when my dad retired, my mom had moved a bunch of my old dolls. They were in a big round barrel kind of thing made out of cardboard. The little cellar thing flooded and most of them, the dolls all got ruined. But my Aunt Isabel grabbed a couple of them and said, "Oh, I think I can save these two." So she saved a little one and then she saved a bigger doll, a good-sized doll.

She gave me this doll in the 1990s, 20 years ago or so. My mother must have taken this doll from me and hidden it. It was a doll that had joints at the arms and at the knees. Once I saw this doll, I remembered that I had been obsessed, going over and over and over this crack on the back of the knee with a pencil. I never knew why I was doing it but it was like I *had* to do it. I had some OCD stuff going on over the years. Washing my hands all the time, changing my clothes, doing this to my dolls. Anyway, I turned the doll over and there were those pencil marks from all those years before. It was so validating. It was also, you know, kind of symbolic of things that had happened, as far as violent things.

And once there had been a little kid, maybe a year and a half old. Sometimes they would kill cats or something on me. I was completely not expecting this, completely not expecting it. It was like there was a hole in the universe. They held this baby over me (you're going to think I lost my mind) and cut off its leg at the knee. It fell on me. When this came back to me, I just started screaming and it was so embarrassing because this woman was giving me bodywork and I didn't have any control over this. Afterward I was just kind of saying, *Oh my God, why would I see that? Why would I feel that?*

I have no idea how they got away with this. Unless it was kids within the family who had had these kids. This would've been pretty hard to come up with, to stage, because it was so physical. It's possible, I hope, that it really wasn't even real. Even if it seemed so real to me. I would hope so. But it's one of the things that is the most chilling because it was so horrible, so ghastly. I mean I can hear this child just scream and scream and then I think I passed out.

My mother and my aunt (one of the bad aunts) brought me a baby doll when I was in the hospital to get my tonsils out. I considered my mother being with this aunt and the baby doll a betrayal. It was like this was symbolic of the stuff that was going on. And I threw this doll across the room. I remember I was a little girl who was longing for dolls, longing for dolls—and I picked up the doll and I just threw it and as loud as I could yell with my throat just being done with surgery I screamed, "I hate you, go away!"

When I think of some of the stuff I had seen with babies and stuff, for them to give me a baby doll just felt like evil. I don't think my mother knew. They came to the hospital together because my aunt drove and my mother didn't, and brought me this doll. I think my aunt bought the doll, too. So it had this double meaning. I was so angry.

My mother would ask—I remember I was 5 or 6, and she said, "Is anybody doing anything you don't like, like touching you in ways you don't like? It could be a man or a woman or a boy or a girl." I still remember her saying that. And I just turned to ice inside. I said, "No, leave me alone." I was just so angry that she asked me. Because the threat, of course, is if you tell anybody anything, your mother was going to be hurt. So when she asked me that, I just completely froze: "Never ask me that again." And then I would obsess worrying about my mother. It was so painful. One time when I was about 13, my parents went away to go visit this aunt, a couple of hours drive away, and then came back the next day. And by the time they came back, I had paced the floor for the 24 hours. My mother was gone. When she came back, they had pulled up on the sidewalk and I was so worked up that I ran outside and collapsed. I had been pacing literally for hours and hours and hours. I collapsed and just starting sobbing. She said, "What in the hell happened? Are you okay?" And I said, "I was sure you were going to be dead." I was just sure she was going to die. And then she did die: Right after she went to my evil aunt's daughter's wedding. She came to my house out here and was diagnosed with cancer. She died three weeks later. That was very sad. My older brother had been threatening to kill her. He was violent. He had become violent. He would come up and try to strangle you and you'd say, "Quit fooling around," hoping that he was fooling around. You never knew what to expect from him.

As a kid, he hit me so many times that I finally developed a cyst on my arm and had it removed. He still broke the stitches many times because he couldn't remember not to hit me on that arm. I later realized that he had kept me sane because we'd go out to play and I would go to the side of the house and say, "Okay, I'm just going to stand here. I would go into just kind of staring into space, not doing anything for hours. And he got to where he would just come and he would tease me and he would hit me until finally I would do something back. He would smile. I remember him just looking at me just so happy that I had come alive again. He thought I was dying because I would just be shut down. I realized later that he was a real ally, even though he drove me crazy as a kid. He kept me from going under.

He died when he was 39. He was schizophrenic for about 6 years and then he started to drink because he said he couldn't deal with the voices in his head. He drank himself to death in 10 years. I said, "You know... you know you're killing yourself?" And he said, "Yeah." And I said, "Do you have to? And he said, "Yeah." I said, "Okay. If you have to, you have to. Some things you just can't live with."

I spoke with a medium on the phone once. She said that she thought it was my brother coming through and she said he doesn't want what happened to him to happen to me. And it made sense. It made me believe that she was kind of getting something. I mean we loved each other a lot. When I would tell him I wouldn't give him my address, he would say, "Why?" I would say, "Because, Jimmy, you are not in control of yourself. The last thing you want to do is hurt me, I know that." And he would say, "Well, yeah." And I'd say, "So it's okay, right? We'll talk on the phone. I'll come visit you. But it's not good for you to have my address." I took care of both of us. And I'm so happy he never had to spend time in prison. He was terrified of being locked up. I don't think he ever killed anybody, which was always my fear. He was homeless for a while. He lived with my parents. He moved back in with my mom and dad in San Mateo for a couple years, and then he lived in Arizona until he died. My dad moved out of the house, though. He couldn't live with them. My brother stayed there and got some dogs and wrote poetry, read books, and died.

*****

I got these other dolls after I started having some of this memory stuff come up. I fell in love with dolls again, of course. This one, the bride doll with the high heels, I just love her, she's so beautiful. They are so cool. And people have given a few to me. This was one I might've had that got saved.

Here's the one I had when I was ten. She's tall. And my little black doll is one of my favorites. I have Indian dolls. We went back to Arizona when I was a kid, so I would get Indian dolls. She's held together quite nicely for her age. I was always very gentle with my dolls.

I didn't have any kids. I really wanted kids. I would've tried to be a good mom. Although I knew when I was in my early 20s that sometimes I had this attitude about children like, *why don't they just shut up and disappear?* I think this is because my survival was shutting up and disappearing. So I always assumed children didn't want my attention. It shocked me when they did. It took me many years to get it that children love adult attention. They love attention and they love *love*. I think you get where you don't even know if you can trust yourself if you haven't been able to trust many people.

I just wanted to give everybody a really wide berth. But then my ex-husband had two kids and he and his wife made me one of their godmothers. Now they are grown up and I adore them both. I was able to be more affectionate as time went on. It was a process, but it's good.

John's in a nursing home now with a stroke. We go up every week to Sacramento to see him. I adore him. He *so* saved my life. I married him when I was 18. He got me away from all those people and took care of me. One of the first times we ever went out, I was trying to throw myself out of the car onto the freeway, but he wouldn't let me and he stayed with me. I said to him, "You know, it must be a karmic connection. Otherwise, if you had been sane in a regular world, you would've run the other way. You would've never been drawn to me. That night, he said he drove around the block the whole night worrying about me.

Oh yeah, and then Janice coming into my life... I have been so lucky with relationships, people who have treated me really beautifully. I left John in large part because I was afraid of what would happen to him. That was always the threat. First it was my mother, then it was my husband. And if I'd had them, my kids. So no husband, no kids. I just tried to sign off on that one. No boyfriend.

I was with him for 10 years. If I hadn't met John, I don't think I would have ever gotten involved with men. I was more drawn to women even as a teenager. It's safer in a lot of ways. You don't get pregnant, which was one of the things that I was really freaked out about.

The last 24 years have been really challenging times. It still is in a lot of ways. But I feel like I have so much more peace and eventually I would like to write about some of this stuff that I have gone through. Just the way that the mind can be manipulated. I find it fascinating. And my cousin Jamie told me that her mother has always really been into NLP, neurolinguistic programming stuff. I thought that kind of makes sense.

I always thought I must have been a bad person in another life, but a woman I'm working with said to me, "I'm not getting that. I think you are innocent and that you really wanted to come in and help stop this line of abuse in this family." I think because of my mother that even though it was traumatic, in some ways she was also really there for me and did everything she could. I think feeling loved is the essence of strength and being able to love. That's what gets taken from a lot of kids: the ability to care about anything.

You know, what's funny is that I was born 3 months premature in June. I was supposed to be born in September and I weighed 2 lbs. 2 oz. Babies didn't live at 2 lbs. 2 oz. in the late 1940s. I mean they just didn't. My grandmother kept saying to my mother, "Pearl, there's no way she's going to live, you just have to forget it and let it go. But my mother said, "I always wondered why she argued so strongly that you weren't going to be able to live." Because at 6 months that was the whole deal with the ritualistic abuse. It wasn't really killing anybody in their minds, because I wasn't going to live after that. I thought about that later and it creeped me out. The evil aunts had induced labor at 6 months for the kids like me and my cousin Jamie or they would do a C-section so that the baby would live for a little bit. They assumed that the baby wouldn't be able to live anyway once it was outside the womb, so therefore it didn't matter what they did to it. That was their kind of thinking. So my grandmother told my mother that the baby (me) was not going to live. How did she know? And nobody knew my mother was pregnant which made me wonder if she wasn't being set up too. I mean I just don't know.

She went into labor, gave birth to me, and then I lived. So I think it made them nervous from the beginning that I could survive being 3 months premature. This wasn't supposed to happen. Someday maybe I will know the whole truth of it. You know what I mean? I like to think that after you leave your body you have access, without all the physical pain and emotions and everything.

I remember being on the ceiling looking down watching things like that. As an adult I was able to leave my body sometimes. It was scary when I realized I was out of my body. I thought, *I've got to get back in.* But I think people really do that. It's not just near-death experiences. I think when you are being subjected to a lot of pain and a lot of horror, that it is a near-death experience even if you're not really going to die from it. However, you feel like you're going to die from it. I felt like writing a book just of my dreams, my nightmares. It would truly be a horror story. I could do 300 pages of nightmares.

YOU REMIND ME

These three stories are about loss: a sibling, a cousin, a mother. Dolls, or a bear in one case, helped the children hold on to the memory of a loved one, no matter under what circumstances.

Diane G's 2nd Story

I have another story that's based on this photograph of my sister and me. She's 2 and I'm probably 5. We both have our Ginny dolls. We're standing on the front porch holding our Ginny dolls in front of us in the wintertime with our wool leggings and coats that matched. The Ginny dolls were something that my sister and I both had. We didn't share very much, but we shared the clothes for them and we played with them. I wasn't really that into dolls. So that other doll and this doll were one of the few dolls that I had. I still have them today.

After my sister passed, I took it from my mom's house and her doll sits on my dresser next to mine, but it's always been missing its left leg. I'm not sure how it happened but when I brought her home, she was missing her left leg. I happened to find a partial Ginny doll at the flea market that had a left leg, so I pulled the left leg off that one. I haven't put it on to her yet, but when I have her on my dresser, I have her sitting with her leg under her. When you put it under her, it crashes into the other one and the leg looks kinda long, so I bent it and made it so it looks like she's got one leg out and one leg bent. I just need to find a doll doctor to put it back together because it's sad. But she sits up there and she's very sweet. Jill's (my sister's) doll is blonde and she's wearing a Brownie dress.

My favorite toy was an erector set. Now you know where I was coming from. But Jill was always kind of the sweeter of the two of us. Her doll just looks very sweet. Mine's got dark hair and mine just looks... I don't know, not as cute.

I know Erica through the theatre community. She is a storyteller extraordinaire. Her story has historical significance as well as heart-wrenching truth.

Erica

It was a German-made bear. So he had the longer nose, the longer, narrower nose, not the American teddy bear kind of ridiculous look. He looked more like a real animal. Or more like Pooh bear. His arms and legs turned completely around because they were on a cardboard wheel. I'm not saying it right, but the arm ended in a piece of cardboard and you could spin the arm around because of that, the legs too. In the days when I was little, you know, in 1940, he was a very moveable doll. A doll with a lot of abilities. And it had lots of hair, it was very furry and it felt good.

I used to like to cut his hair. He never had a name. He didn't need a name. I'm not sure why he didn't need a name. Anyway, I also beat him up when I got mad. But I don't think I did it when I was really little—that was later when I was 7 or 8 or 9. Maybe I stopped doing it by then. But maybe like 6, 7, 8. I would throw him across the room, you know, to hurt him. And then I would jump on him, and I would scream if nobody else was around, if I could get away with it.

I shared the room with my mother and my father slept in the living room. My mother had a single bed on one wall and I had a single bed on the other wall. It was a long, rectangular room. Their things, the wardrobe and the dresser and so on, were on the wall on her side of the room. My things were on my side of the room.

It really wasn't about being crowded into the room. It was about how awful it was. How awful my parents' marriage was, how much they didn't like each other, how they fought every night, how terrible the war was, because the war was still on. The war wasn't over until I was 8.

I don't think I knew yet what happened to Julich in the sewers of Budapest. But I found that out—probably not right away— after the war ended, because it took a while for all of the contacts to reach people who survived. He was my father's sister's son. Is that a first cousin? Yes, I think that is.

I was born in Vienna and when I was maybe a little older than a year, say 15 months old, the Nazis came into Vienna and took over. They began installing the Nuremberg laws in Vienna. The Nuremberg laws were racist laws. You couldn't have a mixed marriage between Christian and Jew. You couldn't work for a Christian if you were Jewish, you couldn't work for a Jew if you were Christian. It was the separation of the races.

And, it escalated from there to public humiliation, particularly community figures. My grandfather, my mother's father, was chosen because he was a very well-loved figure in his neighborhood. He was the grocer. He gave credit to everybody. This was not a rich neighborhood. This was a lower middle-class neighborhood, and it was integrated Christian and Jewish. Nobody had any trouble with that, ever.

My grandfather treated everybody alike. He gave them credit if they needed credit. If it was a hard time for them, he didn't make them starve. So they liked him. And he was fair, you know. And he was generous. So my parents were fair and generous. Then the Nazis came and the soldiers came and pulled him out of his shop. They handed him a toothbrush and made him get down on his hands and knees and gave him a little container of water, or maybe he had to go get the water, and he had to scrub the sidewalk with a toothbrush.

And of course, the Nazis probably picked the perfect time of day when people were either going to work or coming home from work. And people just looked the other way. That was the idea. That was the purpose. To show people that they didn't have the balls to stand up for one of their own. Their own neighborhood. They wanted to prove that the Nazis could come to their neighborhood and show the Jew where he stood. And then, of course, they made everybody sell everything that they owned. They would assign your apartment to somebody with all of its contents.

I don't know whether we left before *Kristalnacht* or immediately after, but I know we didn't stay a moment longer than that. They hired hoodlums, gangs, and paid them to go around and destroy. I mean they had already written *Jude* on people's shops, on all the windows of business places where the public could see that it was owned by a Jew by scrawling in paint across it—*Jude*. Now they escalated one more step and that was to damage the places, especially the synagogues. They smashed up a bunch of other places as well. And there were film crews, Nazi government photography crews, going around filming all of this destruction. So it would be on record, what they had done, this wonderful thing that they had done, the ethnic cleansing that they had been doing. And the synagogues were burned as well and smashed about, as well as hacking into them with axes.

So that's when we left. And we all left. My mother and her sister and their families and her parents. My mother's sister, Annie, went with her husband and her daughter, who was 5 years older than me. She was 7 and she had been thrown out of school. They went to Paris where my mother and her sister had a brother, their baby brother, who had been living there for years.

So, because he had been living there for years, he could help them find a place to live and he could probably help them get from visitor status to permanent status. That was the idea. Meanwhile, we were going to Czechoslovakia, which was, in those days, a rich country and a democracy. The Czechs hated the Germans and had done so for maybe 100 years.

The Czechs weren't going to be like the Austrians. They weren't going to just lay down and welcome the Nazis in. They were going to fight. So it was a safe place—and not a safe place—to go to. But it was certainly a country we could legally enter because my father was born in Czechoslovakia, so he was a citizen and that meant that his wife was a citizen and his baby was a citizen. Also his wife's parents were citizens. They were part of the extended family, which was recognized in Europe. Oh goodness. My father had four sisters and a brother, so there were 6 children in his father's family household. We were welcome to come and stay with grandpa Yaakov and so were my grandparents, my Viennese grandparents, but they got their own apartment. This was probably because his kids were arriving from all over Europe and they didn't want to be in that whole *mispoche*, another family. So they got their own apartment somewhere nearby. It was a small town.

Then my mother got the phone call from Rudy, from Paris, the unexpected phone call. I think before that my mother had gotten in line (there were lines everywhere) I don't know where. The government was distributing guns and gas masks. And my mother got in line for four guns and four gas masks and one for a baby. Two for her parents, one for her husband, and one for herself.

I don't know whether she went for four guns, but she got in the line and found out that they didn't have any gas masks for babies or children. Which was like, excuse me, how can you fight a World War I-style battle without a gas mask for a kid? Typical.

Anyway, probably the thing with the gas masks had happened earlier and put a bad taste in her mouth and then she got the phone call and, I told you about party lines and how everybody could listen in?

Well, there were all these people who betrayed people. Informers, that's what they were called. And they would listen on the phones for people to say something. So my uncle Rudy talked as if it was just a regular day, but it was going to be his birthday party and that he hadn't seen them in a long time and he was sick and tired of it and he wanted to see us, and she should bring the baby. How dare she keep him from his niece? And he said, "You should bring the husband, because there's never enough men around."

He said he likes the husband because they can play tennis together or whatever. And that she should come tomorrow. She should come right away because the party was soon and she knew that meant *leave now*. They hadn't heard yet, in Czechoslovakia, what had happened. But they had heard it in Paris.

What had happened was a meeting between the prime minister of England and Hitler. The prime minister was old. He was elderly and Hitler was not. Hitler made the old man wait until midnight before he would agree to meet with him. So he really had the old man off his footing, and, once he did, he threw a tantrum in the meeting and used vile language such as this old British aristocrat had never heard and was so obnoxious that the Brit bent over backwards to get some kind of graceful peacefulness going, some diplomacy in the meeting. So he gave Hitler everything Hitler wanted. Hitler knew just how to play him.

Anyhow, so then came the sudden departure. And that sudden departure, he had heard it, but he couldn't tell her what he had heard. So he knew that they had to get out and get out fast before they shut down the train service between Czechoslovakia and France. And the train service went through Germany.

So I'm sure there was talk at Grandpa Yaakov's house among the sisters and brothers who were already there, and Grandpa Yaakov and my parents got ready to leave. My mother went to her parents to prepare them to leave with us. We were all going to ride the train together. But her parents refused to do that. They said they were too old. I think that my grandmother might have been like 58 or 60. Imagine.

They just wouldn't go. My mother never had what it took to stand up to something like that and be really persuasive and determined to win. She was too much of a middle child.

Anyhow, she gave in and I don't know whether she took me with her or whether I stayed with my father at my grandfather's house. But my mother and her mother slept in the same bed that night, in each other's arms crying. And they knew that they would never see each other again. And they didn't ever see each other again, and that grandmother ended up riding the cattle cars.

First she was placed in Theresienstadt, not truly a death camp, although it was a concentration camp. It was the showplace for the international Red Cross and anybody who came poking around the camps would get to see this place where Jews wrote poetry and gave concerts and painted paintings and did the things that Jews do. The people who got to go there were the people who were good at things. My grandma Olga was a good seamstress. And her sister, Olga's sister Emma, went also to Theresienstadt but she was not really smart. She was somewhat retarded. And because of that, they selected her out for Auschwitz, the death camp. I don't know what happened with my grandma Olga, but I bet that she selected herself out to go with her sister. People often did that. They changed being in the living line to the line of the dead. They didn't get to change from the line of the dead to the line of the living.

I found out about her through the Swiss government, which had lists of people who were in the cattle cars and died in transit and were delivered and died in location. Her name was there, and her sister Emma's name. But I didn't get that information until long after I was grown up.

So we went to the train station, and I don't know if we went by ourselves and we met my father's sister and her husband, her name was Edith and his name was Ferri. They lived in Budapest and their son was Julich. Or, I guess, Julius. He was 12.

I don't know how it all happened. And I don't know where the packing went on or who did it. But I kind of think, in my imagination, that we rode to the train station together in the back seat of the car, the women and children in the back seat and the two men up front and that Julich showed me his teddy bear. I thought his teddy bear was wonderful. He loved how much I loved his teddy bear and how much I admired him for having it.

He let me play with it and I loved it. And it was like seventh heaven. I had no idea how horrible things were in that moment. I'm sure his mother saw this going on. I was the only other child in that family. His mother and my father—they each had only one kid.

There must have been something about bonding the cousins and bonding the heirs-to-be. Because when we got to the train station and we were saying goodbye, my aunt said, "Son, give her your teddy bear." And I'm sure he didn't want to give it away. But he was probably a very good boy.

Anyway, I got it. And I'm sure I didn't abuse that teddy bear until I was 6 or 7. At that point, when I got it, I was only 2½, maybe not even 2½. And then the teddy bear got to live in Paris in a furnished room. And then he got to live on a ship that went through Haiti to Cuba. And he might've even gotten to meet some Haitians while he was on the ship, because the Haitians liked me a lot and they played with me a lot and they were very noble people, as my mother said.

She said they had much better manners than the European immigrants who were on the ship. And she refused to eat at the European tables. She would eat only with the Haitians because they were mannerly. So she took me, I'm sure, with her. Where she ate, I ate. And so the Haitians felt fine about playing with the kid, you know. I was an amusement for them.

And then, in Cuba, I guess he got to meet my cousin Peter and my cousin Charlotte, who probably didn't appreciate him nearly enough. And he probably got to meet my best friend next door with whom I had banana sandwiches often with the bananas from the tree out back.

I think that I began giving him haircuts when I learned how to cut with a scissor in preschool. In Brooklyn. He went through haircuts from the time I was 5 until I was 8, probably, and then I don't think I gave him haircuts any more after that. And there was a very special scene with him for me. I could throw him around because he wasn't like my other dolls. He wasn't American. He knew how bad it was. He knew how awful life was. He knew why I would be really angry to be alive. So he didn't begrudge me beating him up.

I wasn't a grownup beating him up, so I wasn't that strong. Anyhow, I don't know when he went out of my life but he sort of became, you know, just something I had. And I don't even know where he lived in my room when I was a teenager. Maybe in a box. But he never got thrown out because, of course, after the war, not right away after the war, maybe not 1945, but maybe 1947, I would've been 10 years old, we found out what happened to Julich. We finally had contact.

And I can only imagine, or no, I can't imagine, how my aunt and uncle must have felt, the desperation they must have felt about putting their child in a place where they couldn't get food and water to him. Where he would die. And I can't really go to what it must've been like in that sewer.

Julich was 15 when the Nazis arrived. My uncle Ferri was an engineer and he built bridges in Budapest. And because of that, he knew the people who were engineers and built the sewers. And somebody told him that would be a good place to hide his son. And that he could access it by this particular manhole cover, this section of sewer, which might have also been dry and rat free and so on. Anyhow, who knows? They put the kid down there, and for a long time they were able to get food and water to him.

I imagine that he was not alone. I hope not. But I imagine not. And then the Nazis must've found out about it through an informant and so they came with a tank and they placed the tank on top of the manhole cover. And there must've been something about the sewer structure that the boys, or the boy, couldn't get out from there and go to another section of sewer.

I could never throw the teddy bear out because I couldn't throw my cousin out. And it was the one thing, the one thing that linked me to him. Then I had a couple of kids. By now this teddy bear was really old and badly needed to be repaired. He kind of disintegrated over the years. And so my mother, who was a wonderful seamstress, did a wonderful job of restoring the outside and stuffing. She used whatever she could with whatever she had, which wasn't as good as what the Germans used, but it sufficed for the arms and legs. And then the boys, of course, had a teddy bear. And I didn't pay any attention to what they did with the teddy bear. And I didn't tell them about the teddy bear when they were little. And the teddy bear got more beat up than he had ever been before. And they got bored with him, too, when they were ready to be teenagers. And so he went in a box.

And every now and then, when I would open the box, I would realize I couldn't throw him out. But I didn't want him around the house. For what? So I put him back in the box. And then along comes my granddaughter Elizabeth who, oddly enough, I think is my mother reincarnated. She looks like my mother, she loves to knit like my mother loved to knit. And she's getting to have the wild life that my mother never got to have.

Anyhow, Elizabeth was with me and she was helping me in the garage, and I had the teddy bear in the steamer trunk that is filled with the things that I don't know what to do with but can't throw out. And she saw the teddy bear and, being me, I said, you want to know the story? So I told her the story of the teddy bear.

And then when I told her how old he was now—I'm 76, he's 88. An 88-year-old teddy bear. Anyway, she told me I had to fix him up, I couldn't just leave him be. I had bought the baskets that come from the Philippines. Every now and then I see some great baskets and they are always half off. I love to buy them and then I don't know what to do with them. But occasionally I give them, like when I give gifts, I put the gifts in there. And it makes a nice presentation. That's my excuse for buying them. And there's this great big basket I bought and never found a gift to put in it. It just fits the teddy bear. So I put the teddy bear in there and I put the teddy bear on top of the big file cabinet in my workroom. And then I put all of my Jewish *Yahrzeit* candles around the teddy bear so that he is holding everybody's death dates in his aura.

And you only get to see him in profile now. He looks very noble. He was lucky, that teddy bear. He escaped. I think that is the story.

I know Maria through the improv community. Her story is about growing up lesbian in a Latina community in Texas. Her poignant attachment to her doll, who represented her mother to whom she was greatly attached, is a big part of her story.

Maria

This is my story about my mom's doll when I was growing up in Dallas. She would make dolls out of rags and things. We moved to the United States from Mexico in 1971. I have six older brothers, three older sisters, and one younger sister and brother. I don't remember if my older sisters were into dolls or not. My little sister, Laura, was very girly, but I don't remember her having many dolls. We played with action figures and small figurines. We didn't have very many actual dolls. One time I went to Mexico and got a really nice native-looking crafted doll and I loved that doll.

When I decided I wanted to come to California my mother wasn't very happy about it. One of my older brothers had moved to Ohio, but then he's a man, so it was okay for him to go. I visited Santa Cruz and it was so much freer for my sort here than in Texas, especially back in the late '90s. I was tired of being closeted and teaching high school in Texas. A relationship had just ended and I just wanted some movement in my life. I'm sure you're aware about how Mexican families or Hispanic families aren't too keen on people leaving, but my mother let me go because she knew that's what I wanted to do. It was very difficult for her because she likes to keep a watchful eye on us, so when I was leaving she gave me this doll, her doll, and she said, "This is me." And I kept it.

When my mom died, I couldn't bear to see it and I just put it away. I don't even know where. Just a few months ago, we were kind of fixing stuff around the house and my friend Martin found it. And now, I guess it was like good timing because it seemed like I could go on again with my life. Before all this time I had been mourning my mom, and I suddenly found her doll again. Sadly, she's not in great shape, but I'm glad to have her back. It's not an incredible story, but it's something I found solace in. My mom died 11 years ago. I did not take her death well.

About the Author

Helene Simkin Jara is an actor, director and writer. She has been published in The Porter Gulch Review, La Revista and Mindprints, Phren-Z, Serving House Journal and Nerve Cowboy. In 2003, she was awarded best prose in the Porter Gulch Review for her short story, "Josefina" and once again in 2009 for her play, FUBMC. In November of 2006, her play "The Tongue" was be part of a festival at the African American Shakespeare Company in San Francisco. In 2007, her poem, "The Difference" was nominated for a Pushcart Prize. She wrote her first book in the third grade and stupidly gave it to her teacher, whom she despised. That is her only regret in life so far. She has self-published a book called Because I Had To, a collection of short stories, poems, plays and monologues. It was on the best seller list on Kindle, July 2014. She just published True Doll Stories We Remember and is about to publish a collection of short stories called Turn Left at the Gorilla and Go Down the Hall.

Put The Word
In Your Mouth

Believe God, Agree with His Word,
Declare His Word, and Change Your Life!

Angeline L. Williams

Foreword by Pastors Wilbert and Dr. Demona Warren

Put The Word In Your Mouth:
Believe God, Agree with His Word,
Declare His Word, and Change Your Life!

Copyright © 2018 by Angeline L. Williams
ISBN-13: 978-0-615-43175-8

Published by Redemption Books
http://www.redemptbooks.com

Book Design by Williams DocuPrep
http://www.williamsdocuprep.com

Table of Contents

Table of Contents 1

Dedication...4

Foreword..5

Introduction..7

The Transformation Chamber............................16

Blessing Blockers 23

    Pride..28

    Fear 32

    Disobedience...37

    Ungratefulness...41

    Unforgiveness 48

    Failure to Build God's House 51

    No Seed Sown, Eating God's Tithe................. 56

Renewing Your Mind......................................61

The Power of God's Word 66

Decree the Promise, Not the Problem! 77

Prophesying to Dry Bones................................ 108

Standing on God's Word 118

The Sword of The Spirit..................................136

The Spoken Blessing!.................................144

Faith Builders 157

Promises for Provision 164

Promises for Healing 174

Promises for Protection........................ 182

Promises for Strength............................ 188

Scripture Prayers & Confessions 191

    Faith Confession...............................192

    Favor 193

    Forgive Someone...............................194

    Forgiveness for Speaking Negatively 198

    Healing (Yours) 200

    Healing (Someone Else) 203

    Healing from Addiction..................206

    Hearing God's Voice 208

    Loss of a Loved One 209

    Marriage Restoration...................... 210

    Military Members, and Families 213

    Nation, Country...............................216

    Pastor and Church........................... 218

    Protection..220

    Provision 222

Receive the Holy Spirit 224

Right Attitude 225

Salvation of the Lost 226

Strength 228

Salvation of Unsaved Family 231

Wisdom and Guidance 233

Your Home 234

Your Children, Grandchildren 236

About The Author 237

Other Books By Author 239

Dedication

To my daughter, Pastor Eboni Davis: I appreciate you encouraging me to use the creative gifts God endowed me with. Although you are not here to share in the joy of this book being published, I know you are rejoicing with me in heaven. One day we will again join hands and praise God together. I love you Eboni.

To the greatest sons, a mother could have KaTarus and Antwaun: Thank you for being the blessings that you are. I will forever be grateful to God for sharing you with me. I will never stop telling you how much God and I love you.

To the reader: Praise the Lord! God has put this book in your hands because He wants you to experience all the benefits of the finished work of Christ. If you take heed to what God is saying in this book, your life will never be the same! If we never meet on this side, we too shall rejoice together and glorify Christ in heaven.

Foreword

As pastors, our heart's desire is to help encourage the growth of individuals, the family, and the church to educate, edify and embrace the future of the Christian community with grace, faith, hope and love.

In the book, *Put the Word in Your Mouth*, Evangelist Angeline Williams shares her personal testimony of how God taught her about the importance of putting His Word in our mouth. Angeline candidly teaches on how to stand on God's Word, trust and believe that God hears us and will answer.

Chapter by chapter, we found the book biblically sound, informative, thought provoking, easy to understand and to the point. We were inspired by its step by step format with God's promises, prayers, and scriptures for anyone who desires to grow and build their faith and knowledge through the Word of God – a book that contains everything a believer needs to know and then some.

This book is not fluff—it is a straight-forward, practical guide of how to make things happen by speaking the Word of God out of your mouth.

Pastors Wilbert and Demona Warren,
Grace Temple Christian Ministries

Introduction

"The thief comes only to steal and kill and destroy. I came that they may have life and have it abundantly." — John 10:10 (ESV)

The Bible is so much more than just a great read. When we actually choose to use it as God intended we discover that this timeless book is more powerful than we can imagine. At least I did. It deals with anything we have going on in life, even though it is thousands of years old.

The Word of God is so amazing that every time that you read the Bible, God can speak to you and touch you in a new way, no matter how many times you've read the same scripture. This is why we need to learn how to use the Bible as God intends. And God intends for His Word to be in your mouth as well as your heart.

Like every other God-given tool there are people who misuse God's Word because they either misunderstand the scriptures, or they take God's principles and try to put a worldly spin on them. This unfortunately has turned a lot of Christians away from teachings on faith and putting God's Word in your mouth. But that doesn't change God's intent or the power of His Word. God's Word is meant to be spoken every day, into and over any circumstance you have going on in your life that needs to be changed.

Put the Word in Your Mouth is the result of a word I received from God in prayer. During that time, I was a single parent in a new city with no family and three small children. I attended a local church which I supported whole heartedly with my tithes, offerings and time. I really wanted to please God.

I was doing everything I thought I needed to do to be a good Christian. I taught Sunday School, directed the choir and ministered to everyone God brought across my path that He said to speak to. Yet, it appeared that I was not receiving the blessings I felt I should have. I struggled greatly financially, and nothing seemed to break for me.

"Lord I believe Your Word is true. Why am I struggling so much and not experiencing what Your Word says", was my constant prayer.

Honestly, even when I asked the Lord what the problem was, I answered my own question with my wrong thinking or I relied on the opinions of others. Have you ever done that? I worked temporary jobs during that time, so I would change jobs often. There was never enough money, so we moved a lot, and our struggle was visible.

Rumors began to spread about me in my church that I was doing all sorts of ungodly things. Some of the seasoned saints said God had cursed me because of some hidden sin I was involved in. They told me that I needed to repent and confess my sins. Others said that my family, and I were under a generational curse. Others said that I didn't have enough faith.

I believed what was said about me; that God was against me, but I could not figure out why because my whole life was church and work. I would go home from Church and Bible Study every week broken and discouraged and cry most of the night. I wanted to give up on life, but I couldn't because of my children.

I constantly confessed any sin I thought I had committed or would commit. I prayed for more faith. I was in the prayer line almost every week trying to get free from whatever was holding me back. I went through my family lineage praying and breaking every curse I thought any family member might have committed that had been handed down to me and my children. Still no change. Rather than things getting better, they got worse.

My thoughts were a constant bombardment of discouragement and disappointment. I prayed the same prayer over and over, "Lord, I believe Your Word is true. Why am I struggling so much? Am I cursed? Are you angry with me?" I didn't even realize at the time how whiny I must have sounded to Him. One day I stayed quiet and still long enough to hear the Lord speak. He said,

"Daughter, put the Word in your mouth." It wasn't a loud, boisterous word, it was gentle and loving, yet it cut to the very core of my being.

As I meditated on what I had just heard I was led to Joshua 1:8:

"This book of the law shall not depart out of thy mouth; but thou shalt meditate therein day and night, that thou mayest observe to do according to all that is written therein: for then thou shalt make thy way prosperous, and then thou shalt have good success." — Joshua 1:8

Then I was led to Proverbs 18:20-21:

"A man's belly shall be satisfied with the fruit of his mouth; and with the increase of his lips shall he be filled. Death and life are in the power of the tongue: and they that love it shall eat the fruit thereof." — Proverbs 18:20-21

Lastly, I was led to Mark 11:23 where Jesus says:

"For verily I say unto you, that whosoever shall say unto this mountain, Be thou removed, and be thou cast into the sea; and shall not doubt in his heart, but shall believe that those things which he saith shall come to pass; he shall have whatsoever he saith."
— *Mark 11:23 (KJV)*

Although I had read each scripture before, this time it was like they exploded inside me. The words became Rhema, they entered my heart, and I understood something that I had never seen before. Now I could see why things were so arrayed, and why I was not receiving the blessings God's Word said I should have. No longer could I blame my lack of education, my past, my family or anyone else.

No, I was the culprit. I had been speaking against the Grace of God in my life and every blessing God had spoken over me. I had also been asking God to provide things that He's already provided. What I was lacking was the knowledge in how to access what was rightfully mine.

What I learned that day was just the beginning of what God would share with me. Over the years, the Lord has continued to teach me about the power of His Word, the power of faith in His Word, the power of my thoughts, and the words that I allow to come out of my mouth. I suspect that I will be learning more on this subject until the day I go home to be with the Lord.

We are in a spiritual war and one thing I've noticed is that Satan tries to discredit every tool God has given us to defeat him in our life and live victoriously. Confessing the Word of God is such a tool. Satan has twisted the Word of God since the Garden of Eden, however, when Believers started understanding the power of confessing God's Word into their life new man-made doctrines started popping up to cast doubt on the truth of God's Word.

Since there is so much controversy regarding speaking and confessing the Word of God, I want to clarify something before we move on. In this book I am in no way saying that we can manipulate God with our words or create things out of the blue. God is sovereign, so it would actually be pretty crazy to think that the created could control the Creator.

If you've read or heard any of the controversy and deception from the enemy's camp, I want you to put that out of your mind and focus on God's Word. Rely on the Holy Spirit to lead and guide us into all truth.

As you read and study this life changing message, with the Holy Spirit's help I believe your thoughts about yourself and God will be replaced with Kingdom thoughts, resulting in a closer walk with Christ. As you grow closer to Him, you will automatically begin to walk in the blessings Christ afforded us at the Cross.

My Prayer for You

Father, I pray for every person that reads this Message. I ask You to help them understand what You are speaking. Give them a renewed hunger to eat more of your Word. Let Your Word be the source of all that they say and do. Write Your truth upon their heart so that it may flow out of their mouth in abundance. May the reader receive healing in mind, soul, and body. In Jesus' name, I pray. Amen.

The Transformation Chamber

"Then Jesus was led by the Spirit into the desert to be tempted by the devil.
— Matthew 4:1

When God delivered Israel out of Egypt His intent was to lead them into the land "flowing with milk and honey" which He'd promised Abraham in Exodus 3:8. There is a great lesson in the Exodus story for us today. Most people think the Exodus story is about God delivering the Israelites from Egypt, and it is, but it is also a type and shadow of God's delivering people from the bondage of sin.

After leaving Egypt, the Israelites were driven into the wilderness to be tried and purged. They failed the test and their wilderness experience stretched to forty years.

All Believers go through wilderness seasons. Some more than others. It is not a joyful time, but it is a necessary time. While going through these times it may seem that we are being attacked on every side, as if God is far, far away, as a dear friend of mine who has gone on to be with the Lord described it, but the Word of God assures us that He is a very present help in times of trouble.

Strangely, these experiences often come right after great spiritual breakthroughs like it did with the Israelites.

Disobedience is a disservice to God, and to ourselves.

The Bible says Moses led 600,000 people out of Egypt. So, it is not hard to imagine why when God called Moses to lead them, he gave every excuse he could think of to get out of what the Lord wanted him to do. He said he didn't feel worthy, the people wouldn't believe him, and he wasn't good with words. Finally, he said, "Just send someone else." This time God responded in righteous anger and called Aaron to serve alongside his brother.

Many of us use similar excuses to avoid acting on the commands of God. We say we have no train-ing, no funds or no help. We want to pray about it, seek guidance and sleep on it, but if our boss at work asks us to do something, we do it right away, no questions asked. Is this reluctance to obey God merely a smoke-screen for unbelief?

God didn't accept Moses' excuses and He won't accept ours either. God basically told Moses, "it's not about who you are and what you think you can or can't do, but whose you are. "I AM that I AM."

Our flaws and inabilities don't stop God from calling us to do His work, but pride will. He uses imperfect people with a humble heart all the time to work His perfect plan through them. We may not even see ourselves as humble, but God does.

Life is filled with crooks and curves, trials, and temptations. You may get some bumps and bruises. However, through Christ, who lives inside you, you can do all things, especially those things that God has ordained you to do! As you learn and grow in Christ, you may miss a step or two here and there. If you do, just keep going!

It would be nice if He did, but God does not shield us from the consequences of our actions just because we are His children. He doesn't tell us we will never have pain, but He says He will give us peace, purpose, and power in the pain. Failure is not final for us, because the Holy Spirit is constantly working in us to carry out God's purposes.

Psalm 37:23-24 reminds us that the steps of a good man are ordered by the Lord, and He delights in his way. Though he fall, he shall not be utterly cast down; for the Lord upholds him with His hand. So if you fail or fall, view the defeat as a stepping stone knowing that God is working for your good in every situation. It may hurt, but with the Holy Spirit analyze the problem and find out why the fall happened and then act on that. Take the lesson and move on.

If the failure or lack of success is because of circumstances beyond your control, ask God what He wants you to learn and trust Him to bring good out of it. God's plan either way is for the failure to become a stepping stone to great success. So do not remain where you have fallen.

The world expects Christians to be perfect and as soon as one of us makes a mistake they are ready to pounce on us and call us hypocrites. Don't you do that to yourself or any other Christian. Donnie McClurkin said it best in song when he sang, "We fall down, but we get up." Your fall didn't surprise or shock God. He wants you to rise up, turn your eyes toward the prize and continue to aim for the goal.

Our flaws and inabilities don't stop God from calling us to do His work, but pride will. He uses

imperfect people with a humble heart all the time to work His perfect plan through.

The Apostle Paul set his mind to finish no matter what obstacles were in front of him or what the failures were behind him. He said in Philippians 3:13-14. "But one thing I do: Forgetting what is behind and straining toward what is ahead, I press on toward the goal to win the prize for which God has called me heavenward in Christ Jesus."

Press means to "pursue, to follow after, or to press forward." We can look back and praise God for our past successes, but we cannot live on yester-day's blessings. Leave the past in the past. Constantly focusing on past failures, struggles, obstacles and sins keeps us in the past and prevents us from moving forward.

During their travels in the desert, God gave the Israelites fresh manna for food in the desert daily for 40 years. The manna stayed fresh, so long as the people gathered it up according to His instructions (Numbers 20:11). God wanted them to learn to depend on Him for their supply.

God has promised to supply all our needs through His riches in Christ Jesus (Philippians 4:19). Sometimes the supply may seem slow, but it comes. A common catchphrase among the Body of Christ is, "He may not come when you want Him, but He's always on time."

We must depend on God alone for our provision and gather or count our blessings every day. We cannot get stuck in pause, we must press forward toward the goal. God assures us that He knows what we need before we ask, so we don't have to worry about provision. Scripture tells us to seek God and His kingdom by putting Him first and trust in His faithfulness to provide what we need (Matthew 6:33). When we do, He will provide.

Blessing Blockers

*"Examine yourselves, whether ye be in the
faith; prove your own selves."*
—2 Corinthians 13:5

*"For if we would judge ourselves, we
should not be judged."*
—1 Corinthians 11:31

The Israelites were the rightful owners of the Promised Land long before they entered it, because God had given the land to their Father Abraham and his descendants (Genesis 12:7). After 40 years of wandering in the wilderness and learning how to trust God Joshua was told to lead them into their inheritance.

Although God said the land belonged to the Israelites, it was occupied by powerful nations that had lived there a long time. They did not know

God, and they were not going to just give up their land, which meant that Israel would have to fight to take possession of it.

The naysayers in the Israelite camp became fearful and wanted to give up, but Joshua refused to back down in fear. He knew and believed that the covenant promise God made to Abraham hundreds of years earlier was still in effect, and that God would honor His Word. Had Joshua listened to the naysayers around him, the Israelites probably would have never possessed their inheritance.

As born again Believers, we are adopted children of the Living God. We are joint heirs with Christ. We have a great inheritance on earth, and in heaven (Romans 8:16-17). That alone is enough to praise God for, but it also means that as heirs of God and joint-heirs with Christ, we inherit-ed what belongs to God, and God owns the world and everything in it (Psalm 24:1). So if the earth is the Lord's and everything in it, then the heirs of the Lord will inherit the earth and everything in it.

Paul said it like this: *"For all things are yours, whether Paul or Apollos or Cephas or the world or life or death or the present or the future—all are yours, and you are Christ's, and Christ is God's"* (1 Corinthians 3:21–23).

So, what is our inheritance? In Ephesians 3:8, the Apostle Paul refers to our inheritance as *"the unfathomable riches of Christ."* Peter describes our inheritance as *"exceedingly great"* (2 Peter 1:3-4). Someone has estimated that in the Bible there are at least 30,000 promises that belong to the children of God.

All of God's blessings are ours in the Covenant of Grace, but having the title to our inheritance is not the same thing as possessing it. We must take possession of what is rightfully ours (Joshua 21:43). We must claim our inheritance by faith! Of course, Satan tries to prevent you from doing that.

Since God has blessed you, Satan cannot curse what the Lord has blessed, so he continually tries to get us to curse ourselves. He uses blessing blockers and strongholds to get us to sin against

God, and to get us off focus hoping we will just give up, cave in and quit on God. Blessing blockers and strongholds prevent you from seeing the Truth (Jesus Christ), receiving God's love, and having healthy relation-ships. These things can be emotional, spiritual or physical.

Because a person has been conditioned to think and act a certain way, most blessing blockers are unrecognizable right off. We can go through life with hurt and pain (real or imagined) embedded in our heart, soul, and emotions and not even realize it. I call them splinters in the heart.

When we have a splinter in the heart we may think everything is okay and then one day someone makes a comment, or we are hit with a pressure or trial and suddenly those coping and defense mech-anisms that we've used for so long are not working! Our immediate reaction is to pull away and withdraw or we might verbally or even physically lash out!

God wants His children to be delivered from every bondage. He wants us to deal with our heart splinters. When He wants to heal us in a certain area, He will allow a few splinters to surface. However, many of us try to protect the wound and blame others for the pain, instead of acknowledging it and giving it to God to address it, remove and heal it. I've been there several times. I finally learned to stop fighting God and let Him have His way. I am still a work in progress, but I am a lot more peaceful than I used to be.

This chapter is about dealing with those splinters that block our blessings. While going through this section you may get a bit uncomfortable, and you might want to skip over this section, but please don't, God may just be cutting away some blessing blockers that have attached themselves to your soul to hinder your growth in Christ. Let Him do the work.

You may even be wondering what all this has to do with putting the Word of God in your mouth. Well, if you don't identify and deal with those strongholds or mindsets, and that keep you sinning and speaking curses into your life you will never change the way your life is going.

God's Word is alive and powerful! It will deliver us from gripping fear (Psalm 34:4). It will deliver us from depression and loneliness (Isaiah 41:10). It will deliver us from difficult situations and every bondage. If you study His Word, meditate on it, confess it and live by it, it will change you, and you will experience all that He has for you. You will develop the closest and most intimate relationship with Him a person can have! So, buckle your seat belt and go for the ride.

Before we move on let's pray:

Search me, O God, and know my heart! Try me and know my thoughts! And see if there be any grievous way in me, and lead me in the way everlasting! — Psalm 139:23–24

Pride

Pride is arrogant and self-worshipping. It is an attitude of independence from God. It keeps men from crying out for a Savior. The psalmist says in Psalm 10:4, "The wicked in his proud countenance does not seek God; God is in none of his thoughts."

The Bible says God hates pride and will work against the proud to humble them. Proverbs 15:25 says, "The Lord will destroy the house of the proud," and 1 Peter 5:5 tells us that God resists the proud.

When God showed me that I had pride in my heart, I was surprised because I thought I had dealt with pride years ago. I considered myself to be pretty humble. I guess that's because pride is easier to see in others than in ourselves.

Could some of the trials and tribulations I was enduring be because God was opposing me? What a sobering thought! Had I allowed my relationship with Christ to suffer because I failed to deal with my pride? I thank God for the opportunity to repent and ask for help to deal with pride, especially that hidden pride.

Listen, if you think you have no pride, that's a good indication that you have it. Since we know God resists the proud we should quickly humble ourselves so God doesn't have to do it for us.

"And whoever exalts himself will be humbled, and he who humbles himself will be exalted." —Matthew 23:12.

This scripture is talking about not thinking too highly of yourself, but thinking too poorly of yourself can also be proudful. I read somewhere that humility is not thinking less of yourself, but rather thinking of yourself less. Jesus said in Matthew 6:33, "But seek first the kingdom of God and His righteousness, and all these things shall be added to you."

There can be no real prayer, no real repentance without humility. God required the people of Israel to humble themselves before they prayed and repented. He said,

"If My people who are called by My name will humble themselves, and pray and seek My face, and turn from their wicked ways, then I will hear from heaven, and will forgive their sin and heal their land." — 2 Chronicles 7:14

Humble means to bend the knee or to place oneself under another. God was going to destroy the city of Nineveh because of their wickedness. In His mercy, He sent Jonah to warn them to repent (Jonah 3:4).

Verse 5 says the people of Nineveh believed God, humbled themselves and proclaimed a fast, from the greatest to the least of them. The king got wind of it and he too humbled himself and proclaimed a fast. When the people humbled themselves, God sent them a revival. He can, and will do the same for us when we make His priorities our priorities. Until we admit to ourselves that we have a pride problem, we will not be able to over-come pride.

The number one way to kill pride is to yield to the will of God. How do you know His will? It's in His Word. Take your eyes off yourself and place them on the Lord. Prioritize the "Kingdom of God" over the "Kingdom of self."

Fear

There are three kinds of fears that we should be aware of: healthy fear, harmful fear, and holy fear. Two of these fears are mentioned in the Bible:

- the fear of the LORD, and

- the Spirit of Fear.

Healthy fear is known as the "fight or flight response." This is the body's natural, built-in stress response to perceived threat or danger. This type of fear is normal and can save your life in a dangerous situation.

The fear of the LORD is a reverence and awe for God. It is an attitude of trust in the Lord. It motivates us towards holy living, reverence of God, and righteousness. Proverbs 1:7 tells us that the fear of the LORD is the beginning of knowledge, so this type of fear is also healthy.

There is also what some call a fear of God that is ungodly. This ungodly fear of God is the result of a wrong perception of God. God does not want His children afraid of Him.

The unprofitable servant in Matthew 25:25 is an example of an ungodly fear of God. When asked what had he done with the talent he was given, his excuse was he was afraid so he hid the talent. Fear of the master stopped him from producing and deprived him of his destiny in the Kingdom of God.

Then there is the *Spirit of Fear*. This fear does not come from God either, but from Satan. The spirit of fear is a door opener to other demonic spirits. It is a tormenter and crippler. Its goal is to keep you from fulfilling your destiny in the Kingdom.

"For God hath not given us the spirit of fear; but of power, and of love, and of a sound mind." —2 Timothy 1:7 (KJV)

Knowing that God has not given us a spirit of fear is the beginning of deliverance from the spirit of fear. When Paul wrote the Book of Second Timothy, it was a difficult time for the Early Church. Satan was trying to block the spreading of the Gospel. He was using the Emperor Nero to perse-cute Believers through gruesome and cruel me-thods. Timothy, the pastor of the church of Ephesus was concerned and felt he and his church was in danger too. Paul wrote Timothy a letter to encou-rage him. Timothy, he said:

"I remind you to stir up the gift of God which is in you through the laying on of my hands. For God has not given us a spirit of fear, but of power and of love and of a sound mind." —(2 Timothy 1:6-7)

In other words, Timothy remember who you are and whose you are! Stir up the Christ inside you and do not be afraid.

The Greek word for "sound mind" is sophroneo. Sophroneo is combined from the words sodzo and phroneo. Sodzo means to be saved, rescued, pro-tected or delivered. Phroneo is defined as to have understanding, to be wise; to be of the same mind.

So with this understanding 2nd Timothy 1:7 could be translated like this:

"God has not given you a spirit of fear, but a spirit of power and of love and a mind that has been delivered, rescued, protected, and agrees with God."

As a Believer you have the mind of Christ, which agrees with God now.

"For "who has known the mind of the Lord that he may instruct Him?" But we have the mind of Christ." —1 Corinthians 2:16

"(10) and have put on the new man who is renewed in knowledge according to the image of Him who created him" — Colossians 3:11

You don't have to accept whatever pops into your head, or what Satan and his imps whisper to you. You can choose what you allow into your mind. You should stop wrong thinking before it takes root in your spirit.

Scripture tells us to cast down arguments and every high thing that exalts itself against the knowledge of God and to bring every thought to the obedience of Christ (2nd Corinthians 10:5-6). If you guard your mind with the Word of God, you will find yourself thinking differently, which will result in you acting and reacting differently.

I've found that gathering scriptures on certain circumstances and then reciting them over and over increases my faith and sows the Word in my heart. Then when fear, worry, or doubt starts to talk to me the Word is stored in my heart, ready to be con-fessed and bring life and light to the darkness trying to surround me.

For instance with fear I might confess something like:

"God has not given me a spirit of fear. He has given me the spirit of power and love and a sound mind. My mind has been delivered, rescued, protected, and agrees with God."

Or something like:

I have the mind of Christ. Satan has no power over me. Greater is He that is in me, than he that is in the world. I will fear no evil, for the Lord is with me. His Word and His Spirit comforts me. I am far from oppression. No evil shall befall me, neither shall any plague come near my dwelling. For God has given His angels charge over me, and they keep me in all my ways. What ever I do for the Kingdom of God flourishes and prospers. (Romans 12:2; 1 John 4:4; Isaiah 54:14; Galatians 1:4; Psalm 1:3, 91:11)

Doing this helps me focus on Christ and on things above (Philippians 4:8). It reminds me of what has been accomplished on my behalf at the Cross, and then the spirit of fear, and the negative thoughts are expelled. You should try it, you will be astonished at how much it helps.

Disobedience

"If they obey and serve Him, they shall spend their days in prosperity, and their years in pleasures." — Job 36:11

Obedience is key to receiving the blessings and promises of God. Submission to God's will for our life is so important, that until we really grab hold of this concept God can't bless us the way that He wants to. How do you know God's will? God's will is revealed to us in the Bible, so you will have to study and meditate on His Word.

Psalm 37:23 tells us, "The steps of a good man are ordered by the LORD: and he delighteth in His way." In Jeremiah 29:11 God says, "For I know the thoughts that I think toward you, says the Lord, thoughts of peace and not of evil, to give you a future and a hope."

God is omnipotent and all knowing. He owns tomorrow. He knows what we need and He knows the traps and snares Satan has set up to trip us up and harm us. When He tells us to do something, it is because He loves us and wants to protect us and guide us into what is best for us.

Also, God has an eternal plan and as Believers, we are a part of that plan. He wants to use us to reach the lost and dying, by representing Jesus Christ and sharing the Gospel. As ambassadors of

Christ, it is our responsibility to obey what He asks us to do fully, not half way.

First Samuel chapter 15 gives us an example of how serious God is about us being obedient to His will. God wanted to punish the Amalek nation for what they did to Israel. He gave King Saul specific instructions to completely destroy the entire Amalekite nation. Saul was to kill the men, women, children, babies, cattle, sheep, goats, camels, and donkeys. It sounds cruel, but this is what God wanted.

Saul slaughtered everyone, but King Agag, and he also kept the best animals and everything else that appealed to him. He destroyed only what was worthless or of poor quality. Then he lied and said he had carried out the Lord's command. God got angry and told the prophet Samuel to tell him, "Hath the Lord as great delight in burnt offerings and sacrifices, as in obeying the voice of the Lord? Behold, to obey is better than sacrifice, and to hearken than the fat of rams" (1 Samuel 15:22). Saul's disobedience cost him his destiny as king and he ended up committing suicide (1 Samuel

31:3–6). Almost isn't good enough when it comes to obedience.

Disobedience is an act of rebellion. Rebellion is sinful and a form of idolatry. Disobedience shows a lack of trust in God. Disobedience basically says to God, "I don't like your plan, my plan is better so I'm going to do it this way."

When we walk in deliberate disobedience, we are giving in to the kingdom of darkness, and reject-ing God's wisdom, opening ourselves up to all Satan has to offer. Remember, Jesus said that the thief only comes to steal, kill and destroy (John 10:10). Regardless of how good sin looks or feels it is de-structive and leads to death.

Remebter that obedience and blessings go hand-in-hand! There are several scriptures that confirm this. Here are a few to meditate on: Psalm 112:1-3; Job 36:11; Deuteronomy 28:1-14; Isaiah 48:18; Isaiah 1:19; Acts 5:32; Romans 2:13; John 9:31.

Ungratefulness

Have you ever done something for someone from the kindness of your heart, and then the person acted like you owed it to them, and wouldn't even say thank you? It's just plain old good manners to say thank you when someone shows you kindness, right? Nevertheless, we should never be surprised when we encounter such rudeness, it's a common attitude of the times we live in. In Paul's letter to Timothy, he said that ingratitude would be one of the evils found in the last days (2 Timothy 3:1-5).

When we read the story of ancient Israel, we see the perfect example of how ungratefulness looks and what happens to ungrateful people. Three days after crossing the Red Sea, the Israelites complained against Moses. "Why have you brought us out here to die in this wilderness?" they cried (Numbers 21:5). They had forgotten the oppression they were under in Egypt. They had forgotten the terrible plagues God brought upon Pharaoh for their benefit. In just three short days they forgot how they walked through the Red Sea on dry land.

They were not thankful for God's miraculous deliverance, and their ingratitude led to most of them never receiving the blessings God had already given them. Scripture says, "their bodies were scat-tered in the wilderness" (1 Corinthians 10:5).

The Israelites were like many of us today. Once they were free, they expected all their problems to be solved at once, so when things didn't go the way they thought they should they discounted all that God had done. When I first got saved I had this disillusionment too. I naively expected that nothing evil would ever touch me again. There were many times when this deception caused me to complain.

I remember one particular time there had been a rash of break-ins in the parking garage in the apartment building I lived in. When I heard about what was happening, I prayed over my car and fully expected that no evil would befall it. One morning after that when I got to my car, I saw that someone had tampered with the door lock and I realized that they tried to break into it. I immediately got angry and began to complain and accuse God of not pro-tecting my car.

After a few minutes of fussing, it dawned on me just how silly and ungrateful I was being. I realized that I was acting like a spoiled ungrateful brat, just like the Israelites. My car had not been stolen or destroyed and my key still worked. I was able to get in my car, start it up and drive to work. I realized that the angels of God thwarted the thief's plan. A grateful person would have been praising God. I felt horrible! I am so glad God is merciful. I asked God to forgive me, I repented and changed my un-grateful attitude to one of praise. Glory halleluiah! I'm so glad for those new mercies every morning!

Often when trials come, we question why God would allow us to go through such a thing. Truth is, God never promised that we wouldn't endure trials. However, He did promise that He would be with us during the trial.

To God an ungrateful attitude is evil! God called the Israelites an "evil congregation" for their sinful ingratitude (Numbers 14:27). He got so angry with them that He wanted to kill them all off, but Moses prayed for them and God decided not to kill them. But He said the complainers would not enter into The Promised Land.

Have you ever grown tired of the provision you asked God for? Say a house, a car, children, or a spouse and began to complain about it? Then soon it became difficult to pay the rent or mortgage, the car started having mechanical failures, you and your spouse started arguing more and more, and the more you complained the worse things got in your life? Is this where you are right now?

Ecclesiastes 10:12 says, "The words of a wise man's mouth are gracious, but the lips of a fool shall swallow him up." The words we speak can block or open up our blessings. God is pleased when we "offer the sacrifice of praise with the fruit of our lips" (Hebrews 13:15).

In Psalm 107:22, we are commanded to offer "sacrifices of thanksgiving, and declare His works with rejoicing." Praising God and confessing His promises has helped me many times over the years. I am reminded of one particular time where praising God brought breakthrough. Years ago, my children and I were living in an extended stay motel. My hours at work had been cut and the weekly rent was eating up most of my paycheck.

One week I couldn't make the rent which needed to be paid by checkout time. I was worried, and I didn't know what to do. I was praying and was reminded of the phrase, "when the praises go up the blessings come down." So, I started singing praise songs and praying scriptures from the book of Psalm. It was tough at first because my flesh wanted to focus on the situation, but I kept going and the praise took over and my faith kicked in.

After about an hour the phone rang. It was my son whom I hadn't talked to in several months, which was also weighing heavy on my heart. I was so happy to hear his voice. That phone call itself was an answered prayer. I reluctantly told him what was going on and he said that he would wire us some money to take care of the rent. So we had the money for another week.

That same day, I got a phone call from my pastor who said a former colleague of his had recently come into some money. He said God told him to sow into a single mother and her children. My pastor told him about me and my situation. That man paid for the room for a month and then helped us get into an apartment. Everytime I share this story my eyes fill up with tears of gratefulness to God for His faithfulness.

God inhabits the praises of His people. When we praise and worship Him, the presence of God fills every situation that we are facing, and once God's presence comes in, nothing contrary to God's will can stay around. We will experience victory!

Praise is a powerful weapon. It is so powerful that it caused the prison doors to open for Paul and Silas and several other prisoners. Also, a Philippian guard and his family became Believers (Acts 16:23-26). Paul and Silas knew that praising God would bring them into God's presence and power. The Bible says in Psalm 22:3, that God inhabits the praises of His people. And look what Psalm 149:5-9 says,

"(5) Let the faithful rejoice that he honors them. Let them sing for joy as they lie on their beds. (6) Let the praises of God be in their mouths, and a sharp sword in their hands— (7) to execute vengeance on the nations and punishment on the peoples, (8) to bind their kings with shackles and their leaders with iron chains, (9) to execute the judgment written against them. This is the glorious privilege of His faithful ones. Praise the Lord!" —Psalm 149:5-9 (NLT)

The scripture says, "Let the praises of God be in your mouth, and a sharp sword in your hands." The praises of God and the effective use of His Word are two powerful and effective weapons to aggressively oppose the kingdom of Satan. When we praise God, we humble ourselves and center our attention upon the Lord with expressions of love, adoration, and thanksgiving.

Praise is something we offer to God because we believe in Him, love Him, and believe He is worthy of our praise. Don't let thankfulness and praise be something you only do at church. Make them a part of your everyday lifestyle. Include them in your daily prayer life and when the enemy comes a calling, get to praising God and send him running.

Unforgiveness

In Matthew 6:9-13, Jesus teaches us to pray, "And forgive us our debts, as we forgive our debtors." And when the prayer was finished Jesus added this warning:

> *"For if ye forgive men their trespasses, your heavenly Father will also forgive you: but if ye forgive not men their trespasses, neither will your Father forgive your trespasses"* — *Matthew 14-6:15*

Look how the Message translation says it:

> *"In prayer there is a connection between what God does and what you do. You can't*

get forgiveness from God, for instance, without also forgiving others. If you refuse to do your part, you cut yourself off from God's part." —*Matthew 6:14-15 (MSG)*

Refusing to forgive others after God has forgiven our massive debts towards Him shows a lack of appreciation of how much God has forgiven us. In Matthew chapter 18, Jesus tells talks about the servant who owed millions of dollars to a king. The king canceled his debt when he asked for mercy. This same servant then threw a fellow servant that owed him only a few hundred dollars in prison. He did not appreciate that the king had forgiven his great debt. When his fellow servants saw what he did, they got upset and told the king.

The king summoned the man and said, "You evil servant! I forgave your entire debt when you begged me for mercy. Shouldn't you be compelled to be merciful to your fellow servant who asked for mercy?" The king was so furious that he sent the man to the torture chamber until he had paid every last penny due.

Jesus says in verse 35, "So My heavenly Father also will do to you if each of you, from his heart, does not forgive his brother his trespasses." Unforgiveness blocks the flow of God's blessings and hinders your prayers. Matthew 5:23-24 says, "Therefore if you bring your gift to the altar, and there remember that your brother has something against you, leave your gift there before the altar, and go your way. First be reconciled to your brother, and then come and offer your gift."

Peter asked Jesus, "Lord, how many times shall I forgive my brother when he sins against me? Up to seven times?" Jesus answered, "I tell you, not seven times, but seventy times seven."

Forgiveness is not excusing the action. In fact, in order to forgive, we must acknowledge the hurt a person has caused us. For-giveness is primarily for your own benefit because as long as you are feeling like a victim, you will hold on to bitterness.

Several studies have shown that bitterness and the anger and depression that accompany it can be linked to health issues like cardiovascular problems and a weak immune system. You will also open a door for the enemy to come in and cause havoc in your life. Just being a Christian will bring enough persecution in your life, you don't need to help Satan out by walking in unforgiveness.

Failure to Build God's House

The task was to rebuild the Temple that had been destroyed when the people of Judah were taken captive into Babylon. God made it clear that He wanted the Temple rebuilt. He even set things in order so the task could be completed, but because the people ran into opposition they reasoned that God didn't want the Temple built yet.

They shut God's business down and their desires took precedence over the things of God! They were living like they could do life without God. Because of their selfish living, they suffered in every area. It is never God's will that His children suffer, so He sent Haggai to talk with them.

"(5) Now, therefore, thus says the Lord of hosts: Consider your ways. (6) You have sown much, and harvested little. You eat, but you never have enough; you drink, but you never have your fill. You clothe yourselves, but no one is warm. And he who earns wages does so to put them into a bag with holes.

(7) "Thus says the Lord of hosts: Consider your ways. (8) Go up to the hills and bring wood and build the house, that I may take pleasure in it and that I may be glorified, says the Lord. (9) You looked for much, and be-hold, it came to little. And when you brought it home, I blew it away. Why? declares the Lord of hosts. Because of my house that lies in ruins, while each of you busies himself with his own house.

(10) Therefore the heavens above you have withheld the dew, and the earth has withheld its produce. (11) And I have called for a drought on the land and the hills, on the grain, the new wine, the oil, on what the

ground brings forth, on man and beast, and on all their labors." —Haggai 1:5-11 (ESV)

Some people think, or are even taught that if opposition comes when we are trying to fulfill something God has asked us to do, it means that we either missed God or it is not time yet. I disagree with that theory because whenever we make a commitment to the Lord, we will face opposition in one form or another.

For instance, you might be laughed at and called a "Bible Thumper" or "holier than thou" for using the Bible as a resource for daily living. Or you may be ridiculed for trusting in God in a difficult situation. It's all a part of the enemy's strategy to get you off focus!

I mentioned earlier how much I used to cry at the way I was treated. My pastor said to me, "Angeline, God has called you as His prophet. You cannot be a soft weeping prophet. Sometimes prophets have to share a hard word that God gives. God is going to toughen you up so that you will be able to speak what He says". Not long after that, I started enduring a lot of scorn and ridicule. I didn't understand what was happening at the time and I definitely didn't like it, but I am thankful for the persecution now.

Unfortunately, many Christians can't handle scorn and ridicule, and they surrender at the slight-est bit of opposition. Nehemiah prayed specifically about the problem he faced, and he continued to build (Nehemiah 4:4-5). If we are sure of what God said, when we are confronted with opposition, we must maintain our determination and continue God's work while we pray.

Jesus said in Matthew 6:33, "But seek first the kingdom of God and His righteousness, and all these things will be added to you." Is God saying through Haggai and Jesus that we should neglect our daily duties like going to work and taking care of our families? Of course not, but for the Christian, the things of God should be top priority. Christian-ity and Kingdom living isn't a philosophy, it is a way of life.

Take an honest look at your current priorities. Where are you investing most of your time, money, and energy? Are you too busy building up your life to take care of the things of God? Has God asked you to do something that you have placed on the shelf for a better time? Are you waiting for everything to fall into place before you get started?

The people of Judah faced opposition, so they concluded that God did not want His temple rebuilt at that time. They were incorrect.

Listen, as long as we are on this side of heaven we will face opposition. Satan is always going to try to stop you from completing your assignment. He tries to get you focused on self-seeking and self-gratifying things so you won't have time for the things of God. Don't let this happen. Make God's business a priority, and He will take care of your business.

I do not believe that just because you are saved and worship God that you will amass great wealth. I do believe if you worship God and put Him first in your life He will meet your needs and give you the desires of your heart. We are assured of that in Philippians 4:19, but keep in mind that God's idea of what we need might be different from ours, and His timing will be different from our timing as well.

If you feel like you work and work and can't ever seem to get ahead, as if your pockets have holes in them, I encourage you to consider your ways. Ask God to show you if, and where you are lacking in putting Him and The Kingdom first and then do what He says.

No Seed Sown, Eating God's Tithe

"While the earth remains, seedtime and harvest, cold and heat, winter and summer, and day and night shall not cease." — *Genesis 8:22*

God set up the universe and holds it in place by His Word. He set certain things in place to keep things flowing smoothly. Like the Law of Gravity, and the body being capable of healing itself, and every man is appointed to die, there are also moral and spiritual laws that God has written into His creation. The fact that someone does not believe in God or His laws, does not prove that they do not exist or that they do not work. We can ignore the laws God has given to govern our lives, but when we ignore God's counsel we bring about our own ruin. One such law that God has declared for how our world will be run is "seed time and harvest time".

Galatians 6:7-8 says, "Do not be deceived, God is not mocked; for whatever a man sows, that he will also reap. For he who sows to his flesh will of the flesh reap corruption, but he who sows to the Spirit will of the Spirit reap everlasting life."

Seeds reproduce after their own kind. We reap only what has been sown. If we sowed apple seeds in the past, we will reap apples today. As the saying goes, "What goes around comes around".

If a rich farmer and a poor farmer sow the same amount of seed in the same soil they will receive the same size harvest. If we sow to the Spirit, we reap of the Spirit. If we sow to the flesh, we reap of the flesh. If we sow good, we will reap good. If we sow evil, we will reap evil.

Many people look at Believers who are on fire for God and think that they have some special anointing. They don't realize that these people have sowed tremendously into the Spirit or that they spend most of their time with God in prayer and in His Word. They are thirsty for the things of God and the things of the world will never quench that thirst. Who we are today is a result of the seeds we sowed yesterday.

Many people believe tithing and giving is an Old Testament ritual and is no longer required under the New Covenant. While it is true that tithing is not mentioned as an instruction or a law, in the New Testament the apostles did encourage Believers to give financially. Second Corinthians chapter six tells us that God loves a cheerful giver.

"(6) But this I say: He who sows sparingly will also reap sparingly, and he who sows bountifully will also reap bountifully. (7) So let each one give as he purposes in his heart, not grudgingly or of necessity; for God loves

a cheerful giver. (8) And God is able to make all grace abound toward you, that you, always having all sufficiency in all things, may have an abundance for every good work." — 2 Corinthians 9:6-8 (NKJV)

Remember, there can be no harvest without planting. Nothing multiplied by nothing equals nothing. Its just that simple.

Well, those are the blessing blockers I want to share. There may be others that you need to deal with, so ask God to reveal if He would like you to release something and then release it to Him. It may even take some time to deal with them all. The point is that you want to live holy and righteous.

"(3) But know that the Lord has set apart[a] for Himself him who is godly; the Lord will hear when I call to Him. (4) Be angry, and do not sin. Meditate within your heart on your bed, and be still. Selah (5) Offer the sacrifices of righteousness, and put your trust in the Lord."

I often relate the Christian growth process to layers of an onion. As we grow in Christ, God removes all those stinky layers off of us and heals the area where they used to be. The Israelites had to conquer many cities and overcome many obstacles as they learned to trust God. It's all about *your* freedom! You have to choose to be free. You have to choose to renew your mind daily.

Renewing Your Mind

"And do not be conformed to this world, but be transformed by the renewing of your mind, that you may prove what is that good and acceptable and perfect will of God."

—*Romans 12:2 (NKJV)*

New King The primary way Satan is able to keep Believers from walking in the victory of our new life is by bombarding our minds with negative thinking. He knows our thoughts are a guiding force in our lives, and they open the door to our heart, so he puts a lot of effort into putting bad thoughts into our minds. This is why God tells us in Romans 12:2 that we need to renew our minds.

Renewing your mind is critical to walking in victory in Christ. When I was a teenager, I received salvation. However, that was only the beginning of my Christian experience. It was several years before my life began to change, mainly because I needed to renew my way of thinking.

When we get saved, our spirit is redeemed and reborn instantly. It belongs to God. Although we are a new creation in Christ, we don't immediately stop sinning. Anyone who leads you to believe they did is not being honest. Some sinful habits may have disappeared, but there were some areas where we had to continue to apply Christ's redemptive work. And no matter how long we have been saved, there are some areas where we must continue to apply Christ's redemptive work!

Where our mind goes, our actions will soon follow.

The struggle with temptation, bitterness, hope-lessness, frustrations, depression, fear, and evil thoughts is real because the old way of thinking has not gone away. We must continue to apply Christ's redemptive work in our lives.

Behind every sin is a belief. Where our mind goes, our actions will soon follow. If you lie and cheat it's because you believe lying and cheating will cause you less pain than being honest. It's a lie, but you believe it, so you do it.

God wants us to live an abundant victorious life (John 10:10). If a Christian is not actively trying to renew their mind by reading and hearing the Word of God this Christian will not grow in the ways of the Lord and will find themselves doing Satan's will (2 Peter 2:19).

Romans 6:16 says it like this: "Do you not know that to whom you present yourselves slaves to obey, you are that one's slaves whom you obey, whether of sin leading to death, or of obedience leading to righteousness?"

If we want to live the life God has purposed for us then we need to renew our minds with His Word. God can't renew your mind for you, it is something that you will have to do. But the good news is God has given you the tools to do it. Romans 12:1-2 gives us some instruction on renewing our mind:

"... present your bodies a living sacrifice, holy, acceptable unto God, which is your reason-able service. (2) And be not conformed to this world: but be ye transformed by the renew-ing of your mind, that ye may prove what is that good, and acceptable, and perfect, will of God." —Romans 12:1-2

Philippians chapter four gives us more instruc-tion on renewing our mind:

"(8) Finally, brothers, whatever is true, whatever is honorable, whatever is just, whatever is pure, whatever is lovely, what-ever is commendable, if there is any excel-lence, if there is anything worthy of praise, think about these things. (9) What you have learned and received and heard and seen in me—practice these things, and the God of peace will be with you." —Philippians 4:8-9 (ESV)

And then Hebrews 3:1 gives us some instruction on renewing our mind as well:

"Therefore, holy brethren, partakers of the heavenly calling, consider the Apostle and High Priest of our confession, Christ Jesus,"
—*Hebrews 3:1 (ESV)*

Notice each of the above scriptures say YOU must do something:

- YOU consider Jesus (Hebrews 3:1)

- YOU think about these things (Phil 4:8)

- What YOU have learned, received, heard and seen put into practice. (Philipians 4:9)

- BE TRANSFORMED by the renewal of YOUR mind. (Romans 12:2)

As you continue to read, meditate upon, and apply God's Word in your daily life, you will change from the inside out. You will begin to reflect God's character, and through you others will see that the Lord is good!

The Power of God's Word

*"For I am not ashamed of the gospel of Christ,
for it is the power of God to salvation for
everyone who believes, for the Jew first and also
for the Greek."*
— Romans 1:16

The Bible is a collection of sixty-six books, written over a period of 1600 years by 40 different men from diverse backgrounds. God used a doctor, fishermen, shepherds, soldiers, kings and princes from 13 different countries and three different continents to tell the greatest story of all time. This remarkable masterpiece has stood for over 2,000 years and is the number one bestselling book of all time.

For me, the Bible is amazing in the fact that although the Bible was written thousands of years ago, today it speaks to the world's circumstances, and to our own personal needs and circumstances.

As remarkable as the Bible is, the Word of God is mocked, criticized and challenged constantly. Nonbelievers say they reject the Bible because it was written by man to control people and should be dismissed. I shouldn't be amazed because I know who and what is behind the hatred, but I am, especially since so much gibberish written by man is readily accepted.

When I first started reading the Bible it just seemed like a bunch of rules and regulations, especially the Old Testament. Many passages in the Old Testament literally scared me, but the more I read and studied the Word of God, the more I recognized how powerful and truthful it is. I've come to realize that God's Word is so precise that even the periods and commas have a meaning.

Jesus is the Word of God. In John 1:1 we read, "In the beginning was the Word, and the Word was with God, and the Word was God." Then in John 1:14 it says, "The Word became flesh and made His dwelling among us." Jesus Christ, the Son of God is the dominating figure in the Bible from beginning to end.

Second Timothy 3:16 says,

"(16) All Scripture is given by inspiration of God, and is profitable for doctrine, for reproof, for correction, for instruction in righteousness, (17) that the man of God may be complete, thoroughly equipped for every good work."

Inspired means "God breathed". God has given us the instructions in His Word to live a victorious life. If we study and meditate on the Word we will come to live the abundant life Jesus talks about in John 10:10. I've heard it said that a Bible that is falling apart usually belongs to a person who isn't.

The Holy Spirit is the One who gives life. Jesus said, "It is the Spirit who gives life; the flesh profits nothing. The words that I speak to you are spirit, and they are life" (John 6:63).

The following verses talk about the supernatural power in the Word of God.

Isaiah 55:11: So shall My word be that goes forth from My mouth; it shall not return to Me void, but it shall accomplish what I please, and it shall prosper in the thing for which I sent it.

Jeremiah 23:29: Is not My Word like a fire?" says the Lord, "And like a hammer that breaks the rock in pieces?

Psalm 119:50: This is my comfort in my affliction, for Your Word has given me life.

Jeremiah 15:16: "Your Words were found, and I ate them, and Your Word was to me the joy and rejoicing of my heart ..."

Matthew 4:4: But He answered and said, "It is written, 'Man shall not live by bread alone, but by every Word that proceeds from the mouth of God.'

Jesus says in Matthew 24:35, "Heaven and earth shall pass away, but my words shall not pass away." God is faithful to His Word! You can trust it and Him! His Word is eternal and forever settled in heaven (Psalm 119:89). Everything in life may change, but God's Word remains constant. His truth never changes.

"The grass withers, the flower fades, but the word of our God will stand forever." — *Isaiah 40:8 (ESV)*

"But the word of the Lord endures forever."... —*1 Peter 1:25*

Forever means without beginning or end. Settled means to be firmly fixed so that an object cannot be moved. The Word of God can be rejected, but it cannot be overturned. It can be doubted, but it cannot be defeated.

God's Word will transform you, and your situation if you apply it.

I am convinced that the power of God's Word is unmatched. Scripture says it is alive and quick, and powerful, and sharper than any two-edged sword and it cuts with accurate precision

(Hebrews 4:12). God's Word is so powerful and authoritative that angels move at His command (Hebrews 1:14).

The Word of God has the ability to completely change and transform you if you are willing to accept and work with the truths contained in it. It has the power to save, deliver and set the captive free. Paul said, "For I am not ashamed of the Gospel of Christ: for it is the power of God unto salvation to every one that believeth; to the Jew first, and also to the Greek" (Romans 1:16).

The Word of God produces faith. Romans 10:17 says, "So then faith cometh by hearing, and hearing by the word of God." So, if faith cometh by hearing and hearing comes by the Word of God, then faith comes by the Word of God. Jesus says that you shall know the truth and the truth shall make you free (John 8:32).

As a child of God, we are responsible for not just being hearers of the Word, but doers also. This is why we must meditate on the Word of God and learn the meaning of the divine truths in it so we can apply them in our daily lives. It's one thing to read His Word, and another thing to study His Word.

The Word of God is full of His creative power. When God speaks amazing things happen. Over and over in Genesis chapter one, we see the words, "And God said" and whatever God said became reality. God said, "Let there be light" and light became. God said, "Let the earth bring forth plants" and it did. God said, "Let there be living creatures", and they were so, and then finally, God said to the Trinity, "let us make man in our own image".

The Word of God can be doubted, but it cannot be defeated. It can be rejected, but it cannot be overturned.

Look at the power in those three words, "Let there be." *Let* means do not prevent or forbid, and to allow. Some synonyms of "let" are: allow to, permit to, give permission to, authorize to, sanction to, grant the right to, license to, empower to, enable to and entitle to. I am often led to use the word "let" in my prayers and I am convinced that it opens up blockages.

Genesis 1:27 says, "God created man in His own image; in the image of God He created him; male and female He created them. God breathed into his nostrils the breath of life; and man became a living soul" (Genesis 2:7). When the first man Adam sinned by yielding to the devil's temptation of his divine nature was lost. Praise God Jesus' finished work on the Cross made it possible for everyone who believes to regain this divine nature!

The image of God is not our bodies, it is His character. Being made in God's image means we can function like Him in thoughts, words and actions. Out of all God's creations, man is the only creature that has the ability to speak words. God extended His divine nature to us out of love.

"But to all who believed him and accepted him, he gave the right to become children of God." —John 1:12 (NLT)

If you are truly born again, then the seed of God has been deposited into your spirit man. As sons and daughters of God, we are to become imitators of God. We are to copy Him and follow His example. God expects us to think, speak, and act like Him (Ephesians 5:1). When God shows us love, we can love Him back. When God speaks to us, we can understand what He says and respond; when God tells us what to do, we can either accept the request and obey, or we can reject the request and disobey. Only humans are able to relate to God in this way. What an amazing act of grace it is that God chose to create us in His image!

Worry blocks the flow of God's blessings into our lives.

In the parable of the sower, Jesus says that the seed being sown is the Word of God. Jesus is the One who sows the seed. The soil is the heart of man. The Word of God is being sown into the heart of man.

(4) And when a great multitude had gathered, and they had come to Him from

every city, He spoke by a parable: (5) "A sower went out to sow his seed. And as he sowed, some fell by the wayside; and it was trampled down, and the birds of the air devoured it.

(6) Some fell on rock; and as soon as it sprang up, it withered away because it lacked moisture. (7) And some fell among thorns, and the thorns sprang up with it and choked it. (8) But others fell on good ground, sprang up, and yielded a crop a hundred-fold." When He had said these things He cried, "He who has ears to hear, let him hear!" —Luke 8:4-8 (NKJV)

Notice the seed sown in the good soil is the same as all the other soils. However, this soil has less rocks and thorns, less cares and worries and less distractions, so there is more room for the seed to work and produce.

In Matthew 6:27, Jesus asked the question, "And which of you by being anxious can add a single hour to his span of life?" What Jesus was saying is that worry adds nothing to our lives. In fact, worry blocks God's flow of blessings (Read Matthew 6:25-34).

Like natural plants, some seedlings will grow faster than others. We may not see the harvest immediately, but every day the seed is sprouting and growing even when we do not see visible proof (Mark 4:26-29). Also, like natural plants the seed requires watering. Watering is accomplished by hearing the Word of God, understanding it and confessing it out of your mouth in faith. This is the key to making soil suitable for growth.

"This Book of the Law shall not depart from your mouth, but you shall meditate in it day and night, that you may observe to do according to all that is written in it. For then you will make your way prosperous, and then you will have good success." —Joshua 1:8 (NKJV)

It is not enough to read God's Word. You must hear it, understand it, and speak it. By hearing it and speaking the Word, you plant it in your heart. The more you speak the Word, the more your faith will grow. Nothing builds your faith as quickly as speaking and hearing God's Word.

Decree the Promise, Not the Problem!

"And He has made My mouth like a sharp sword; in the shadow of His hand He has hidden me, and made me a polished shaft; in his quiver he has hidden me." — Isaiah 49:2

While it is true that the devil is trying to destroy us, sometimes it's not the devil that harms us. It's our beliefs and the words we speak into our own lives. According to scripture, death and life are in the power of your tongue. What you say can and will be used against you.

Here are some scriptures that caution us about what we say:

Matthew 12:37: *"By thy words thou shalt be justified, and by thy words thou shalt be condemned."*

1 Peter 3:10: *"He who would love life and see good days, Let him refrain his tongue from evil, and his lips from speaking deceit."*

Ephesians 4:29: *"Let no corrupt commu-nication proceed out of your mouth, but that which is good to the use of edifying, that it may minister grace unto the hearers."*

Proverbs 6:2: *"You are snared by the words of your mouth; You are taken by the words of your mouth."*

As you can see, God is serious about what comes out of our mouth, which is probably why the Psalmist declared, "I will guard my ways, lest I sin with my tongue; I will restrain my mouth with a muzzle, while the wicked are before me" (Psalm 39:1).

He understood that what you say can and will be used against you! That's true in human courts of law, and it's also true in the court of Heaven.

Satan knows the Scriptures probably better than any person on earth, and he also knows how difficult it is for us to control what we say. He seeks to exploit our weakness, attack our character and commitment to God, and use our words and actions against us (Job 1:6-12). But one thing to keep in mind is that Believers have the ultimate weapons: the power of the Word of God, and the blood of Jesus that has covered our sin.

So Satan can't get anywhere with God concerning us, but that doesn't stop him. Just as God's angels heed the voice of God and do His work, Satan's fallen angels go about heeding his voice and working for him. They use our words against us. With that in mind, we must be careful of what we speak.

Speaking phrases like, "this makes me sick" or "you make me sick" can bring on illness. When you talk like this you give pain permission to come and bring pain.

Remember words are seeds, so the harvest may not come right away, but if you keep watering those seeds they will grow. Think about it. Does every sin or imperfection immediately lead to visible con-sequences? No. That's not how the spiritual world works. Sometimes it's instant, and sometimes there is a delayed reaction, but the harvest will come.

In fact, after doing something wrong, it may even seem that you have a streak of good luck, giving you a false peace about the wrong done, but understand that Satan is a taker not a giver. That false peace and seemingly good luck will eventually unravel. You are going to eat the harvest of your words. So, the question is: do you want a harvest of life or death?

What have you been eating lately? Jesus said in Matthew 12:35, "a good man out of the good trea-sure of the heart bringeth forth good things: and an evil man out of the evil treasure bringeth forth evil things." What comes out of your mouth depends on what's filling your heart. A loving heart produces a gracious tongue, but a critical heart produces a criti-cal tongue. A peaceful heart produces a reconciling tongue, but a bitter, self-righteous heart produces a judgmental tongue.

There was a woman who had a dream in which an angel escorted her to Heaven. The woman was taken to an exquisite mansion. When she walked into the foyer, she noticed the house was filled with doors to the right and to the left.

Curious, the woman asked the angel, "What are all those doors?"

The angel replied, "Let's open them and find out."

First, they opened the door to their right, and inside there was "a great idea" that would have more than replaced the job the woman had lost years before. "But," the angel uttered to the woman, "you said and believed that nothing good would ever happen to you again."

Within the next door was "a wonderful new friendship."

"However," the angel explained, "because someone betrayed you long ago, you became so bitter and discouraged that you stopped saying and expecting that great things were in your future."

The following door contained "a golden oppor-tunity."

"Yet," the angel described, "due to past set-backs, you continually declared it was, 'too late' and you were 'not qualified enough' to accomplish new dreams."

In her dream, the woman was shown that she continually used negative words of doubt and fear. So when she came to a door, because of doubt and fear, she missed out on the joys, blessings and opportunities behind the doors.

We are called to walk by faith, not by sight. I'm not saying that we are to suppress our feelings or pretend the problem doesn't exist, but constantly rehearsing or talking about the problem will only make us more fearful and bring more problems with it like stress which is harmful to the body. Have you noticed that when problems come, the more you talk about them the worse things become? Misery sure does love company, doesn't it?

Instead of complaining about the problem, we can use our God-given authority in Christ and speak the answer not the problem. The answer is in the Word of God.

Job 22:28 says, "Thou shalt also decree a thing, and it shall be established unto thee: and the light shall shine upon thy ways." A decree is an order, a law, or a command set forth by someone in authority that must be followed by those under the decree. Once a decree is made, it cannot be changed until after the one who made it has died.

In the biblical days when a king made a decree it was final. It couldn't be changed and had to be obeyed or punishment was done for disobeying the decree. This is the reason Daniel was cast into the lion's den, and Shadrach, Meshach and

Abednego were cast into the fiery furnace; because they disobeyed the king's decree.

So if a worldly king's decree carries that much weight and power, how much more weight and power does the King of Kings decree carry. We are the kings that Jesus is king over. Before ascending to heaven, Jesus gave authority to the disciples and all Believers after them to be applied at the leading of the Holy Spirit. Believers have authority on earth to enforce the decrees and covenants that God and Jesus have spoken on the earth.

"(18) And Jesus came and spoke to them, saying, "All authority has been given to Me in heaven and on earth. (19) Go therefore and make disciples of all the nations, baptizing them in the name of the Father and of the Son and of the Holy Spirit, (20) teaching them to observe all things that I have commanded you; and lo, I am with you always, even to the end of the age." Amen."—Matthew 28:18-20.

And He said:

"And these signs will follow those who believe: In My name they will cast out demons; they will speak with new tongues; they will take up serpents; and if they drink anything deadly, it will by no means hurt them; they will lay hands on the sick, and they will recover." —Mark 16:17-18

The kingdom of Satan has been destroyed,

"(15) Having disarmed principalities and powers, He made a public spectacle of them, triumphing over them in it." — Colossians 2:15

We have been raised and seated with Christ Jesus,

"and raised us up together, and made us sit together in the heavenly places in Christ Jesus," —Ephesians 2:6

Now we are co-heirs with Christ.

"and if children, then heirs—heirs of God and joint heirs with Christ, if indeed we

suffer with Him, that we may also be glorified together." —Romans 8:17

As a joint heir with Christ Jesus, you inherit everything that He is and all that He has.

Love has been perfected among us in this: that we may have boldness in the day of judgment; because as He is, so are we in this world. —1 John 4:17

As Jesus is, so are we in this world. We have been baptized into His body. Isn't that amazing? Wherever we go, He goes because He lives in us. We don't have to *try* to be like Jesus, WE ARE LIKE HIM. I'm not saying we are little Gods. I'm saying that the same Spirit that raised Christ from the dead has raised us from the dead also. The old man has passed away and we have become new and now we sit in Christ. Now we must renew our minds with the Word of God, and then the Word and the Holy Spirit will help us to live out our new character.

Understand that we are not called to copy the works of Christ, we are called to yield to His life in us, so that the Father's will might be done on earth as it is in heaven.

In John 14:12 Jesus says, *"Truly, truly, I say to you, whoever believes in me will also do the works that I do; and greater works than these will he do, because I am going to the Father."* We are able to do more works by way of the Holy Spirit. The Holy Spirit was the key to the early church's growth and He is also the key to everything we do in the Kingdom today. So with that said, how do you see yourself in the kingdom? Do you see living for God as something you do for God, or as something God does through you?

It will take a lifetime to discover everything that Christ has done for us, and can do through us, but the more we come to know Christ, the more we will see Him in all His glory and beauty.

Again, Jesus has turned over authority on this earth to believers. Although Satan would like people to think that he has free reign in this world, he does not. God is sovereign over the earth and everything in it including the devil. First Peter 5:8

says, the devil has to seek whom he may devour. If Satan has as much power as he wants us to believe he has, then he would not have to seek whom he may devour, he would just devour everyone he came across. Satan can do no more than God permits or what we yield to him.

"And the Lord said to Satan, 'Behold, he is in your hand, but spare his life.'" —*Job 2:6*

"(31) And the Lord said, "Simon, Simon! Indeed, Satan has asked for you, that he may sift you as wheat. (32) But I have prayed for you, that your faith should not fail; and when you have returned to Me, strengthen your brethren." —*Luke 22:31*

Jesus prayed that Peter's faith would not fail and He is ever interceding for you and me too.

The believer's authority is rooted in Christ's authority. We have Christ's Spirit dwelling in us. We are raised and seated with Christ. I keep saying this in different ways because I want you to understand who you are. This is our legal position.

Because of our position in Christ we have the authority to act on His behalf. Jesus said,

> *"Behold, I give you the authority to trample on serpents and scorpions, and over all the power of the enemy, and nothing shall by any means hurt you." —Luke 10:19*

> *"(18) And Jesus came and spoke to them, saying, "All authority has been given to Me in heaven and on earth. (19) Go therefore and make disciples of all the nations, baptizing them in the name of the Father and of the Son and of the Holy Spirit, (20) teaching them to observe all things that I have commanded you; and lo, I am with you always, even to the end of the age. Amen." —Matthew 28:18-20*

There is power in the name of Jesus. His name has authority in heaven, on earth, and under the earth. Philippians 2:10 says that at the name of Jesus every knee should bow, of those in heaven, and of those on earth, and of those under the earth.

He commissioned us and gave us the power and authority to use His name and to function in this world just as He functioned when He was here:

"(17) And these signs will follow those who believe: In My name they will cast out demons; they will speak with new tongues; (18) they will take up serpents; and if they drink anything deadly, it will by no means hurt them; they will lay hands on the sick, and they will recover.

(19) So then, after the Lord had spoken to them, He was received up into heaven, and sat down at the right hand of God. (20) And they went out and preached everywhere, the Lord working with them and confirming the word through the accompanying signs. Amen." — Mark 16:17-20.

Did you see that? The Lord sat down at the right hand of God, the disciples went out and preached the Gospel *(spoke and confessed what they believed)* and the Lord Himself bore witness with what they spoke. In other words, what they spoke, He did.

While on earth, Jesus taught His disciples about faith and authority. He showed that authority doesn't ask or beg, it enforces and commands! Look how Jesus spoke to a fig tree that was not bearing fruit in Mark 11:

*"(12) And on the morrow, when they were come from Bethany, he was hungry: (13) And seeing a fig tree afar off having leaves, he came, if haply he might find any thing thereon: and when he came to it, he found nothing but leaves; for the time of figs was not yet. (14) And Jesus answered and **said unto it**, No man eat fruit of thee hereafter for ever. And His disciples heard it." —* Mark 11:12-14 (KJV)

Notice that Jesus didn't stand there and beg or ask anything of the fig tree, neither did He lose focus of where He was going. He used His authority and spoke "no man eat fruit from you ever again" and they kept walking. This is our example.

The next day Jesus and His disciples walked by the same fig tree, and the disciples noticed that the fig tree was dead. Peter said to Jesus, "Rabbi, look! The fig tree you cursed has withered." Jesus answered:

> *"(22) ... Have faith in God. (23) For verily I say unto you, that whosoever **shall say** unto this mountain, Be thou removed, and be thou cast into the sea; and shall not doubt in his heart, but shall believe that those things which **he saith** shall come to pass; he shall have **whatsoever he saith.** " —* *Mark 11:22-23 (KJV)*

Wow, what a promise! Now, watch this:

- Numbers 23:19 talks about the words that proceed from the mouth of God. The Word says, "God is not a man, that he should lie ... hath he **spoken**, and shall he not make it good?"

- In Matthew 12:34 Jesus said, "out of the abundance of the heart the mouth **speaketh**."

- To the father of a sick child in Mark 9:23, Jesus said, "If thou canst **believe**, all things are possible to him that **believeth**."

- In Revelation 12:11 John wrote about how believers overcame Satan as he accuses believers before God day and night. He said "they overcame him by the blood of the Lamb, and by the **word of their testimony**".

So if what comes out of our mouth is what is in our heart? If it determines our future? If what God says is true, and we know it is, then we must be careful of what we are taking in, and we must renew our minds. Jesus believed what He said. What He spoke came from His heart. Notice in Mark 11:22-23 Jesus mentions doubt and believe only once, but He mentions the word "say" or "saith" three times. This leads me to believe that both faith, and confession are important.

Faith is more than a feeling. Neither is it wishing and hoping. Faith involves knowledge, agreement, and trust, and it also is responsive. Here is what I mean: we must have knowledge of some-thing before we can put faith in it, and we must believe and agree with that knowledge before we can act on it. For instance, if we believe a stove top is hot, we will not place our hand on it. If we believe a chair will hold us up, we will sit down on it.

The actions that result from our faith in God should be no different from those of our other beliefs. If we believe God is who He says He is, and that the Bible means what it says, we will act accord-ingly.

What does this look like in the natural? Peter's walking on water is a great example:

" *(25) Now in the fourth watch of the night Jesus went to them, walking on the sea. (26) And when the disciples saw Him walking on the sea, they were troubled, saying, "It is a ghost!" And they cried out for fear.*

(27) But immediately Jesus spoke to them, saying, "Be of good cheer! It is I; do not be afraid." (28) And Peter answered Him and said, "Lord, if it is You, command me to come to You on the water."

(29) So He said, "Come." And when Peter had come down out of the boat, he walked on the water to go to Jesus. (30) But when he saw that the wind was boisterous, he was afraid; and beginning to sink he cried out, saying, "Lord, save me!" (31) And immediately Jesus stretched out His hand and caught him, and said to him, "O you of little faith, why did you doubt?"

(32) And when they got into the boat, the wind ceased. (33) Then those who were in the boat came and worshiped Him, saying, "Truly You are the Son of God." —Matthew 14:26-33

The scripture says in the middle of the night Jesus came walking on the sea. Mark says, when the disciples saw Jesus walking up to the boat they thought He was a ghost, and they were terrified (Mark 6:48–50). I'm not putting the disciples down, because had I seen a figure walking up towards my boat in the middle of the ocean I would have been calling on Jesus for sure. Don't beat yourself up if fear shows up. Call on Jesus to help you. Fear and faith cannot live in the same heart. One will suppress the other. Let faith be the suppressor.

Notice that when the storm came fear immediately struck the disciples, and even though they knew Jesus, they did not recognize Him walking towards them. Fear is a blessing blocker, and it will block the presence of the Lord. This is why we must not entertain fear, we must cast it down. We'll talk more about that later.

But, why didn't Jesus just wait until morning to meet up with them? I believe He wanted them to see that what they feared most was under His feet. He wants us to trust that He will always come to us during the storms of life. His action confirms God's word in Isaiah 43:2,

"When you pass through the waters, I will be with you; and through the rivers, they shall not overflow you. When you walk through the fire, you shall not be burned, nor shall the flame scorch you."

How many times have we found ourselves in the midst of a terrible life storm and cried out, "Lord help me!" Peter could have done this. He could have said, "LORD, if it's You, please come to our rescue" or "can you please stop this storm" But that's not what Peter said. Peter shouted, "Lord, if it is You, command me to come to You on the water."

Peter was able to trust Jesus like this because he knew Him. He had a close personal relationship with Him. He believed Jesus was the Son of God, and that with Him he could do anything. So when Jesus bid him to come, he acted on his belief, and stepped out, and did the miraculous. His faith was responsive, but the moment he took his focus off Jesus, and put it back on the storm, he began to sink.

This is what happens to so many Believers. God tells us to do something, and we get zealous, and step out in faith. Then Satan comes to steal the word. Our finances are attacked, or sickness hits, or some other obstacle comes, and we panic, and take our eyes off Jesus. And many just simply lay their vision down thinking they missed God.

Jesus wants us to step out of our comfort zone, and completely trust in Him. So, what are you most afraid of at this moment? Whatever it is know that Jesus is above it. All financial, physical, emotional, and family problems or any other problem is under His feet, which means it is under your feet too because you are seated in Him (Hebrews 2:5-8).

You have the power, and dominion, and the legal right to legislate, and cause change. Use it.

When life tosses a storm your way, like Peter, cry out, "Lord, please help me to come near to you", and if you sink or fall He will be there to offer a hand to help you get back on your feet. Just don't give up. Difficult experiences such as illness, financial hard-ships, and loss of loved ones can draw us closer to Jesus, if we don't give up.

It takes faith and action to walk in the authority Christ has given us. James 2:17says, "faith without works is dead." In other words works or action must follow faith.

As Believers, we are a part of the Army of the Lord. We are a powerful force to be reckoned with. We are peculiar people doing mighty exploits for the glory of God. We are not here to blend in, we are here to take over. And, we do all of this by faith in God, being obedient to God, and declaring His Word. As we do the Angels of God stand ready to hearken to the voice of His Word, and carry out the decrees according to God's instruction. (Psalm 103:20)

You are God's hands and feet in the earth. In the early church God turned the world upside down with His mighty power flowing through yielded ves-sels, and now that mantle has fallen upon us. Jesus said the fields are ripe, and ready for harvest. It's our turn now to do our part, and allow God's mighty power to flow through us.

Even if you are not called into the five-fold ministry, you have a tremendous role in the Kingdom of God. If you would just put God's Word in your mouth, and declare the Word of God into your community, your family, your workplace, the gro-cery store, the doctor's office or where ever you are you can change the atmosphere, and bring life to dead situations, and places. With God's Word in your mouth you are armed, and dangerous to the forces of darkness.

God wants to resurrect some dry places, and situations in your world, and He wants to use you to do it, but you must come to the understanding that it's not for others to do the work. The work is for you. The assignment is yours. It must be you. You and I have a mandate from God to speak His Word into the seemingly hopeless situations around us and bring His Life into those situations. The Holy Spirit will help us do the work! He is our teacher and He brings His Word back to us.

God said in Acts chapter two,

"And it shall come to pass in the last days, says God, that I will pour out of My Spirit on all flesh; your sons and your daughters shall prophesy, your young men shall see visions, your old men shall dream dreams."
—*Acts 2:17*

The Spirit this scripture is talking about is the Holy Spirit. God is a Consuming Fire, and everything associated with Him has fire connected to it. The fire of the Holy Spirit will destroy the works of the devil.

On the day of Pentecost a flame of fire sat upon every person's head in the room, and they we filled with the Holy Spirit (Acts 2:3). The Holy Ghost came as a rushing mighty Wind, and Fire. Cloven tongues like fire sat upon each of them, and they were all filled with the Holy Ghost, and began to speak with other tongues as the Spirit gave them utterance.

The fire is the Holy Spirit, the power of God. On that day they spoke in other tongues, and they received power. The Holy Ghost Baptism is a baptism of Fire. The Holy Ghost in your life means that you receive God's power for the service that takes place in the life of the Christian.

> *"But you shall receive power when the Holy Spirit has come upon you; and you shall be witnesses to Me in Jerusalem, and in all Judea and Samaria, and to the end of the earth." —Acts 1:8*

Strong's definition of Power is: force, ability, strength, specifically miraculous power. So, when Believers are baptized with the Holy Ghost they are filled with the supernatural force, ability, and strength of God. The same miraculous power that raised Jesus Christ from the dead comes inside you.

When the Holy Spirit comes He will clean His house. John said, "His winnowing fan is in His hand, and He will thoroughly purge His floor" (Matthew 3:12). He will burn up everything that is of the world, the flesh, and the devil. His floor is where he walks; He walks in you, and He walks in me. This is why the chapter on "Blessing Blockers" is so important. If you brushed over or skipped over this section, please go back, and let the Holy Spirit do what needs to be done.

With the power of the Holy Spirit, and God's Word in your mouth you are armed, and dangerous to the kingdom of darkness.

Maybe at one time you had the Fire, but you've cooled off. Now is the time for a fresh anointing of the fire of God. Repent, and ask God to refresh you.

Maybe you've never experienced the Fire of God. This is your time to be filled with the Holy Spirit. The same way you received Christ is the same way you receive the Holy Spirit, by faith.

The infilling of the Holy Spirit can take place at the moment you confess faith in Christ, but more often it occurs after the salvation experience

(Acts 10:44-46, Acts 11:15-16, Acts 8:12-17). Although we are filled with the Holy Spirit by faith alone, there are a few things you must do in preparing your heart for the filling of the Spirit.

1. **You must have accepted Jesus Christ** as your personal Lord, and Savior.

2. **You must ask**. The Bible says, "Ask, and it will be given to you" (Luke 11:9).

3. **You must surrender** to God, and desire to live a life that will please the LORD. Jesus promised, "Blessed are those who hunger, and thirst for righteousness, for they will be filled" (Matthew 5:6). Paul admonishes in Romans 12:1, "I beseech you therefore, brethren, by the mercies of God, that you present your bodies a living sacrifice, holy, acceptable to God, which is your reasonable service".

4. **You must believe** you have received the Holy Spirit from God. The apostle Paul said to the Galatians, "Did you receive the Spirit by the works of the law, or by hearing with faith?"

5. Finally, **you must exercise** what God has given you. The Bible says those baptized with the Holy Spirit on the day of Pentecost "began to speak with other tongues, as the Spirit gave them utterance" (Acts 2:4). They spoke the words that the Spirit gave them. They they acted on faith, and spoke what they heard.

Now, if you are ready, you just have to ask God to baptize you in the Holy Spirit. Just lift your hands, open your mouth, and tell God you want the Fire. You can pray something like:

"Heavenly Father, I recognize my need for Your power to live this new life. I want the baptism of the Holy Ghost and Fire. I ask You to baptize me now in the Holy Spirit. By faith, I receive the baptism in the Holy Spirit right now. Thank You for baptizing me. Holy Spirit, You are welcome in my life. May the anointing, the glory, and the power of God come upon me, and into my life right now. May I be empowered for service from this day forward. In Jesus' name I pray. Amen."

Now, having asked, and received, begin to practice the power of the Spirit by praising God out loud in whatever words come to you. Thank Him, and worship Him. Yield your voice to Him, and speak whatever comes to you. It may be one syllable or it may just be utterings, but praise Him in the utterings, no matter how silly you think you sound. Keep speaking until you become more comfortable. Keep praying in your prayer language every day, and God will strengthen you.

It is possible you didn't feel anything, and no new language came out. Understand that receiving the Holy Spirit has nothing to do with initial feelings or what happens on the outside. God's Word said that if you asked, you would receive. That means by faith you have received the Baptism in the Holy Spirit.

Also, there are many people who receive the Baptism in the Holy Spirit, and do not pray in other tongues right away. Don't be discouraged, it will come. Just continue to pray, and praise God each day. Yield your voice to Him, and speak whatever comes to you.

Can you imagine what would happen if a group of Holy Ghost filled Believers got on one accord, and actually worked the Word, and began to consis-tently declare the promises of God over their families, ministries, city, government, and lost fam-ily, and friends ? Satan can! Just something to think about.

Jesus said in Matthew 18:20, *"For where two or three are gathered together in My name, I am there in the midst of them."* When Jesus comes on the scene things have to change.

You have the legal right to legislate, and cause change to come into your life based on the power, and dominion God has given you. Remember to speak the answer not the problem. Ask the Holy Spirit for guidance as you search the scriptures on what to decree in your life, and on behalf of your families, ministries, city, government, and nation, and then do it.

Prophesying to Dry Bones

"This is what the Sovereign Lord says:
Look! I am going to put breath into you,
and make you live again! I will put flesh
and muscles on you, and cover you with
skin. I will put breath into you, and you
will come to life. Then you will know that I
am the Lord."'
—Ezekiel 37:5-6 NLT

In Ezekiel chapter 37 the Spirit of God took Ezekiel to a valley filled with dry bones, and asked him, "Son of man, can these dry bones live?" In the natural it didn't look like any life could bloom in that wasteland of bones, but Ezekiel knew enough about God to know that anything is possible with Him. So he answered, "O Lord, you know".

God said in *Ezekiel 37, "Prophesy to these bones, and say to them, 'O dry bones, hear the word of the Lord! Thus says the Lord God to these bones: "Surely I will cause breath to enter into you, and you shall live. I will put sinews on you, and bring flesh upon you, cover you with skin, and put breath in you; and you shall live. Then you shall know that I am the Lord."*

Ezekiel prophesied as God commanded Him, and breath came into the human forms, and they stood up, and became fully alive. The Bible says they were "an exceeding great army" for the Lord.

Prophesying is speaking what God says, whether in His Word or through a Rhema word over a person or into a situation. Ezekiel prophesied the Word of God over the dead, dry bones, and literally called them back to life. He commanded them to hear the word of the Lord. The Word of the Lord carries the life, and authority of the Lord.

You may be thinking, but God spoke directly to Ezekiel. And to that I say God is speaking directly to you too through His Word. God says that He will watch over His Word to perform it. When we decree the Word of God, we are giving voice to His Word.

Job 22:28 states that you have to speak, and make a decree, and when it is established light will shine on your way. So if you don't issue the decree, nothing will be established, and the darkness will remain.

Many times we say our lack of supply, power, or understanding is the will of God, but that is contrary to what He says in Psalm 34:10: *"those who seek the Lord shall not lack any good thing."*

James 4:2 says "you do not have because you do not ask." You see, you must open your mouth, and speak. Ezekiel obeyed God, and decreed the life of God into those dry bones, and they began to come together, and he kept decreeing until he had bodies all around him.

If we believe God for salvation from sin, we can believe God for salvation from the results of sin.

I'm sure at first he felt a little strange talking to bones, but as he spoke, there was a noise, and a rattling, and the bones came together. There have been times when I've prophesied into situations that seemed impossible, and I can tell you it can be difficult to get past what you see with your physical eye. That's why you will need the Holy Spirit!

It may be a fact that you have an illness, but the truth is, God is the God who heals (Exodus15:26), and by the stripes of Jesus we were healed (Isaiah 53:5). It may be a fact that you have no job, and no money, and a mountain of bills right now, but the truth is God supplies all of your needs (Philippians 4:19). Truth is God gives you the power to get wealth (Deuteronomy 8:18).

Ezekiel was obedient in the middle of a dead situation. This is an example of what you can, and should do in the midst of what seems to be defeat! When you obey, and decree God's Word over and into your situation, you become the anointed breath of God to overcome that circumstance.

The moment you decree His established and settled Word, at God's command, the angels go forth, and bring fulfillment of that Word (Psalm 103:20). The angels obey the voice of His Word, not your thoughts, so you must open your mouth, and speak.

One of the most powerful things you can do to transform your life is to speak, and decree God's promises in your prayers, and over, and into whatever area of life you are struggling in. Why is it so important to include Scripture promises in our prayers? Second Corinthians helped to open my understanding:

> *"For all the promises of God in Him are Yes, and in Him Amen, to the glory of God through us."* —2 Corinthians 1:20 (NKJV)

Many people have a problem with us applying the promises in the Old Testament to our daily life today. They believe because these promises were given to Abraham, Moses, David, Joshua or the people of Israel that we cannot believe them for us today. That we cannot declare them, or apply them in prayer to our own situations. However, that is not what the above scripture says, is it? The Scripture says ALL THE PROMISES of God in Him are Yes. In who? In Christ! Are you in Christ? Jesus is the fulfillment of ALL THE PROMISES of

God, and He is also the key to receiving ALL THE PROMISES of God.

Paul quotes some promises God made to the people of Israel in the New Testament in Second Corinthians chapter six,

(16) "... As God has said: "I will dwell in them, and walk among them. I will be their God, and they shall be My people. (17) I will be a Father to you, and you shall be My sons and daughters, says the Lord Almighty." — 2 Corinthians 6:16-17

He was referencing what God said in Leviticus 26:12: *"I will walk among you, and be your God, and you shall be My people"*;

and in Jeremiah 32:38: *"They shall be My people, and I will be their God."*

Then Paul said in chapter seven,

"Therefore, since we have these promises, dear friends, let us purify ourselves from everything that contaminates body and

spirit, perfecting holiness out of reverence for God." —2 Corinthians 7:1 NIV

The requirements to receive God's promises are part of Christ's finished work on the Cross. Jesus fulfilled the requirements so all you have to do is believe, and decree them. Because we are in Christ, we are heirs to His promises for every area of our lives.

"Now to Abraham, and his Seed were the promises made. He does not say, "And to seeds," as of many, but as of one, "And to your Seed," who is Christ." — Galatians 3:16

"And if ye be Christ's, then are ye Abraham's seed, and heirs according to the promise." —Galatians 3:29

Jesus teaches us to pray,

"may your kingdom come, may your will be done on earth as it is in heaven." —Matthew 6:10 NET Bible

What's in Heaven? The Bible lets us know in heaven there is no sadness, no hurt, no sickness, no lack or anything else that has to do with the curse of sin. This is God's will for you in heaven, and this is God's will for you on earth too. You don't have to wait until you get to heaven to experience God's will for your life.

Whether it is salvation, healing, the baptism in the Holy Spirit, or some other promise or gift God has provided we receive it all by faith. The psalmist said in Psalm 27:13 declares, "Yet I am confident I will see the Lord's goodness while I am here in the land of the living."

The same faith you used to receive salvation opens the door for the benefits of salvation.

Just as we believe God for salvation from sin, we can believe God for salvation from the results of sin. Right now as a Believer you are seated in Christ in heavenly places. It is not God's will for you to lack in any area of your life.

"Beloved, I pray that you may prosper in every way and [that your body] may keep well, even as [I know] your should keeps well and prospers." —*3 John 1:2 AMP*

How much harder, or how much more time does it take to speak the promise rather than the problem? The promises of God are His will for your life. Don't let anyone talk you out of what belongs to you. Where the Spirit of the Lord is, there is liberty! Freedom belongs to you, whether it is from depres-sion, addiction, fear, anxiety, or any other issue, freedom is yours by way of God's promises.

God's Word has the answer for every problem we will encounter, but if we don't believe it, and apply it in our lives it cannot benefit us.

Financial provision, deliverance from sin and evil, a good marriage, physical and mental health and healing, and much more are the blessings, and gifts that God promises to provide for those who believe in Him. God's Truth is supreme. When you stand in confidence, and speak God's Word to the seemingly hopeless, dead situations in your life, all of a sudden you will see things start to come together. The impossible starts to happen.

In Genesis, God saw darkness, and called forth what He wanted to see. Likewise, you can speak, and declare the promises in God's Word into the dark areas in your life, and even in the life of others, and bring life, and light to them. It may not happen immediately, but keep speaking the promises of God, and you will see them manifested in your life.

Right now, if you realize that you have been speaking against God's grace over your life you can pray, and repent. God will forgive you, and place those words into the sea of forgetfulness, and they will never again be able to rise to create havoc in your life.

Standing on God's Word

"Let us hold fast the profession of our faith without wavering; (for he is faithful that promised)" —*Hebrews 10:23 (KJV)*

One day God asked me, "Daughter do you think I'm wise?" I sat there dumbfounded for a minute, wondering why He would ask me such a question. "Yes God, You are wise. Why do You ask me that? Is something about to happen? Should I be preparing for something", I replied. I never got an answer, but I sensed that God just wanted me to trust Him with something that was coming.

As I look at this earth, I realize that no one else could've created the earth and the universe but God. As I look at me, I realize that no one else could have created me but God. With all that I've come through no one else could have shielded and protected, and brought me through but God. My answer to the question do I think that God is wise is a resounding yes!

With so many things going on in the world, now more than ever before, believers must take hold of the Word of God, and refuse to let it go, especially in personal difficult times. We must trust Him, and pay attention to His instructions.

You can complain, and remain, or you can be thankful, declare, confess, and overcome. The choice is yours!

God's Word has the answer for every problem we will encounter, but if we do not apply it in our lives it will not benefit us. What good does the medicine do us if we do not take it? We must be like the writer of Psalm 119 who said: "Your Word is a lamp to guide my feet, and a light for my path.

The Bible says we are to walk by faith, not by sight. Jesus said, "the just shall live by faith, and on every word that proceeds out of the mouth of God." Faith is not limited to physical sight. Faith is not a feeling, faith is an action. It is believing the pro-mises in your heart, and confessing them with your mouth as you are led by the Holy Spirit.

We need faith to survive in this world. Without faith, we couldn't go to the grocery store, send our children to school, drive our cars, fly in an airplane, or move from one moment to the next without second guessing everything we do. Because of faith, we can expect things to turn out all right for us no matter what the situation might be. Faith is an important part of everyone's life. Our faith in God is what connects us to God. With so much uncertainty, and so much evil in the earth today, I can't imagine living in this world without faith in God.

We don't know when our last breath will come. Our bodies are dying from the moment we are born. I don't care how well you eat or how much you work out the death process continues from day one until God saves us. On the day we receive Christ as Lord, and Savior, our spirits are reborn, but the flesh keeps on dying. This flesh will one day go back to the dust from whence it came, and our spirit will go back to God.

Sickness can hit any of us, without notice, if it does we need faith to fight for healing. My daughter was only 34 years old when she was stricken with inflammatory breast cancer. She was 35 when she went home to be with the Lord. She ate healthy, and worked out several times a week.

We believed God for her healing on this side, but He decided to take her home. If I didn't know that she believed in Christ, and lived a life for the Lord, I don't think I would have been able to endure her leaving. Since she was a believer, by faith I know I will see her again when I get to heaven.

Since my daughter has gone home to be with the Lord, I have gotten several prayer requests for healing from people with different types of cancer. I've prayed for them as led by the Holy Spirit. Some have been healed instantly, some over time, some are still standing for healing, and some have received the ultimate healing like my daughter did.

Since my daughter has gone home to be with the Lord, I have gotten several prayer requests for healing from people with different types of cancer. Some have been healed instantly, some over time, some are still standing for healing, and some have received the ultimate healing like my daughter did.

In the midst of writing this book I was diagnosed with breast cancer. One night about two months before the diagnosis, at the end of Bible Study, a prayer request came forth from a member whose sister had been diagnosed with breast cancer. She was due to have surgery that week. In the closing prayer, God touched my mouth, and had me pray for her. I declared His Word regarding healing, spoke healing to her body, and God used me to prophesy that she would be healed, and she would not have any chemo or radiation therapy.

Not long after that, again, as we were closing out Bible Study the member shared the testimony of what happened. Their family member did have the surgery. The doctors got all the cancer, and she did not need chemo or radiation therapy. I was so happy that I burst into an uncontrollable cry for several minutes. It was like I had received the healing myself. Driving home, I asked, "Lord, why was I crying so hard?" I didn't get an answer, but I just kept praising God for what He had done.

A couple of weeks after that, I started having breast pain at night that would wake me out of my sleep. I would pray, and the pain would go away, but it kept coming back. I sensed something was wrong, so I went to the doctor, and she referred me for a mammogram.

During this time I constantly thought about my daughter's battle with cancer, and how thankful we bother were that I was there to walk by faith with her. A few days before the mammogram I was talking to God about what was going on. I sensed that I did have cancer. I am not married, I live in a city where I have no immediate family other than my young grandchildren, and I felt so alone.

"Lord I've gone through so much, and I've had to do it all alone. After seeing Eboni go through this, Father I can't go through this alone too. I know You've been here all the time, but Father, I need someone to walk with me. Please don't let me go through this by myself", was my cry.

God gave me a rhema word. He clearly spoke in the midst of my tears and said,

"You have sown prayer, and you will reap prayer. You have sown healing, and you will reap healing."

Those words comforted me more than I can say. I shared this experience one night in Bible Study. Those who were there prayed with me, and assured me that I would not walk through the battle alone.

I went for the mammogram which came back showing three spots on my right breast. I was scheduled for a biopsy, and the biopsy showed stage one breast cancer. Breast surgery was the first recommended stage of treatment. The next phase would be determined on the pathology report from the tumors.

Dealing with the fact that I had breast cancer was hard enough, but my daughter's leaving was still very fresh. Every step I took in the process brought back memories, and grief. I was in a battle for my mind, and my life. The word God gave me "You have sown prayer, and you will reap prayer. You have sown healing, and you will reap healing", literally carried me through the entire process.

I printed out scriptures on healing, and taped them over my house: on the kitchen cabinets, on the refrigerator, on the front and back door, on the bathroom mirrors, and other places where I frequented during the day, so that if fear or discouragement came I would see it, and confess it to build up my faith. I believed the Word of God, and continually spoke my faith, and praised, and thanked God for His Rhema Word.

> # The more you believe the blessings are yours, the more you will experience them.

Of course, the devil tried to tell me it wouldn't work. He tried to take my focus off healing by putting death on my mind. He constantly told me that I wouldn't be healed. I started dreaming about people who have passed on. Memories of times when people hurt me started coming back, memories of my daughter's illness, and the emotional pain inflicted on her during her illness came back.

Satan was trying to use one his greatest tools, "unforgiveness" to bring death, and destruction. I thank God for the Holy Spirit, and His Word! You see God had already decreed that I would be healed from the cancer, so Satan couldn't stop that. But he could get me to lay my healing down by speaking, and acting against the Grace of God.

No matter what storm you face, the battle is going to be in your mind. Satan comes to steal the Word out of your heart. What he tried with me is an example of the type of tactics he uses to stop us from walking in our authority in Christ. He bombards your mind with thoughts contrary to the Word of God, and He knows that bitterness, and un-forgiveness will block God's blessings.

Don't accept what Satan says. You have the power of God in you to cast down Satan's words of doubt, and unbelief.

The Word of God will work for you, but you have to work it!

Although I had done it several times before, again, I released forgiveness, and healing to the people who hurt me, and my daughter, and prayed for them, and those memories stopped. I prayed, and bound the enemy from my dreams, and decreed peace over my sleep, and those dreams stopped.

I had to constantly cast down Satan's negative thoughts. Every time I got to the point where I was about to doubt, the Lord would remind me of His Rhema Word. Those words would ring in my head, and I would confess them, and thank God for His Word.

God honored my request, and I wasn't alone. My church family was amazing. They honored their word, and they walked through the process with me. My pastors, and a couple of members fasted, and prayed for me. I had several doctor appointments before the surgery, and women from my church took me to my appointments.

My Co-Pastor, a few women from my church, and a dear friend who had just been healed of breast cancer was with me on the day of surgery. My sons were praying for me, and even a couple of my Uber passengers prayed for me. My sisters flew into Atlanta from Miami, Florida to help me the first few days after the surgery. My son came in after they left, and I got to spend Thanksgiving with him and my daughter in law and see my newest grand-daughter the first time.

My medical oncologist even said to me, "Ms. Williams, the fact that you had pain means that God is with you, because pain usually doesn't present itself until a later stage of cancer. God wanted you to know that something is wrong so you can get it taken care of, and be healed."

I am still in awe of the faithfulness of God. He did exactly what He said He would do. I had sown prayer, and support, and I reaped prayer, and support. I have sown healing over the years, and I reaped healing. God honored my faith in action. I did need to have surgery, but I did not have to have chemo or radiation therapy. I am cancer free, and I declare that I will remain cancer free!

When storms come fear will immediately try to come, and take control. Recognize fear for what it is: a spirit (2 Timothy 1:7). The Spirit of Fear masks itself as anxiety or worry. It may even try to tell you that fear is a normal human reaction to such cir-cumstances, but the Spirit of Fear IS NOT a part of the blessings God has given us.

Remember the Spirit of Fear is a blessing block-er. It is a work of the enemy. Jesus has destroyed the works of the enemy at the Cross! So cast fear down. The best way to cast down, and fight fear is by de-claring the Word of God! This is what Jesus did, and this is what you should do.

Like I said earlier, we all have faith in some-thing, but what our faith is in, depends on what or who we are listening to. If we listen to the world, then chances are our faith will be in the world's system, and the world will dictate our thoughts. Remember, where our thoughts go our actions will follow.

I don't know if you've noticed yet, but you cannot depend on the world's system. It will let you down every time. However, if we depend on the Word of God, and what He has spoken then we will operate in an entirely different realm, the realm of great faith, and the promises of God will be manifested in our life.

Jesus said, "Have faith in God" (Mark 11:22). He is Greater than any problem or obstacle you will ever face! With faith in God, we are able to see the invisible, achieve the unattainable, move the un-movable, survive the unthinkable, and thrive in the midst of the impossible.

Hebrews 11:6 says,

"But without faith it is impossible to please Him, for he who comes to God must believe that He is, and that He is a rewarder of those who diligently seek Him."

Faith comes by hearing the Word of God (Romans 10:17). The Word of God is a faith builder. The more you hear it, the more encouraged in your faith you will become. This is why it is important to attend a good church where the Word of God is taught.

Also, with today's technology, God has made the Word so available to you that there is no excuse not to immerse yourself in the Word. There is Christian television, YouTube, and other online videos, and many other places to get the Word of God in you. You are good ground, you need to cultivate your soil with the Word, and the Word will yield proportionally to what was sown.

"But he who received seed on the good ground is he who hears the word, and understands it, who indeed bears fruit, and produces: some a hundredfold, some sixty, some thirty." —Matthew 13:23 (NKJV)

In Luke chapter seven is the story about the centurion soldier who believed that Jesus could heal his servant. The story is the perfect example of what faith in action looks like.

The centurion told Jesus, "Just say the word, and my servant will be healed. I am not worthy to have you come under my roof. I too am a man under authority, with soldiers under me. I say to one, 'Go,' and he goes; and to another, 'Come,' and he comes; and to my servant, 'Do this,' and he does it."

Apparently, the centurion had observed Jesus' actions, and heard Him speak, and as a result had come to believe, and understand Christ's position, and heavenly authority. Although he himself was a man of authority, the Bible says he felt unworthy to have Jesus come into his house. He humbled him-self to Jesus' heavenly power.

The Centurion was convinced of the authority of Christ's Word. He believed that if Christ would just give the command, healing would respond. He did not need to see anything or feel anything. He rested solely upon the premise of the spoken Word. Jesus marveled at the centurion's understanding of faith.

In fact, He turned to the crowd that was follow-ing Him, and said, "I say to you, not even in Israel have I found such great faith." Great faith is believing who God is, trusting in the dependability of His Word, and accepting it as fact above any other evidence or circumstance.

Hebrews chapter 11 talks about some people who had great faith. Regardless of how illogical God's request was, each person mentioned took God at His Word. They obeyed His command, and because of their obedience God was able to do exactly what He promised.

For instance, God told Noah to build an ark because He was going to bring a massive flood. Noah took God at His Word, and built the ark. He told Abraham to leave his homeland, and go to a place where he would receive his inheritance. Abraham took God at His Word, left his familiar surroundings, and moved to a new land, and God fulfilled His promise.

God told Sarah that she would conceive a son even though she was well past child bearing age.

She too took God at His Word, and God fulfilled His promise.

God is wise, and intentional. He has a purpose, and a plan for everything that takes place in our life, even our so-called mistakes. Nothing catches Him off guard. From the beginning He has planned for us to experience certain things that will help cultivate our godly character, so others might be introduced to Jesus through your example. What an honor it is for someone to see Christ in you!

The story of Joseph is a great example of this. I don't have to tell you there are some evil people in this world who will seek to harm you. Sometimes these evil people are close family members, as was the case with Joseph. His half brothers hated him, and they would have killed him had not the slave traders come by at just the right moment, and they realized they could make some money.

What a remarkable story. If you haven't done so, I suggest you read Joseph's story (Genesis 37-45). Like me, you may see yourself in the story.

Although Joseph had the dream, he didn't know how things would turn out when his brothers sold him. He didn't know that God would raise him up as Pharaoh's right hand. Joseph's trust in God is what carried him through all those bleak days in the dungeon. God used all Joseph went through to build his character and save lives.

> *"You intended to harm me, but God intended it all for good. He brought me to this position so I could save the lives of many people." —Genesis 50:20 (NLT)*

Trusting God during a trial does not mean we should passively sit by, and watch the situation. No, not at all! Paul said that we are to be strong in the Lord, and in the power of His might. He tells us to put on the whole armor of God, that you may be able to stand against the wiles of the devil (Ephesians 6:10-11).

The Sword of The Spirit

"And take ... the Sword of the Spirit, which is the Word of God" —Ephesians 6:17

When I was crying out to God for change in my life He said to me, "Daughter, put the Word in your mouth". When I studied the scriptures God gave me, I realized that He had given me all the tools I needed to change my circumstances, and it was up to me to utilize them. He was saying that His Word in my mouth has supernatural power, and I needed to learn how to use it to fight the unseen enemies that were attempting to stop me from fulfilling God's plan for my life.

When Paul talks about the Christian armor in Ephesians chapter six, he uses the Roman soldier's uniform to indicate that Believers are in a spiritual battle, and God wants us to be prepared to fight. He lists the powerful supernatural weapons that

God has given us, so that we can stand up to everything the enemy throws our way.

He said to the Ephesians,

(10) Finally, my brethren, be strong in the Lord, and in the power of His might. (11) Put on the whole armor of God, that you may be able to stand against the wiles of the devil. (12) For we do not wrestle against flesh and blood, but against principalities, against powers, against the rulers of the darkness of this age, against spiritual hosts of wickedness in the heavenly places. (13) Therefore take up the whole armor of God, that you may be able to withstand in the evil day, and having done all, to stand.

(14) Stand therefore, having girded your waist with truth, having put on the breastplate of righteousness, (15) and having shod your feet with the preparation of the gospel of peace; (16) above all, taking the shield of faith with which you will be able to quench all the fiery darts of the

wicked one. (17) And take the helmet of salvation, and the sword of the Spirit, which is the word of God; (18) praying always with all prayer, and supplication in the Spirit, being watchful to this end with all perseverance, and sup-plication for all the saints" — Ephesians 6:14-18 (NKJV)

Paul defines the Sword of the Spirit as the "Word of God" (verse 17). Swords are used for close combat, which implies that our battle is up close and personal. The sword is used for offense as well as defense. For defense, the Roman soldier wielded the sword to deflect the enemy's blows. As an offensive weapon, the sword was used to attack the enemy.

The Bible also describes God's Word as a sword in Hebrews 4:12-13,

"For the word of God is living, and powerful, and sharper than any two-edged sword, piercing even to the division of soul, and spirit, and of joints and marrow, and is a discerner of the thoughts, and intents of the heart. And

*there is no creature hidden from His sight,
but all things are naked, and open to the
eyes of Him to whom we must give
account" (Hebrews 4:12-13).*

The authority of the Sword of the Spirit is God Himself. In spiritual warfare the battles are fought with words packed, and backed up with the Spirit of God. Regardless of what comes at us our biggest fight will be in our mind.

*" For though we walk in the flesh, we do
not war according to the flesh. For the
weapons of our warfare are not carnal but
mighty in God for pulling down
strongholds, casting down arguments,
and every high thing that exalts itself
against the knowledge of God, bringing
every thought into captivity to the
obedience of Christ, and being ready to
punish all disobedience when your obedience is fulfilled." —2 Corinthians 10:3-6*

The enemy wants to control your mind, because if he can control your mind, he has full control of you! The strongholds, arguments, and thoughts the scripture talks about are all darts that the enemy uses against us to try to gain control of our mind. Through the Sword of the Spirit, God has given you, and I the power, and authority to reject, and cast down every thought from the enemy!

In Matthew chapter four Jesus demonstrated how to use the Sword of the Spirit when He was attacked by Satan:

> *(3) Now when the tempter came to Him, he said, "**If You are the Son of God**, command that these stones become bread." (4) But He answered and said, "It is written, 'Man shall not live by bread alone, but by every word that proceeds from the mouth of God.'"...*

> *(6) and said to Him, "**If You are the Son of God**, throw Yourself down. For it is written: 'He shall give His angels charge over you,' and, 'In their hands they shall bear you up, Lest you dash your foot against*

a stone.'" (7) Jesus said to him, "It is written again, 'You shall not tempt the Lord your God.'" ...

(8) Again, the devil took Him up on an exceedingly high mountain, and showed Him all the kingdoms of the world and their glory. (9) And he said to Him, "All these things I will give You if You will fall down and worship me." (10) Then Jesus said to him, "Away with you, Satan! For it is written, 'You shall worship the Lord your God, and Him only you shall serve.'" — Matthew 4:4, 7, 10

Notice that Satan starts each of his attacks by saying, "If You are the Son of God." This is similar to the tactic he used on Adam and Eve in the Garden of Eden. "Did God really say"? Just as Satan knew what God said to Adam, he knew that Jesus Christ was the Son of God. Satan's plan of destruction always seems to include one or more of the same elements:

- He challenges who you are in Christ.

- He attempts to cast doubt on the truth, and authenticity of the Word of God.

- He tries to discredit your testimony, and dishonor God.

- He attempts to pull you away from your dependence upon the Father.

- He attempts to distract you from doing the Father's will.

Soldiers must be skilled in handling their weapons or they could be easily killed in battle, so they go through vigorous training on how to use their weapons before they are sent into a battle. Each time Satan challenged Jesus, He readily used the Sword of the Spirit to refute Satan's ploys. He was able to do so because the Word of God was in Him.

Just as Jesus Christ used the Sword of the Spirit to counter Satan's attacks, we must also learn to use the sword of the Spirit. The bible says Satan only goes away for a while, so to overcome in an area you will have to persist in the truth of the scripture you've spoken to him. He's persistent, and you must be too. This is what the Apostle Paul is saying in Hebrews chapter six:

"(11) And we desire each one of you to show the same earnestness to have the full assurance of hope until the end, (12) so that you may not be sluggish, but imitators of those who through faith, and patience inherit the promises." — Hebrews 6:11-12 (ESV)

You have the power, and the authority to use Jesus' name, and God's Word. Empower yourself with the Word of God every day, and take every thought captive that the enemy brings to your mind that is not of God!

The Spoken Blessing!

"Christ hath redeemed us from the curse of the law, being made a curse for us: for it is written, Cursed is every one that hangeth on a tree: That the blessing of Abraham might come on the Gentiles through Jesus Christ; that we might receive the promise of the Spirit through faith." — Galatians 3:13-14 (KJV)

When God put Adam in the garden, He gave him the best, and provided him with more than enough resources for their needs, and for the generations to come. God blessed them, and said to them, "Be fruitful, and multiply." The word fruitful is defined as: "abundantly productive."

"Then God blessed them, and God said to them, "Be fruitful, and multiply; fill the earth, and subdue it; have dominion over the fish of the sea, over the birds of the air,

and over every living thing that moves on the earth." —*Genesis 1:28 (NKJV)*

Blessings must flow outward by action or word. Notice that God spoke, and blessed them. Jesus when sending out the seventy instructed them,

"(5) But whatever house you enter, first say, 'Peace to this house.' (6) And if a son of peace is there, your peace will rest on it; if not, it will return to you." —*Luke 10:5-6*

"Peace be to you" was the common salutation among the Jews, but Jesus wanted to speak according to the power that was working within them through the Holy Spirit, not according to custom. *"And if the son of peace, be there your peace shall rest upon it."* In other words, your prayer for the peace, and prosperity of the family shall be heard, and answered.

The message translation says *"If your greeting is received, then it's a good place to stay.*

But if it's not received, take it back and get out. Don't impose yourself."

The Apostles pronounced blessings over the churches where they preached. John spoke a powerful blessing over Gaius when he said, "Beloved, I pray that you may prosper in all things, and be in health, just as your soul prospers" (3 John 1:2).

Paul declared a blessing over the church in Philippi saying, "And my God shall supply all your need according to His riches in glory by Christ Jesus" (Philippians 4:19).

Jesus pronounced a blessing of deliverance on the Syro-Phoenician woman's daughter,

"(28) And she answered and said to Him, "Yes, Lord, yet even the little dogs under the table eat from the children's crumbs." (29) Then He said to her, "For this saying go your way; the demon has gone out of your daughter." —Mark 7:28-29

The woman received the blessing by faith, and found that her daughter was well when she reached home (Mark 7:30). The centurion also received the blessing by faith, and healing came upon his servant back home (Matthew 8:8–13). These were blessings by proxy, they were received on behalf of another.

There is power in blessing! Once a blessing has been spoken, it will eventually land. The person to whom the blessing is intended is the only one who can shut the door or block the blessing once it has been spoken.

A curse is different. Like a blessing, it is also empowered by speech, however, because of Christ's work of the Cross a curse can be rejected, rescinded, and broken, and you can be redeemed from it, and all of its effects.

God told Abraham "I will bless you ... and you will be a blessing" (Genesis 12:2). The word "bless" comes from the word "barak", which means to kneel, and bless. In the New Testament, the word bless means fortunate or happy. Another biblical definition for blessings is happiness, favor, praise or heavenly reward.

When I think about blessings, a dream I had a few years ago comes to mind. I dreamd I was in heaven walking with Jesus down a very long corridor with huge rooms on each side. I never saw His face, but I knew that it was Jesus.

God wants to use you as a vessel, and a vehicle for His Word.

We walked and talked for what seemed like a good while. I can't remember all of what we talked about, but I was amazed at His wisdom. Every now and then, we would enter one of the rooms. Each room was huge, and filled to the ceiling with beautifully wrapped gifts of all sizes. I watched as angels would rush in, get some of the gifts, and take them away.

"Lord what are these", I asked.

"These are gifts, and blessings for my sheep. Everything they need, and could ever desire," He said.

I was amazed at what I was seeing, at the size of the rooms, at how many there were, at the joy, and excitement on the angels' faces when they would take the gifts. As I looked around I was in total awe!

Then we entered a room that seemed larger than the others. I walked over, and looked at the nametags on the gifts. I saw names of people I knew. I got so excited, and went to grab them up, so I could take them their gifts.

"Stop!", He shouted.

"But Lord, I know these people I can take them their gifts", I said.

"No Angeline you cannot, they have to come, and get their own", He said.

I got so sad. With tears rolling down my face I said, "Lord you know many of these people don't believe, they are not going to come." I could hear the sadness in His voice when He said, "Yes I know, but they are here for them when they are ready. Just share what you saw, and those who have an ear to hear will hear, and come.

I said okay, and we walked out, but my heart was so heavy. I remember praying for the people whose names I recognized that they would hear, and believe.

I woke up, and continued praying because I wanted to know how to get the gifts, and what I should tell people. I know there are many people who don't believe that God shares with us in dreams, or that He will come, and talk with us, but God has declared that He does not change. If He has done it in times past, He will do it again.

I shared the dream as God told me in church one Sunday. Some people looked at me crazy, but one couple got excited, and received what God was saying. They came to church the next week with two testimonies of what happened the previous week.

One testimony was: they were at a stop light, and several hundred dollars flew into their car window. The other testimony was a blessing in one of their children's lives. Both of these testimonies were clearly miraculous events. I was greatful that God honored what He had me share with signs, and wonders. They attributed the blessing to believing, and accepting what God said when I shared the dream.

Jesus said all things are possible to the one who believes. I pray you are one who believes, because I am here to tell you that God has already blessed you, and He wants you to come, and receive your blessings.

Ephesians 1:3 says God has blessed us with everything we need to live an abundant life of faith in Christ. Many people do not believe they are worthy of God's blessings, so they don't accept the blessings. Regardless of where you started or what you used to do, in Christ you have have been blessed with the authority of Christ, and everything else you need to succeed, but if you want to receive a blessing you must accept it.

"Therefore say to them, 'Thus says the Lord God: "None of My words will be postponed any more, but the word which I speak will be done," says the Lord God." — Ezekiel 12:28 (NKJV)

God enforces His Word, and assures us that it does not come back to Him empty. His angels are ready, listening for His spoken Word so they can carry it out (Jeremiah 1:12, Psalm 103:20).

Scripture encourages us to bless others not only with our physical substance, but also with our words. In the book of Numbers God instructed His priests to speak a blessing over the people, and as they spoke the blessing, God followed the words to bring about *the* blessing:

"(22) Then the Lord spoke to Moses, saying, (23) Speak to Aaron and his sons, saying, 'This is the way you shall bless the Israelites. Say to them: (24) The Lord bless you, and keep you [protect you, sustain you, and

guard you]; (25) The Lord make His face shine upon you [with favor], and be gracious to you [surrounding you with lovingkindness]; (26) The Lord lift up His countenance (face) upon you [with divine approval], and give you peace [a tranquil heart and life].' (27) So Aaron and his sons shall put My name upon the children of Israel, and I will bless them." — Numbers 6:22-27 (AMP)

Ephesians 3:16-20 is also a great passage for blessing others with spiritual growth in the Lord. You can declare it something like this:

May God grant you, according to the riches of His glory, to be strengthened with might through His Spirit in the inner man, that Christ may dwell in your heart by faith. May you, be rooted, and grounded in love. May you comprehend what is the width, and length, and depth, and height of the love of Christ which passes knowledge. May you may be filled with all the fullness of God.

Now to Him who is able to do exceedingly abundantly above all that we ask or think, according to the power that works in us.

Another great blessing passage is found in Colossians 1:9-12. You can declare something like this:

May God give you the gift of spiritual insight, and understanding, so that you may see things from His point of view, and so that your life may bring glory to His name, and joy to His heart. May your life bear the fruit of God's Spirit, as you continue to grow in your knowledge, and understanding of God. And may God give you the strength you need to be able to pass through any experience, and endure it with joy, and giving thanks to God who has enabled you to share in the inheritance that belongs to God's holy people.

You can use any scripture promise to use as a blessing, and in prayer. When the Lord directs you to bless or pray for someone be quick to be obedient because God wants to do something in that person's life, and He needs those words to be declared in the atmosphere, so He can work with them to bring about the blessing (Psalm 103:20). Trust the Holy Spirit to direct you to Scripture to use in the blessing you share.

For instance, suppose God leads you to pray or bless someone who struggles with fear. You could use scripture verses that refer to fear, anxiety, peace, and comfort to personalize a blessing for them. If someone is dealing with sickness you could use scripture verses that refer to healing, peace, and comfort to personalize a blessing for them. For provision, you could use scripture verses that refer to provision, prosperity, and wealth to personalize a blessing for them.

When Jesus was instructing the disciples to minister to others in the power of the Holy Spirit, He said, "Freely ye have received, freely give" (Matthew 10:8). Speaking blessings over ourselves, and others should be a part of the Believer's life every day, not just set aside for spiritual moments or times, because every moment can be spiritual when we're blessing each other with goodness, and truth.

Faith Builders

Jesus relied on the Word of God alone to overcome obstacles, including the devil. Here are some scriptures that I use to build my faith, to strengthen my prayers, and to resist the enemy when he comes to challenge my confidence in God. I believe will the strengthen your faith as well.

Hebrews 4:16 (ESV): Let us then with confidence draw near to the throne of grace, that we may receive mercy, and find grace to help in time of need.

Hebrews 12:2: looking unto Jesus, the author and finisher of our faith, who for the joy that was set before Him endured the cross, despising the shame, and has sat down at the right hand of the throne of God.

Isaiah 43:19: Behold, I will do a new thing; now it shall spring forth; shall you not know it? I will even make a way in the wilderness, and rivers in the desert.

Isaiah 55:11: *So shall My word be that goes forth from My mouth; it shall not return to Me void, but it shall accomplish what I please, and it shall prosper in the thing for which I sent it.*

Isaiah 65:24: *It shall come to pass that before they call, I will answer; and while they are still speaking, I will hear.*

James 1:6: *But he must ask in faith without any doubting, for the one who doubts is like the surf of the sea, driven and tossed by the wind.*

James 5:16: *"The effectual fervent prayer of a righteous man availeth much."*

Jeremiah 1:12: *"...I am ready to perform My Word."*

Jeremiah 29:12: *"Then you will call upon Me, and go, and pray to Me, and I will listen to you."*

Jeremiah 32:27: *"Behold, I am the LORD, the God of all flesh: is there any thing too hard for me?"*

Jeremiah 33:3: *"Call to Me, and I will answer you, and show you great, and mighty things, which you do not know."*

Job 22:27: *"You will make your prayer to Him, He will hear you…"*

John 14:13: *"And whatever you ask in My name, that I will do, that the Father may be glorified in the Son."*

John 14:14: *"If you ask anything in my name, I will do it."*

John 14:27: *Peace I leave with you, My peace I give to you; not as the world gives* do I give to you. Let not your heart be troubled, neither let it be afraid.

John 15:16: *"You did not choose Me, but I chose you, and appointed you that you should go, and bear fruit, and that your fruit should remain, that whatever you ask the Father in My name He may give you."*

John 15:7: *If you abide in Me, and My words abide in you, you will ask what you desire, and it shall be done for you.*

John 16:23: *And in that day you will ask Me nothing. Most assuredly, I say to you, whatever you ask the Father in My name He will give you.*

John 16:24: *Ask, and you will receive, that your joy may be full."*

Mark 11:22-24: *And Jesus answered them, "Have faith in God. Truly, I say to you, whoever says to this mountain, 'Be taken up, and thrown into the sea,' and does* *not doubt in his heart, but believes that what he says will come to pass, it will be done for him. Therefore I tell you, whatever you ask in prayer, believe that you have received it, and it will be yours.*

Matthew 18:18: *Assuredly, I say to you, whatever you bind on earth will be bound in heaven, and whatever you loose on earth will be loosed in heaven.*

Matthew 18:19: *Again I say to you that if two of you agree on earth concerning anything that they ask, it will be done for them by My Father in heaven.*

Matthew 19:26: *But Jesus beheld them, and said unto them, With men this is impossible; but with God all things are possible.*

Matthew 21:22: *...whatever things you ask in prayer, believing, you will receive.*

Matthew 9:22: *But Jesus turned him about, and when He saw her, He said, Daughter, be of good comfort; thy faith hath made thee whole. And the woman was made whole from that hour.*

Matthew 9:29: *Then touched He their eyes, saying, According to your faith be it unto you.*

Philippians 1:6: *And I am sure of this, that He who began a good work in you will bring it to completion at the day of Jesus Christ.*

Proverbs 1:33 (NLT): *But all who listen to me will live in peace, untroubled by fear of harm.*

Psalm 91:15-16: *He shall call upon Me, and I will answer him; I will be with him in trouble; I will deliver him, and honor him. With long life I will satisfy him, and show him My salvation.*

Romans 8:31: *What then shall we say to these things? If God is for us, who can be against us?*

Romans 8:38-39: *For I am sure that neither death nor life, nor angels nor rulers, nor things present nor things to come, nor powers, nor height nor depth, nor anything else in all creation, will be able to separate us from the love of God in Christ Jesus our Lord.*

Romans 10:9: *If you confess with your mouth that Jesus is Lord, and believe in your heart that God raised him from the dead, you will be saved.*

Promises for Provision

1 John 3:21-22*: (21) Beloved, if our heart does not condemn us, we have confidence before God; (22) and whatever we ask we receive from him, because we keep His commandments, and do what pleases him.*

2 Corinthians 9:7*: So let each one give as he purposes in his heart, not grudgingly or of necessity; for God loves a cheerful giver.*

3 John 2*: Beloved, I pray that you may pros-per in all things, and be in health, just as your soul prospers.*

Deuteronomy 28:1*: And if you faithfully obey the voice of the Lord your God, being careful to do all His commandments that I command you today, the Lord your God will set you high above all the nations of the earth.*

Deuteronomy 8:18: *But thou shalt remem-ber the LORD thy God: for it is He that giveth thee power to get wealth, that He may establish His covenant which He sware unto thy fathers, as it is this day.*

Galatians 3:13: *Christ has redeemed us from the curse of the law, having become a curse for us (for it is written, "Cursed is everyone who hangs on a tree".*

Galatians 6:9: *And let us not grow weary of doing good, for in due season we will reap, if we do not give up.*

Hebrews 10:35: *Therefore do not throw away your confidence, which has a great reward.*

Hebrews 11:6: *And without faith, it is impossible to please God, because anyone who comes to Him must believe that He* exists, and that He rewards those who earnestly seek Him.

Isaiah 54:17: *No weapon that is formed against thee shall prosper; and every tongue that shall rise against thee in judgment thou shalt condemn. This is the heritage of the servants of the LORD, and their righteousness is of me, saith the LORD.*

James 1:5: *If any of you lacks wisdom, let him ask of God, who gives to all liberally, and without reproach, and it will be given to him.*

Joel 2:25-26: *And I will restore to you the years that the locust hath eaten, the cankerworm, and the caterpiller, and the palmerworm, my great army which I sent among you. And ye shall eat in plenty, and be satisfied, and praise the name of the LORD your God, that hath dealt wondrously with you: and my people shall never be ashamed.*

Luke 6:38*: Give, and it shall be given unto you; good measure, pressed down, and shaken together, and running over, shall men give into your bosom. For with the same measure that ye mete withal it shall be measured to you again.*

Malachi 3:8-11*: (8) Will man rob God? Yet you are robbing me. But you say, 'How have we robbed you?' In your tithes, and contributions. (9) You are cursed with a curse, for you are robbing me, the whole nation of you. (10) Bring the full tithe into the storehouse, that there may be food in my house. And thereby put me to the test, says the Lord of hosts, if I will not open the windows of heaven for you, and pour down for you a blessing until there is no more need. (11) I will rebuke the devourer for you, so that it will not destroy the fruits of your soil, and your vine in the field shall not fail to bear, says the Lord of hosts.*

Matthew 6:33: *But seek ye first the king-dom of God, and His righteousness; and all these things shall be added unto you.*

Philippians 4:19: *But my God shall supply all your need according to His riches in glory by Christ Jesus.*

Proverbs 10:22: *The blessing of the LORD, it maketh rich, and He addeth no sorrow with it.*

Proverbs 16:3: *Commit thy works unto the LORD, and thy thoughts shall be established.*

Proverbs 22:9: *He who has a generous eye will be blessed, for he gives of his bread to the poor.*

Proverbs 3:5-10: *(5) Trust in the Lord with all your heart, and lean not on your own understanding; (6) In all your ways acknowledge Him, and He shall direct[a] your paths. (7) Do not be wise in your own* *eyes; fear the Lord, and depart from evil. (8) It will be health to your flesh, and strength to your bones. (9) Honor the Lord with your possessions, and with the firstfruits of all your increase; (10) So your barns will be filled with plenty, and your vats will overflow with new wine.*

Proverbs 3:9-10*: (9) Honor the Lord with your wealth, and with the firstfruits of all your produce; (10) then your barns will be filled with plenty, and your vats will be bursting with wine.*

Proverbs 8:18-21*: (18) Riches, and honor are with me, enduring wealth, and righteousness. (19) My fruit is better than gold, even fine gold, and my yield than choice silver. (20) I walk in the way of righteous-ness, in the paths of justice, (21) granting an inheritance to those who love me, and filling their treasuries.*

Proverbs 11:25: *The generous soul will be made rich, and he who waters will also be watered himself.*

Psalm 1:1-3: *(1) Blessed is the man who walks not in the counsel of the ungodly, nor stands in the path of sinners, nor sits in the seat of the scornful; (2) But his delight is in the law of the Lord, and in His law he meditates day, and night. (3) He shall be like a tree planted by the rivers of water, that brings forth its fruit in its season, whose leaf also shall not wither; and whatever he does shall prosper.*

Psalm 23:1: *The Lord is my shepherd I shall not want.*

Psalm 35:27: *Let them shout for joy, and be glad, who favor my righteous cause; and let them say continually, "Let the Lord be mag-nified, who has pleasure in the prosperity of His servant."*

Psalm 37:18-19: *(18) The Lord knows the days of the upright, and their inheritance shall be forever. (19) They shall not be ashamed in the evil time, and in the days of famine they shall be satisfied.*

Psalm 37:3-5: *(3) Trust in the Lord, and do good; dwell in the land, and feed on His faithfulness. (4) Delight yourself also in the Lord, and He shall give you the desires of your heart. (5) Commit your way to the Lord, trust also in Him, and He shall bring it to pass.*

Psalm 37:4: *Delight thyself also in the LORD: and He shall give thee the desires of thine heart.*

Psalm 84:11-12: *For the Lord God is a sun, and shield: the Lord will give grace, and glory: no good thing will He withhold from them that walk uprightly.*

Psalm 85:12: *Yes, the Lord will give what is good; and our land will yield its increase.*

Psalm 92:12-15: *The righteous shall flour-ish like a palm tree: he shall grow like a cedar in Lebanon. Those that be planted in the house of the Lord shall flourish in the courts of our God. They shall bring forth fruit in old age; they shall be fat, and flourishing. To shew that the Lord is upright: He is my rock, and there is no unrighteousness in him.*

Psalm 119:105: *Thy word is a lamp unto my feet, and a light unto my path.*

Psalm 115:12-16: *The Lord hath been mindful of us: He will bless us; He will bless the house of Israel; He will bless the house of Aaron. He will bless them that fear the Lord, both small, and great. The Lord shall increase you more and more, you, and your children.*

Psalm 122:6-7: *Pray for the peace of Jeru-salem: they shall prosper that love thee. Peace be within thy walls, and prosperity within thy palaces.*

Matthew 6:31-33: *Therefore take no thought, saying, What shall we eat? or, what shall we drink: or, wherewithal shall we be clothed? (For after all these things do the Gentiles seek:) for your heavenly Father knoweth that ye have need of all these things. But seek ye first the kingdom of God, and His righteousness; and all these things shall be added unto you.*

Romans 8:32: *He who did not spare His own Son, but delivered Him up for us all, how shall He not with Him also freely give us all things?*

Promises for Healing

It is God's will that we are healed. Following are some healing scriptures, and confessions. Highlight the scriptures, and confessions that jump out at you, and speak them to your need, and believe that God will perform His will. Make changes to the confession to make it more real, and personal to you if you need to.

1 Peter 2:24: He himself bore our sins in His body on the tree, that we might die to sin, and live to righteousness. By His wounds you have been healed.

2 Corinthians 12:9: But He said to me, "My grace is sufficient for you, for my power is made perfect in weakness." Therefore, I will boast all the more gladly of my weaknesses, so that the power of Christ may rest upon me.
3 John 1:2: Beloved, I pray that all may go well with you, and that you may be in good health, as it goes well with your soul.

174

Deuteronomy 7:15*: And the Lord will take away from you all sickness, and none of the evil diseases of Egypt, which you knew, will He inflict on you, but He will lay them on all who hate you.*

Exodus 23:25*: Worship the LORD your God, and His blessing will be on your food, and water. I will take away sickness from among you.*

Hebrews 11:6*: And without faith it is impossible to please him, for whoever would draw near to God must believe that He exists, and that He rewards those who seek him.*

Hebrews 13:8*: Jesus Christ is the same yesterday, and today, and forever.*

Isaiah 41:10*: Fear not, for I am with you; be not dismayed, for I am your God; I will strengthen you, I will help you, I will uphold you with my righteous right hand.*

Isaiah 53:5: *But He was wounded for our transgressions; He was crushed for our iniquities; upon him was the chastisement that brought us peace, and with His stripes we are healed.*

Isaiah 54:17: *No weapon that is fashioned against you shall succeed, and you shall confute every tongue that rises against you in judgment. This is the heritage of the servants of the Lord, and their vindication from me, declares the Lord.*

Isaiah 57:18-19: *I have seen his ways, but I will heal him; I will lead him, and restore comfort to him, and his mourners, creating the fruit of the lips. Peace, peace, to the far, and to the near," says the Lord, "and I will heal him.*

James 5:14-16: *Is anyone among you sick? Let him call for the elders of the church, and let them pray over him,* *anointing him with oil in the name of the Lord. And the prayer of faith will save the one who is sick, and the Lord will raise him up. And if he has committed sins, he will be forgiven. There-fore, confess your sins to one another, and pray for one another, that you may be healed. The prayer of a righteous person has great power as it is working.*

Jeremiah 17:14*: Heal me, O Lord, and I shall be healed; save me, and I shall be saved, for you are my praise.*

Jeremiah 30:17*: For I will restore health to you, and your wounds I will heal, declares the Lord, because they have called you an outcast: 'It is Zion, for whom no one cares!'*

Jeremiah 33:6*: Behold, I will bring to it health, and healing, and I will heal them, and reveal to them abundance of prosperity, and security.*

Job 5:26: *You shall come to your grave in ripe old age, like a sheaf gathered up in its season.*

Luke 5:17: *...And the power of the Lord was present to heal them.*

Luke 10:9: *Heal the sick in it, and say to them, 'The kingdom of God has come near to you.'*

Luke 4:18: *"The Spirit of the Lord is upon me, because He has anointed me to proclaim good news to the poor. He has sent me to pro-claim liberty to the captives, and recovering of sight to the blind, to set at liberty those who are oppressed,*

Matthew 11:28: *Come to me, all who labor, and are heavy laden, and I will give you rest.*

Mark 5:34*: He [Jesus] said to her, "Daughter, your faith has healed you. Go in peace, and be freed from your suffering."*

Philippians 4:19*: And my God will supply every need of yours according to His riches in glory in Christ Jesus.*
Philippians 4:6-7*: Do not be anxious about anything, but in everything by prayer, and supplication with thanksgiving let your requests be made known to God. And the peace of God, which surpasses all under-standing, will guard your hearts, and your minds in Christ Jesus.*

Proverbs 17:22*: A joyful heart is good medicine, but a crushed spirit dries up the bones.*

Proverbs 3:5-8*: Trust in the Lord with all your heart, and do not lean on your own understanding. In all your ways acknow-ledge him, and He will make straight your paths. Be not wise in your own eyes; fear*

the Lord, and turn away from evil. It will
be healing to your flesh, and refreshment to
your bones.

Proverbs 4:20-22: My son, be attentive
to my words; incline your ear to my
sayings. Let them not escape from your
sight; keep them within your heart. For
they are life to those who find them, and
healing to all their flesh.

Psalm 103:2-4: Bless the Lord, O my soul,
and forget not all His benefits, who
forgives all your iniquity, who heals all
your diseases, who redeems your life from
the pit, who crowns you with steadfast love
and mercy,

Psalm 107:41: But He raises up the needy
out of affliction and makes their families
like flocks.

Psalm 147:3: He heals the brokenhearted,
and binds up their wounds.

Psalm 34:17-20*: When the righteous cry for help, the Lord hears, and delivers them out of all their troubles. The Lord is near to the brokenhearted, and saves the crushed in spirit. Many are the afflictions of the righteous, but the Lord delivers him out of them all. He keeps all his bones; not one of them is broken.*

Psalm 41:3*: The Lord sustains him on his sickbed; in his illness you restore him to full health.*

Psalm 6:2*: Be gracious to me, O Lord, for I am languishing; heal me, O Lord, for my bones are troubled.*

Psalm 107:20*: He sent His Word, and healed them, and delivered them from their destructions.*

Promises for Protection

1 Corinthians 10:13: No temptation has overtaken you but such as is common to man; and God is faithful, who will not allow you to be tempted beyond what you are able, but with the temptation will provide the way of escape also, so that you will be able to endure it.

1 Peter 1:5: who are protected by the power of God through faith for a salvation ready to be revealed in the last time.

1 Samuel 17:45: Then David said to the Philistine, "You come to me with a sword, a spear, and a javelin, but I come to you in the name of the LORD of hosts, the God of the armies of Israel, whom you have taunted.

1 Thessalonians 5:23-24: (23) Now may the God of peace Himself sanctify you completely; and may your whole spirit, soul, and body be preserved blameless at the coming of our Lord Jesus Christ. (24) He who calls you is faithful, who also will do it.

2 Chronicles 14:11: Then Asa called to the LORD his God and said, "LORD, there is no one besides You to help in the battle between the powerful and those who have no strength; so help us, O LORD our God, for we trust in You, and in Your name have come against this multitude. O LORD, You are our God; let not man prevail against You."

2 Corinthians 12:9: And He has said to me, "My grace is sufficient for you, for power is perfected in weakness." Most gladly, therefore, I will rather boast about my weaknesses, so that the power of Christ may dwell in me.

2 Thessalonians 3:3: But the Lord is faithful, and He will strengthen, and protect you from the evil one.

Deuteronomy 31:6: *Be strong, and courageous, do not be afraid or tremble at them, for the LORD your God is the one who goes with you He will not fail you or forsake you.*

Isaiah 41:10: *Do not fear, for I am with you; Do not anxiously look about you, for I am your God I will strengthen you, surely I will help you, Surely I will uphold you with My righteous right hand.*

Isaiah 50:7: *For the Lord GOD helps Me, Therefore, I am not disgraced; Therefore, I have set My face like flint, And I know that I will not be ashamed.*

John 10:28-30: *(28) And I give them eternal life, and they shall never perish; neither shall anyone snatch them out of My hand. (29) My Father, who has given them to Me, is greater than all; and no one is able to snatch them out of My Father's hand. (30) I and My Father are one."*

Joshua 1:5: *No man will be able to stand before you all the days of your life Just as I have been with Moses, I will be with you; I will not fail you or forsake you.*

Psalm 121:3-8: *(3) He will not allow your foot to be moved; He who keeps you will not slumber. (4) Behold, He who keeps Israel shall neither slumber nor sleep. (5) The Lord is your keeper; the Lord is your shade at your right hand. (6) The sun shall not strike you by day, nor the moon by night. (7) The Lord shall preserve you from all evil; He shall preserve your soul. (8) The Lord shall preserve your going out, and your coming in from this time forth, and even forevermore.*

Psalm 121:8: *The LORD will guard your going out and your coming in from this time forth and forever.*

Psalm 124:1-5: *(1) If it had not been the Lord who was on our side," Let Israel now* *say— (2) "If it had not been the Lord who was on our side, when men rose up against us, (3) then they would have swallowed us alive, when their wrath was kindled against us; (4) then the waters would have overwhelmed us, the stream would have gone over our soul; (5) then the swollen waters would have gone over our soul."*

Psalm 46:1: *God is our refuge, and strength, a very present help in trouble.*

Psalm 56:9: *Then my enemies will turn back in the day when I call; this I know, that God is for me.*

Psalm 57:1: *Be gracious to me, O God, be gracious to me, for my soul takes refuge in You; and in the shadow of Your wings I will take refuge until destruction passes by.*

Psalm 91:3-7: *(3) Surely He shall deliver you from the snare of the fowler and from the perilous pestilence. (4) He shall cover you with His feathers, and under His wings* *you shall take refuge; His truth shall be your shield, and buckler. (5) You shall not be afraid of the terror by night, nor of the arrow that flies by day, (6) nor of the pestilence that walks in darkness, nor of the destruction that lays waste at noonday. (7) A thousand may fall at your side, and ten thousand at your right hand; but it shall not come near you.*

Revelation 3:10: *Because you have kept My command to persevere, I also will keep you from the hour of trial which shall come upon the whole world, to test those who dwell on the earth.*

Promises for Strength

2 Corinthians 12:9-10: *(9) But He said to me, "My grace is sufficient for you, for my power is made perfect in weakness." Therefore I will boast all the more gladly about my weaknesses, so that Christ's power may rest on me. (10) That is why, for Christ's sake, I delight in weaknesses, in insults, in hardships, in persecutions, in difficulties. For when I am weak, then I am strong.*

Ephesians 3:16: *I pray that out of His glorious riches He may strengthen you with power through His Spirit in your inner being,*

Ephesians 6:10: *Finally, be strong in the Lord, and in His mighty power.*

Habakkuk 3:19: *The Sovereign LORD is my strength; He makes my feet like the feet* *of a deer, He enables me to tread on the heights.*

Isaiah 12:2: *Surely God is my salvation; I will trust, and not be afraid. The LORD, the LORD himself, is my strength, and my defense; He has become my salvation.*

Isaiah 33:2: *LORD, be gracious to us; we long for you. Be our strength every morning, our salvation in time of distress.*

Isaiah 40:29-31: *(29) He gives strength to the weary and increases the power of the weak. (30) Even youths grow tired and weary, and young men stumble and fall; (31) but those who hope in the LORD will renew their strength. They will soar on wings like eagles; they will run and not grow weary, they will walk and not be faint.*

Philippians 4:13: *I can do all things through Christ who strengthens me.*

Psalm 118:14: *The LORD is my strength, and my defense; He has become my salvation.*

Psalm 119:28: *My soul is weary with sorrow; strengthen me according to Your Word.*

Psalm 22:19: *But you, LORD, do not be far from me. You are my strength; come quickly to help me.*

Psalm 28:7-8: *(7) The LORD is my strength, and my shield; my heart trusts in Him, and He helps me. My heart leaps for joy, and with my song I praise him. (8) The LORD is the strength of His people, a fortress of salvation for His anointed one.*

Psalm 29:11: *The Lord will give strength to His people; the Lord will bless His people with peace.*

Psalm 46:1: *God is our refuge, and strength, an ever-present help in trouble.*

Scripture Prayers and Confessions

Praying Scripture is a powerful way to pray. As you pray God's Word, you are proclaiming who you are in Christ, and declaring your faith in what God's *established*, and *settled* Word says about you, and the situation.

Following are examples of Scripture based prayers to show how you can use Scripture promises to personalize your prayers to pray, and decree what God has already established in His Word. Read through the prayer the first time. Look up, and meditate on the scripture references, and then pray the prayer out loud as many times as you need to. The point is to come into agreement with God. If the Holy Spirit opens up a scripture reference to you, and you feel led to pray something else, do so.

Faith Confession

In the name of Jesus, I confess that I am strong, and firmly rooted in faith. I am an overcomer. I can do all things through Christ. I seek the Lord, and I will lack no good thing. My God supplies all of my needs according to His riches in glory in Christ Jesus. By His stripes, I am healed. I walk in divine health.

I am anointed, and empowered by God to succeed. Everything I put my hands to for the King-dom of God prospers. Signs, wonders, and miracles are manifested through my life as I attract others to Christ. Now thanks be to God, who in Christ always leads us in triumphal procession.

Scripture references: 2 Corinthians 2:14; 2 Corinthians 5:7; Colossians 2:6-7; Psalm 23:1; Philippians 4:13; Hebrews 2:4; 1 John 5:4; Isaiah 10:27; Colossians 2:2-3

Favor

Father, thank You for righteousness in Christ Jesus. You bless the righteous, and surround us with favor. Favor is as a shield to me. Thank You for going before me, and making every crooked path straight. Thank You that I have favor with You, and man today. Because of Your favor on my life, my enemies cannot triumph over me.

Father, Your word says You take pleasure in the prosperity of Your servant, there I thank You prosperity in every area of my life. I ask You for restoration of everything that has been stolen from me by the destroyer. I thank You supernatural increase, and promotion and that I prosper in every place, and in every situation I am in because the Lord is always with me. In Jesus' name, I pray, Amen.

Scripture references: Psalm 5:12; Psalm 119:89; Psalm 84:11; Isaiah 45:2; Psalm 41:11; Joel 2:25; Isaiah 61:7-8; Jeremiah 30:17; Luke 1:28; Genesis 39:1-6, 21; Psalm 75:6-7; Esther 2:17; Psalm 35:27; 3 John 2; Deuteronomy 8:18; Psalm 112:3

Forgive Someone

Father God, I know You love me, and I love You. Thank you for sending Jesus to the Cross so that I could be free from every bondage including unforgiveness. Father I want to be free of everything that hinders me!

You said in Isaiah 43:25-26, "I, even I, am He who blots out your transgressions for My own sake; and I will not remember your sins. Put Me in remembrance; let us contend together; state your case, that you may be acquitted.

Colossians 3:13 says, "Make allowance for each other's faults, and forgive anyone who offends you. Remember, the Lord forgave you, so you must forgive others." Father I realize that regardless of what evil was done to me it was the enemy trying to destroy my offender, and me. I want to be free from any hurtful or traumatic experience that is holding me in bondage to unforgiveness.

I come to You today asking for forgiveness for them, and for me. I repent of not forgiving, of holding bitterness in my heart, and being upset with people, You, situations, and even myself. Father as you so willingly forgive, I too choose to forgive (_____) completely.

I ask You Father to forgive me for releasing any hurt or anger towards them. Forgive me for any judgmental, and condemning thoughts, words I have spoken to them, and over them. Destroy the destructive seeds, and their harvest that I have planted.

I ask You Father to forgive them, and release them. Let them not be guilty any longer of doing me any harm. I place them in Your Hands Lord Jesus, and I ask You to heal them, deliver them, and set them free, and use them for Your glory.

Father I know that You do not make mistakes. You are perfect in all your ways. Forgive me for holding bitterness, and anger in my heart towards You because of situations, and circumstances that did not work out the way I thought they should have. I forgive myself for letting this hurt control me, and for hurting others out of my hurt. I repent of this behavior, and my attitude.

Let the Blood of Jesus Christ purge me from all unforgiveness, bitterness, resentment, and wrath. Help me to know who I am in Christ that I may walk in Your Love. In Your strength, and provision help me to restore whatever I owe to anyone. Whatever is owed to me by any person in Your strength, and provision may it be released to me, and whatever doesn't come I forgive in the name of Jesus Christ.

Father I receive the finished work Christ has done for healing my emotions, and my physical body. I decree that I am healed in my mind, soul, and body, and command infirmity, and disease to leave from me now in the name of Jesus. I speak restoration, and peace to the areas where the infirmity was.

Thank You Father for giving me beauty for ashes of failure, for replacing mourning, and grief with the oil of joy, and for giving me a garment of praise instead of a spirit of despair. Thank You for forgiving me, and setting me free. I ask You to bind forgiveness in my heart so that when offence comes it will not take root, and I can forgive quickly. In Jesus name I pray, Amen.

Scripture references: Psalm 51:10; 43:25-26; Hebrews 9:14; Isaiah 61:3; Isaiah 53:5

Forgiveness for Speaking Negatively

Father, Your Word says we must give an account of every idle word that we have spoken from our mouth. You said if I confess my sins, You would forgive me, and the blood of Christ shall cleanse me from all unrighteousness. Father, I repent for speaking words contrary to Your will.

Forgive me for speaking lies, for gossiping, backbiting, murmuring, and for complaining. Forgive me for every idle word I have spoken against my pastor, my church, my family, my friends, my co-workers, and associates. Forgive me for not seeing them as the blessing they are in my life. I ask You to bless them Father.

I also ask for You to forgive me for not trusting You, and for speaking words of fear, doubt, and unbelief regarding Your Word, and Your ability to do what You have promised in my life. Father, break the power of these ungodly words from my life. I forgive every person who has spoken ill of me, to me, and over me. Bless them also Father, and break the power of word curses spoken over me by others.

Create in me a clean heart, O God; and renew a right spirit within me. Incline not my heart to any evil thing. Set a guard over my mouth, and keep watch over the door of my lips. In Jesus' name I pray. Amen.

Scripture references: Psalm 141:3-4; 1 John 1:9; Psalm 51:10

Healing (Yours)

Heavenly Father, I praise You for Your Goodness. You sent Your Word, and healed all diseases including (*name of illness*). Your anointing destroys all yokes, and burdens. With You all things are possible. Heal me O Lord, and I shall be healed. Save me, and I shall be saved, for You are my praise. Saturate me with Your presence, love, joy, and peace, and draw me closer to You. Give me more revelation of Your Love. Fill me with Your Holy Spirit, and empower me to do Your work so that my life will bring glory, and honor to Your holy name.

Jesus said in Mark 11:23-24, "whosoever shall say unto this mountain, be thou removed, and be thou cast into the sea; and shall not doubt in his heart, but shall believe that those things which he saith shall come to pass; he shall have whatsoever he saith. Therefore I say unto you, What things soever ye desire, when ye pray, believe that ye receive them, and ye shall have them".

It is written, "Love has been perfected among us. As He is, so are we in this world." Father I believe, and stand on Your Word. I live in Jesus, and Jesus lives in me, therefore sickness, and death is not my portion.

I declare that Jesus has destroyed the works of the devil, and that includes (_name of illness_). I bind up (_name of illness_)'s works, and loose (_name of illness_) from it's assignment against me. My body is the temple of the Holy Spirit, (_name of illness_) cannot stay in my body. Leave now, and take your inflammation, infection, symptoms, and any abnor-malities with you.

Father, thank You for Your restoration power. Let Your healing balm restore any diseased areas in me so that my body will function the way You created it to function. In Jesus' Name I speak restoration, and rejuvenation to my blood, immune, and central nervous systems, organs, tissues, liga-ments, and bones. Harmony, and balance be in every cell of my body. Function the way you were created to do daily in the name of Jesus Christ. I decree I will live a long life, and declare the Glory of the Lord my God, who forgives all sins, and heals all diseases.

Now Lord I pray for my family, and friends that their faith in Your power fail not. I ask for an abundance of strength for them to endure this trying time. I bind up all seeds of doubt, and unbelief regarding my healing, and I declare that these seed will not take root in them or me. I loose the peace of God that surpasses all understanding to keep our hearts, and minds through Christ Jesus. In Jesus' Name, I pray. Amen.

Scripture references: Mark 11:23-24; 1 John 4:17; Isaiah 10:27; 1 John 3:8; 1 Corinthians 6:19-20; Jeremiah 30:17; Philippians 4:7; Psalm 103:3, 118:17; Jeremiah 17:14

Healing (Someone Else)

Heavenly Father, I praise You for Your Goodness. I thank You for this day, and all of my many blessings in Christ Jesus. Thank You for salvation, and all of it's benefits. You sent Your Word, and healed all diseases including (*name of illness*). With You all things are possible. As a believer, and Ambassador of Jesus Christ I pray now according to Mark 11:23-24 that says, "whosoever shall say unto this mountain, be thou removed, and be thou cast into the sea;, and shall not doubt in his heart, but shall believe that those things which he saith shall come to pass; he shall have whatsoever he saith.

You said in 3 John 2, "Beloved, I pray that you may prosper in all things, and be in health, just as your soul prospers." It is also written in Colossians 2:15 that Satan, and his evil hosts were spoiled, disarmed, stripped of their power, and defeated by our Lord Jesus Christ. And then Jesus gave Believers power, and authority over all devils, and to cure diseases according to Luke 9:1.

I speak to all disease, infirmity, and abnormalities in (*person's name*)'s body, and I command you to come out now, and never enter it again, in Jesus mighty name.

Father, thank You for Your restoration power. Let Your healing balm restore the diseased areas in (*person's name*)'s body so that it will function the way You created it to function. I speak restoration, to (*person's name*)'s blood system, immune system, and central nervous system, organs, tissues, liga-ments, and bones in Jesus Mighty Name. I speak harmony, and balance in every cell of (his/her) body. Function the way you were created to do daily in the name of Jesus Christ. I speak life to you (*person's name*)! Live, and declare the Glory of the Lord our God who forgives all sins, and heals all your diseases.

Father I praise You for (*person's name*)'s total healing (mind, soul, and body). Thank You for glorifying Your Goodness. Saturate (*him/her*) with Your presence, love, joy, and peace, and draw (*him/her*) close to You every moment of the day. Give (*person's name*) more revelation of Your

Love. Fill (*him/her*) with Your Holy Spirit, and empower (*him/her*) to do Your work so that their life will bring glory, and honor to Your holy name.

Now Lord I pray for (*person's name*)'s family, and friends that their faith in Your power fail not. Set a guard over the mouth of all who come in contact with (*person's name*), let no words of doubt, and unbelief come out of their mouths, and take root in (*person's name*). Help (him/her) cast down everything that tries to exalt itself against the Word of God. In Jesus name, I pray. Amen.

Scripture references: Colossians 2:15; Luke 9:1; 2 Corinthians 5:20; 3 John 1:2; Psalm 118:17; Psalm 103:3; Psalm 141:3

Healing from Addiction

Father, I thank You for Your grace, and setting my feet on Jesus Christ, the Rock of my Salvation. I am a new creature in Christ, old things have passed away, and all things have become new. I reckon myself dead to sin. Just as death no longer has power over Jesus Christ, sin, and addiction has no dominion or power over me. (addiction) you cannot reign in my mind, soul, and body.

Jesus has destroyed the works of the devil. I have authority through Christ Jesus to execute judgment on all the forces that want me to stay in this addiction. In the name of Jesus I bind up this addiction, and render your power against me destroyed. Where the Spirit of the Lord is there is liberty. I loose the liberty of the Lord in my life!

Father I know that You have plans for good, and not evil for me, and I claim Your plan for my life right now. Spirit of God, search me, know me, reveal to me the lies that I have accepted, and the agree-ments I have made with the enemy in this area because of the lie. *(Pause, and listen to what the Holy Spirit says.)*

Forgive me Father for accepting *(name the lies)*. I renounce those agreements, and I break these agreements now in the name of Jesus Christ. I renounce every claim they have given the enemy in my life. Lord God I ask You to deliver me from the effects of this lie. Father let Your anointing destroy this yoke, and break this stronghold. Set me free, and help me to walk by the Spirit, so I will not fulfill the lusts of the flesh. I declare this sin, and addiction is under my feet, in the Name of Jesus. Amen.

Scripture references: 2 Corinthians 5:17; Galatians 2:20; Romans 8:11; John 10:10; Romans 6:4, 6, 10–11; Colossians 1:13; Ephesians 2:6, 1:21, 6:12; 1 John 3:8; Matthew 18:18; 2 Corinthians 3:17; Jeremiah 29:11; Psalm 149:5–9; Romans 6:14; Galatians 5:16

Hearing God's Voice

Heavenly Father, Thank you for saving me. I bless Your holy name. Father, it is written, "My sheep hear my voice, and I know them, and they follow me. I give them eternal life, and they will never perish, and no one will snatch them out of my hand. Jesus said, "Ask, and it will be given to you; seek, and you will find; knock, and it will be opened to you. To teach me to know Your Voice, and to hear You distinctly, and clearly according to John 10:27.

It is written that we should not believe every spirit, but test the spirits to determine whether the spirits are of God. I ask You Lord to teach me to discern every spirit to know if they are of You, Lord. Draw me closer to You so I will not heed the voice of a stranger. I ask You to do this in Jesus' Name. Amen!

Scripture references: 2 Timothy 1:9; John 10:27-28; Matthew 7:7; 1 John 4:1-2

Loss of a Loved One

Father, I thank You for Jesus my High Priest; who is able to understand, and sympathize with our weaknesses, infirmities, and temptations. I come to the throne of grace with confidence, to receive mercy, and grace to help in this time of grief. It is written that You rescue those that are crushed in spirit. Draw me near to in this time of sadness, and loss. Show me the depths of your love, a glimpse of the kingdom of heaven. Heal my broken heart, bind up these wounds. Lord, You are the Resurrection, and the Life! In Jesus' Name, I pray. Amen.

Scripture references: Hebrews 4:14-16, Psalm 34:18, Ephesians 3:18, John 11:25

Marriage Restoration

Father you said it is not good that man should be alone, and that a man shall cleave unto his wife, and they shall be one flesh. I stand in faith on the authority I have as a believer in Jesus Christ, and pray Your Word over my marriage that (*spouse's name*), and I are no longer two, but one. Therefore, what God has joined together, let no man separate. No weapon formed against this marriage will prosper, and every tongue raised against our reconciliation God is showing in the wrong, for this is my heritage as a child of God, and my righteous-ness is in Jesus.

Lord God I ask that you forgive me for holding bitterness in my heart and not forgiving (*spouse's name*), for releasing any hurt or anger toward (*him/her*), and for being selfish, and not loving the mate that you blessed me with according to Your Word. I repent this day, and I choose to let (spouse's name) off the hook, and forgive (*him/her*) com-pletely, and I ask you to forgive, and release (*him/her*) too. Let (*him/her*) not be guilty any longer of doing me any harm. I place (*spouse's name*), and my marriage in Your hands Lord Jesus that You may heal us.

Father, I ask in Jesus name that You restore to me, and my spouse everything the enemy has stolen including every Spiritual blessing that you blessed us with on the day we were married. Correct past mistakes, right every wrong, reverse all harm, and remove all shortcomings that have blocked us. Let us revisit the opportunities we have missed. Give us everlasting joy, and a double portion of blessing instead of shame, and disgrace. Let us rejoice in our inheritance. By faith I believe, and see everything restored according to Your Word.

Thank You that Your grace is sufficient for those standing for the restoration of their marriage, and that your power is made perfect in weakness, and that the power of Christ is in us. Father strengthen the marriages of our land. Set a guard before my mouth, and keep watch at the door of my lips, train me not to speak against Your favor at work in my life, and marriage.

Lord God, You instituted the family to be the cornerstone of society, restore us to our rightful place, and glorify Your name through this marriage. Father, I ask for a double portion of blessing in this marriage.

I praise You Lord, for keeping the promise You have made concerning me, my marriage, and my home, and for doing as You promised, so that Your name will be great forever. You have said that You will build a home for me, and that it pleases You to bless my marriage. Establish this marriage with blessings forever. In Jesus' name I pray, Amen.

Scripture references: Genesis 2: 18; Psalm 51:1; Mark 11:24; Mark 10: 9; Exodus 12:13; Psalm 42:1-2; Colossians 4:2; 1 Corinthians 10:31; John 16:8; Isaiah 54:17; Jeremiah 1:12; Luke 18:8; Joel 2:25; Isaiah 61:7; Proverbs 6:31; Matthew 16:18; Acts 19:20; John 10:28; Psalm 141:3

Military Members, and Families

Dear Heavenly Father, You are our Refuge, and Stronghold in times of trouble. I come to You to lift up the men, and women of the Armed Forces of the United States of America. I petition You, Lord, according to Psalm 91, for the safety of our military personnel. I ask You to keep them safe from all hidden dangers, and all deadly diseases. Shield, and shelter them with your wings, and let Your faithful promises be their armor, and protection. Let no evil conquer them. Let no plague come near their tent or dwelling. Order your angels to protect them wherever they go, and return them safely to their families.

I pray for strength, and courage for the POWs, and those held hostage, and missing in action, and I ask you to work it out that they may come home. I pray for the protection, and safety of relief workers, and missionaries. I ask You God to pour out Your Glory on our military, and use them as instruments of righteousness.

I pray for the protection of children, and innocent civilians in war torn lands. Lord God make known Your salvation, and Your righteousness in these nations. May they call upon Your name, and be saved.

Father, provide for, and protect the families of our armed forces members. Preserve marriages; cause the hearts of the parents to turn toward their children, and the hearts of the children to turn toward the fathers, and mothers. Uplift, and edify those who have been left to raise children by themselves. Through Your Holy Spirit, comfort the lonely, and strengthen the weary.

Thank You for Your protective hand that shields America. Guide, and direct the leadership of America, and the Military in every way. Destroy the ungodly plans of leadership, and let skillful, and Godly wisdom enter into the hearts of our President, and leaders. Give them hearts, and ears attentive to Your counsel. Make them a people of Your integrity. May they hear Your Voice, and do Your will, that we all may lead a quiet, and peaceful life in all Godliness, and honesty.

Father I give You praise, and declare that we Your people will dwell safely in this land, and prosper abundantly for we are more than conquerors through Christ Jesus, and no weapon formed against us shall prosper. In the Name of my Lord, and Savior Jesus Christ of Nazareth, I pray, Amen.

Scripture references: Colossians 2:15, Ephesians 6:12, Ezekiel 22:30, Malachi 4:6, Psalm 98:2, Luke 2:30-31, John 10:10

Nation, Country

Father, You said in Isaiah 44:3 "I will pour water on the thirsty land, and streams on the dry ground; I will pour my Spirit upon your offspring, and my blessing on your descendants." I ask You Lord God to pour out Your Spirit upon this thirsty Nation. Convict the lost of sin, guide us in truth, teach us how to be Holy for You are Holy, remind us of what Jesus said, and glorify Jesus in this land.

Father, strengthen us and uphold us with Your righteous right hand. You are our Refuge, and Stronghold in times of trouble. Thank You for Your protective hand that shields this nation. Father I prayer for the leaders of our government. I know that their authority comes from You. I pray that they will learn to trust You and seek Your way and instructions. I pray that the authority You've given them to further Your work and protect Your people. Give them the wisdom and foresight to implement plans that will benefit all people.

Thank You Lord for hearing the prayers, and requests of Your people on behalf of this nation. I declare that Your children will dwell safely in this land, and prosper abundantly, for we are more than conquerors through Christ Jesus, and no weapon formed against us shall prosper. Father, let the Holy Spirit cause revival to break forth in this nation. In Jesus' name I pray, Amen.

Scripture references: Joel 2:28, Acts 2:1-2, Mark 11:22-24; John 14:13-14

Pastor and Church

Heavenly Father, I come thank You for the Glorious Gospel, and the Gift of Your Son Jesus Christ. Thank You for my Pastor(s), and my church family. Bless this ministry You have placed in my Pastor(s) hands to prepare Your sheep for the works of service, to the building up of the body of Christ in the faith, and in the knowledge of the Son of God that we may come to maturity, and attain the fullness of Christ.

I ask You to protect my pastor(s), and my church family from the deceitfulness of sin. Let Wisdom, Guidance, Understanding, Counsel, and Might, and the Spirit of Knowledge be with us. May we be filled with humility, have a teachable spirit, a servant's heart, be devoted to prayer, and to the ministry of the Word.

May my Pastor(s) hold fast to Scripture, and stand on Your Word, and only Your Word. Let my Pastor(s) preach the Gospel with the demonstration of the Spirit, and it's power. May my Pastor(s), and church family make an impact for Your kingdom in every place the soles of our feet tread. May many come to know Christ as we share the Gospel of Jesus Christ. I decree that no weapon formed against my my Pastor(s), and church family will prosper, and every tongue rising against us shall be shown to be in the wrong.

Thank You Father for the remnant that You have gathered here from all nations! Let everyone in this congregation hold fast, and follow the pattern of wholesome, and sound teaching in faith, and love in Christ Jesus. May this congregation be abundant, prosperous, and vibrant. Touch everyone who enters this doorway; destroy yokes, and set the people free. Meet their needs according to Your riches in Glory in Christ Jesus our Savior, and Lord. In Jesus' name I pray. Amen.

Scripture references: Ephesians 4:12-13, 6:19-20; 2 Timothy 1:13-14; Isaiah 11:2-3, 54:17; 1 Corinthians 2:4; 1 Corinthians 9:27; Romans 1:11-12; 1 Timothy 3:2-6; Philippians 4:19; Acts 6:4; James 1:14-15; Colossians 4:2

Protection

Father, You declared in Deuteronomy 33:12 that, "The beloved of the Lord dwells in safety. The High God surrounds him all day long, and dwells between his shoulders."

Lord God, You are my hiding place; You shall preserve me from trouble; You shall surround me with songs of deliverance. Show me Your unfailing love in wonderful ways. By Your mighty power rescue me as I seek refuge from the enemy.

Hide me in the shadow of Your wings. Protect me from wicked people who seek to attack me, and from the murderous enemies who surround me. Hide me from the enemy, and all his demon spirits. Let no evil conquer me; no plague come near my home according to Your Word in Psalm 91. Father I declare that You are my vindicator. No weapon formed against me shall prosper; and every tongue that accuses me in judgment you will condemn. This is my heritage as a servant of the Lord.

Father, I thank You for the hedge of protection around me. I declare that God indeed is my savior; I am confident, and unafraid. My strength, and my courage are in the Lord, and He has been my Savior. In Jesus' name, I pray. Amen.

Scripture references: Deuteronomy 33:12; Jeremiah 1:12; Psalm 91; Psalm 18:2; Psalm 91:2; Matthew 6:13; Psalm 32:7; Psalm 17:7-9; Psalm 26:1; Isaiah 54:17; Isaiah 12:2

Provision

Father it is written that You provide for those who fear you. You keep Your covenant. According to Your Word give rain for my land in it's season, the early rain, and the latter rain, so I may gather in my grain, new wine, and oil. Thank You for watching over me, and providing for me every time there is a need. Help me not to be anxious about my food, and clothing, but to trust you will provide. I thank You for supplying all my needs according to your riches in glory by Christ Jesus. In Jesus' name I pray. Amen.

Scripture references: Psalm 111:5; Deuteronomy 11:14; Matthew 6:31-32; Philippians 4:19

* * * * * * * * * * * * * * * * * *

Father, because You are my shepherd, Lord, I shall not be in want. You provide my every need – even to overflowing. Thank You, for taking care of me. It is written that whenever I ask, it shall be given to me, whenever I seek, I shall find, and whenever I knock, it shall be opened to me. Thank You for abundantly blessing my provision, and satisfying me with bread. Thank You for prospering me in all things, and good health, just as my soul prospers. Thank You for helping me to water others. Father, I ask that You restore to me what was destroyed, and provide plenty so I will be satisfied, and praise you for the way you provide for me.

Scripture references: Psalm 23:1; Proverbs 3:9-10; Matthew 7:7; Psalm 132:15; 3 John 2; Proverbs 11:25; Joel 2:25-26

Receive the Holy Spirit

Heavenly Father, I recognize my need for Your power to live this new life. I want the baptism of the Holy Ghost, and Fire. I ask You to baptize me now in the Holy Spirit. By faith, I receive the baptism in the Holy Spirit right now. Thank You for baptizing me. Holy Spirit, You are welcome in my life. May I be empowered for service from this day forward. In Jesus' name I pray. Amen.

Scripture references: Luke 11:13; Acts 2:4; Romans 8:26–27

Right Attitude

Father, You are my God, my Source, my Provider, and my Guide. I humbly ask You to create in me a clean heart, O God, and renew a steadfast spirit within me. I choose to seek Your face. Free me from any thoughts that I have which are contrary to You, and that hinders me from drawing closer to You. One thing I ask from You LORD, is that I may dwell in Your house of the LORD all the days of my life. In Jesus' name, I pray. Amen.

Scripture references: Psalm 51:10; James 4:7; Psalm 27:4; Psalm 27:8; 1 Timothy 6:11; Psalm 27:4

Salvation of the Lost

But you, O Lord, are a God merciful, and gracious, slow to anger, and abounding in steadfast love, and faithfulness. I know all things are possible with You, and that You desire all men to be saved, and come into the knowledge of the Truth. So, in the name of my Lord, and Savior Jesus Christ I bring (___) before You this day pleading, and interceding on their behalf.

Jesus said, no one can come to Me unless the Father who sent Me draws him. I ask that You draw (___) to You. Take the stony heart out of their flesh, and give them a heart of flesh. I also ask You to send laborers across their path who can communicate the Gospel effectively to them.

It is written that if two of you agree on earth about anything that they may ask, it shall be done for them by My Father who is in heaven. Therefore, I ask You to place (___) on the hearts of other intercessors that prayers for them will not cease until Your will is accomplished in their life.

As truth is ministered to (_____) I believe, and decree that their stony hearts will be changed, and their eyes will be opened to the Gospel, and they will choose to come out of the snare of the devil, and make Jesus Lord. Father, I pray not only for their salvation, I also ask You to make them a strong, active Christian, and prayer warrior. In Jesus' name I pray. Amen.

Scripture references: Psalm 86:15; Matthew 19:26; Ezekiel 36:26; 1 Timothy 2:4; John 6:44; Jeremiah 31:3; Matthew 9:38; Matthew 18:19-20

Strength

Father I thank you for renewing my strength as I wait on You. Lord, I thank You that as my strength is renewed I shall rise up with wings like eagles, I shall run, and not grow weary, and shall walk, and not faint. Thank You, Lord, that I can do all things through Christ who strengthens me.

Thank You, Lord, for being my refuge, and strength – a very present help in trouble. My flesh, and heart may fail, but You, Lord, are the strength of my heart, and my portion forever. Lord, I ask You to strengthen me even more with power through Your Spirit in my inner being out of Your glorious riches. In Jesus' name. I pray. Amen.

Scripture references: Psalm 46:1; Isaiah 40:29; Psalm 18:32; Psalm 138:3

Lord, I thank You that Your grace is sufficient for me, for Your strength is made perfect in my weakness. I will gladly boast in my weakness that Your power, Lord, may rest on me. Your joy is my strength. Be gracious, and come quickly to help me. Make my feet like the feet of a deer and enable me to tread on the heights. I long for You, Lord. Be my strength every morning – my salvation in times of distress. For You are my defense, and my salvation.

Thank You, Lord, for giving me strength when I am weary, and increasing me with power when I have no might. Thank You for arming me with strength, and making my way perfect. Thank You for answering me when I cry out to you. You have made me bold with strength in my soul. In Jesus' name. I pray. Amen.

Scripture references: Isaiah 33:2; Habakkuk 3:19; Psalm 118:14; 2 Corinthians 12:9; Nehemiah 8:10; Ephesians 6:10; Psalm 22:19; Psalm 18:32; Isaiah 40:29; Psalm 138:3

Salvation of Unsaved Family

Father God, in the name of Jesus I come before You on behalf of (____). It is written, Lord You are not slack concerning Your promise, but are longsuffering towards us, not willing that any should perish, but that all should come to repentance. May Your Will be done, on earth as it is in heaven in (____)'s life. Please Lord extend mercy to (____), and move upon (*his/her*) heart to accept the Truth of Christ. Bid them to come, and to be relieved of the burden of their sin.

Father, I desire for my entire family to be saved. Show me how to minister to each family member specifically. Show me when to "be merciful to those who doubt, when to save others by snatching them from the fire, and when to show mercy, mixed with fear." Open opportunities for me to share the gospel with my family, and friends, and give me the strength to obey when You open the door.

It is written that the effective, fervent prayer of a righteous man avails much. I thank You for right-eousness in Christ, and I thank You for answering my prayer. In Jesus' name I pray. Amen.

Scripture references: John 14:6; Matthew 11:28-30; John 6:44; 2 Peter 3:9; Acts 16:14; 2 Corinthians 4:4; 2 Timothy 2:25-26; James 5:16; Matthew 6:10; 2 Corinthians 5:21; Jude 22-23

Wisdom and Guidance

Father, it is written that the steps of a good man are ordered by You. Even if I wander off the road, I will hear Your voice behind me saying, "Here is the road. Follow it." You are my strength. You have made my feet like hinds' feet, and You will make me to walk upon high places.

It is written if any of you lacks wisdom, let him ask God, who gives generously to all without reproach, and it will be given him. Father, I want to do what is good, pleasing, and acceptable in your sight. Please grant me divine wisdom, and clear di-rection, and spiritual discernment. In Jesus' name I pray. Amen.

Scripture references: Psalm 25; Psalm 37:23; James 1:5; Colossians 1:9; 3:16, Proverbs 3:5-6; Isaiah 30:21; Psalm 94:18-19; Romans 12:2; Ephesians 1:17-18; Ephesians 2:10; Habakkuk 3:19; Psalm 19:14

Your Home

Father Your Word declares in Isaiah 32:18 that your people shall dwell in a peaceable habitation, in sure dwellings, and in quiet resting places. I stand in faith on Your Word. You are my shield, and my hope. Thank You that Your face is against those who plot evil against me, and for working all things for my good. In all things I am more than a conqueror.

I thank You that I dwell in the shadow of the Most High God, and I am delivered from terror, and darts from the enemy. My adversaries shall bow at my feet, and turn their backs in flight. No weapon formed against me will prosper.

Thank You for Your angels who are encamped around me to shield, and protect me and all that You have placed in my hands. I pray that everyone in this house will lie down and sleep in peace, for You O Lord, make us dwell in safety.

Father let love, joy, peace, patience, kindness, goodness, faithfulness, gentleness, and self-control be manifested in everyone in this home. May we be brought to complete unity in Christ. Give us the widsom, and knowledge to let the world know that You sent Jesus, and have loved them even as You have loved him. In the name of Jesus I pray. Amen

---

Scripture references: I Peter 3:12; Romans 8:33-34; Romans 8:37; Samuel 22:35-41; Psalm 91:5-6; Psalm 91:1; Luke 10:19; Psalm 4:8; Galatians 5:22-23; John 17

Your Children, Grandchildren

Father, in the name of Jesus Christ I lift up my (*son/daughter/children*) before you. Thank You that I have not labored in vain or brought forth children for trouble. May (*he/she/they*) make the Lord their refuge, may no evil befall them, nor any plague come near their dwelling. Give Your angels charge over them, to keep them in all their ways. Destroy the plans of the enemy in (*his/her/their*) life. Let their life be a testament of Your Goodness, and Mercy. Satisfy my (*child, children*) with a long, and prosperous life. Give (*him/her/them*) the strength to do what they need to do each day.

May wealth, and riches will be in their house. Thank You for blessing me, and my offspring. In Jesus' name I pray. Amen.

Scripture references: Isaiah 38:19; Proverbs 1:8; Ephesians 1:18–20; Philippians 4:13; Joshua 1:9; Isaiah 65:23

About The Author

Prophetess Angeline L. Williams is a submitted vessel of God who flows in the ministry gifts of Prophet, Evangelist, and Teacher.

She loves to encourage and empower others to live a God inspired life that far exceeds their limits. Her passion for God and His Word has led to an anointing to preach and teach the word of God with authority, revelation, and deliverance. She was licensed and ordained to preach the Gospel in 2002. Her messages are filled with revelation, personal testimony and a depth of wisdom, and insight resulting from decades of studying God's word, and her relationship with God.

She is also the author of I Don't Believe in Fairytales: Breaking Anti-Marriage and Promises,

Promises, God Keeps His Promises. She is the owner of Williams DocuPrep, where she has been providing self-publishing services to authors, and independent publishers since 2005. To learn more visit her website at www.williamsdocuprep.com.

Prophetess Angeline is available to speak at churches, groups, conferences, and anywhere else God opens a door. Contact her about speaking at your event visit her website at: www.angelinelwilliams.com

"Let us not become weary in doing good, for at the proper time we will reap a harvest if we do not give up." — Galatians 6:9

Other Books By Author

Available online where books are sold.